A PERILOUS PLAN

Melanie Dickerson

GraceFaith Press

Copyright © 2021 Melanie Dickerson

All rights reserved

The characters and events portrayed in this book are fictitious. Any similarity to real persons, living or dead, is coincidental and not intended by the author.

No part of this book may be reproduced, or stored in a retrieval system, or transmitted in any form or by any means, electronic, mechanical, photocopying, recording, or otherwise, without express written permission of the publisher.

ISBN: 9798476328766

Cover design by: EDH Professionals, Erin Dameron-Hill

Printed in the United States of America

To Aaron
I have found the one
my soul loves

CONTENTS

Title Page
Copyright
Dedication
A Perilous Plan
CHAPTER ONE 1
Chapter Two 13
Chapter Three 25
Chapter Four 37
Chapter Five 44
Chapter Six 55
Chapter Seven 64
Chapter Eight 71
Chapter Nine 81
Chapter Ten 92
Chapter Eleven 100
Chapter Twelve 110
Chapter Thirteen 119
Chapter Fourteen 126
Chapter Fifteen 138

Chapter Sixteen	147
Chapter Seventeen	158
Chapter Eighteen	166
Chapter Nineteen	179
Chapter Twenty	189
Chapter Twenty-One	197
Chapter Twenty-Two	205
Chapter Twenty-Three	218
Chapter Twenty-Four	228
Chapter Twenty-Five	237
Chapter Twenty-Six	245
Chapter Twenty-Seven	256
Chapter Twenty-Eight	264
Chapter Twenty-Nine	273
Epilogue	278
A Treacherous Treasure	280
Want to Help an author?	285
Want to stay in the know?	287
Discussion questions	289
About The Author	291

A PERILOUS PLAN

*Imperiled Young Widows
Regency Romance series*

by Melanie Dickerson

CHAPTER ONE

Early Autumn, 1810
London, England

Penelope knew better than to wait for her husband, as David rarely came home before dark, and sometimes he did not come home at all.

This was not how she imagined married life.

She was supposed to assume he was at his club, but she'd heard the gossip. He had secret trysts with a paramour. He had as good as admitted it—but the whispers said that there was more than one.

And although she knew all that, here she sat in the drawing room, alone, hoping he'd be home for supper and she would get a chance to talk to him, to explain to him how she felt, how much she loved him and longed for his love in return.

If she could just say the right words, could just make him understand, he would realize what his absence, his silence, did to her.

She had no near examples of married couples living pleasantly or contentedly together. Her own parents had died before she was five years old, and her grandmother, who had been her guardian for the rest of Penelope's childhood, had always lived apart from her husband, to the point that they no longer spoke and made sure they were never in the same house together.

Penelope had vowed never to let that happen to her.

She was determined to make a love match, that whomever she married would love her and she would love him. So when her grandmother urged her to marry David Hammond, the Earl of Hampstead, after a short acquaintance, she initially refused.

"What?" Grandmother's face went a shade of purple as she stared down at Penelope.

Penelope had been reading a book in the sitting room. "It is so sudden. Can we not postpone the wedding for a few weeks so that we can become more acquainted, to let affection grow?"

"Selfish, ungrateful girl!" Her grandmother, who was taller than the average woman, appeared to be staring down her long nose at Penelope. "Do you not know that a young woman who receives an offer of marriage from a handsome earl does not wait for affection to grow?" The last few words fairly dripped with derision.

Penelope's stomach churned. She tried to think of something to say, knowing that when Grandmother had made up her mind about something, Penelope had never been able to change her mind.

"After your father married your mother—a Frenchwoman—he virtually ruined your chances to marry well. Do you not know that a wealthy earl, and a young one at that, is the best match you could ever hope to make? Indeed, I never dared hope you could land someone the likes of the Earl of Hampstead! And now you refuse?" She drew out the last word as if it was three syllables long.

It seemed she could never be cleansed of the sin of being half French.

A day or two of her grandmother making snide comments and treating her coldly and Penelope gave in. She was disappointed that it was not a love match, but husbands and wives frequently grew to love one another. She had read about it in stories and even in history, where arranged marriages turned out happily for everyone. She was determined to love her husband, and she prayed he would love her in return, that her marriage would be happy, and that she might finally have someone to love—and someone who would love her.

But within the first week, even the second day, as David brusquely brushed her off to go to his club, or when he went out on business that he claimed was "Parliamentary" in nature, only to discover that Parliament was not sitting that day.

She felt as if she was shrinking, a tiny, invisible thing, not even a person.

She was his wife, but she was nothing to him.

If he did not wish to be with her so early in the marriage, would he want to be with her when she was becoming wrinkled and gray?

"David, what do you do when you go to your club?" she'd asked him in the first month after their wedding, while they ate supper in the formal dining hall in their house in St. James Place.

"You do not wish to hear about that, my dear." He said "my dear" with the coldest stare she'd ever seen. "Men do . . . manly things." Then he shoved another bite of roast beef and gravy in his mouth.

Her husband was not a particularly handsome man, with pale eyes and bushy black brows and a large belly. But she had not minded about that. If he had been handsome, he would have expected his wife to take great pains about her appearance as well. She was considered a beauty by some, but there were prettier young women who would be more than happy to be married to an earl of the relatively young age of her husband, who was now thirty-seven. And she would not always be twenty-three.

She loved him. He was her husband. She tried to be pleasing and attentive to him, but he never even seemed to notice, rarely showing her the least bit of attention in return.

This had gone on for five years. Five long years. Would things ever be good between them? Or would she always feel this desperation to make him notice her? To make him love her? It was so painful to be always seeking love, practically begging for it, but never receiving it.

There. A noise from downstairs. Was that David? Footsteps coming. It certainly was him.

Her heart fluttered. This was the night she would speak to him. She would explain how she felt, be honest and vulnerable with him, and he would finally listen to her and understand. He would finally realize how much she loved him and that all she wanted was his love. Any man would melt at such a declaration, would he not?

She had just enough time before supper was announced.

He was walking past.

"David?"

He stopped and turned his head to look at her. "Good evening, Lady Hampstead. I shall be down for supper." He continued past the doorway.

"David, please wait."

Slowly, he stepped back into the doorway. He glanced at her, then looked away again. "Did you run out of pin money again?"

"No, I simply wish to speak with you."

"Speak with me?"

"You are my husband. Cannot a woman speak with

her own husband?"

"What is it, Penny?" He frowned on one side of his mouth and slumped his shoulders, as if annoyed by something frivolous.

She cringed at him calling her Penny. That was a pet name for people who loved her, and he obviously did not. Besides, he had once insinuated that her name was annoying because it was too long. He only called her Penny because it was short. Easy. Convenient.

"I just want to say that I would like more of your company. I love you and I would like to see more of you, spend more time with you."

Her insides trembled as she waited for his reply.

"What is this about? You are not making sense." He shifted his feet and squinted as if he was impatient to move on.

"I am here alone nearly all the time. You pay no heed to me nor to my wishes. I desire just a small portion of your attention, but to no avail. I don't understand why you stay away from me, as if I'm hideous."

Tears stung her eyes. This was not the way she had intended to speak to him. She knew from experience that criticism made him clench his teeth and say something infinitely cruel. But she couldn't help herself.

"You are so dramatic." He stared at her with a look of mild surprise.

"Am I odious to you? Do you hate me?" She nearly choked on her own tears.

"Now you're being hysterical. Why would I wish to spend my time with a hysterical woman? Very tiresome. Very unbecoming."

Heat filled her head. Again with telling her it was her fault!

"There is no one here to be becoming for! You're my husband but you're never here. You ignore me and coldly dismiss me day after day." She felt almost out of control as the words flew from her mouth, pent-up emotion spilling forth. She was even raising her voice. Her grandmother would strongly disapprove, and by the look on David's face, he did as well.

"I shall send for the doctor to bring you a tonic." He was all calm disapproval.

"No. I don't want a tonic. I want a husband who loves me."

"You are not making sense. Hysterical. I shall tell the servants you will dine in your room tonight."

"You will do no such thing." She never stood up to him like this. She was afraid, afraid of how he would react, but she couldn't seem to stop. "All I wanted was to have my husband's attention for a few minutes." She could no longer keep the tears in check, and sobs prevented her from saying anything more.

"My attention?" He said, his eyes widening, leaning away from her, his upper lip curling in a look of contempt.

She shook her head, struggling to control her tears so she could speak.

"You know I hate you blubbering. Surely you are not becoming one of those overly emotional women who —"

"I just want your love, David. Your love."

"If that is what you desire, Penny . . . I am willing to turn a blind eye if you wish to take a lover. All I ask is that you use discretion." And with that he turned and continued down the hall. "Have my supper sent to my room."

Penelope's chest was hollow, her body numb. Her tears were gone now as she made her way to her own bedroom and closed the door behind her.

She had to force the air through her constricted throat. "He hates me," she whispered. "My husband hates me."

A sharp ache went through her. If only she could hate him back, then the unbearable pain would go away. But she didn't hate him—she didn't know why—perhaps because she was trapped in this marriage, with a man whom she had vowed to love until death, and he was her only chance at ever being loved.

She hadn't wanted to believe he would never love her. If she told him that all she wanted was his love . . . if she told him how much she disliked his staying away . . . if she just said the right things . . .

Now she could no longer deny that he didn't care. And if he didn't hate her, he might as well, because he'd just killed her greatest dream—to love and be loved.

Her chest ached so much. Was she dying? Perhaps it would be best if she was.

~ ~ ~

The next day was Sunday, and just as if nothing amiss had been said between them, David joined her downstairs when it was time to walk to church.

He said not a word as he carefully pulled on his gloves and reached for his walking stick. Then he held out his arm to her.

"Shall we?"

At his cool, uncaring manner, Penelope felt the tears flood her eyes, but David didn't even look at her.

She took his arm and they walked out onto the street and started toward the steeple not far away, as if they were a happily married couple strolling to church in contentment and harmony.

A lump formed in her throat from the tears she was desperately holding back.

No one wanted to see her tears, least of all David. He'd probably think she was trying to shame him into an insincere apology, or that she wanted to embarrass him in public. So she forced herself to think of something else, of the leaves on the trees in Hyde Park, beginning to turn bright colors. Of her mare, Chestnut. Her horse nuzzled her every time she came near her.

Even her horse gave her more affection than her husband.

But that made the tears prick her eyelids again.

David's arm was warm. Was he having an affair, giving his warmth to some other woman? Or did he even feel love at all? She'd heard the rumors that he had had a paramour for a short time in the first year of her marriage, but he'd told her—in a very cold way—that he had ended it because the woman no longer pleased him. She had been daft enough to tell herself that was because he realized he loved his wife. But soon there were rumors of another woman.

He'd never said or done anything to make her feel loved or comforted or cherished. But she'd chosen to live in denial of the truth as long as she was able.

A tear fell. She quickly flicked the saltwater drop with her finger, then rubbed the evidence away with her finger, as though something tickled her cheek.

She had to master her thoughts, turn her mind to something besides her pain.

Autumn leaves. Her mare. Her new friend Camille. Church. People whom she had seen for the last five years of her marriage but who had never spoken to her.

Why was life so cold?

Autumn leaves in Hyde Park. Chestnut's nibbling lips when he took the carrot from her hand.

Finally, they arrived at the church door. David smiled at the rector and even began a conversation with another gentleman, as cheerful as could be. She waited as the men exchanged stories about shooting parties.

Perhaps she could go home to her grandmother. But Grandmother was just as cold as David. In fact, in her mind, she associated the two of them, sometimes even remembering something they'd said but forgetting which of them had said it. "Penelope, no one wants to be subjected to your emotions." Was that Grandmother when Penelope had shed a tear explaining to a visitor that her dog had died? Or David, when her voice had hitched as she spoke of her friend who was dying of consumption?

They were entering the church when Penelope's foot caught on the last step. She stumbled. David squeezed her arm, hard, and yanked up on it with more force than necessary, as she had already steadied herself.

David abruptly let go of her arm and walked away.

Of course he would ignore her. He probably thought she was trying to embarrass him by stumbling. Why couldn't he understand that not everything was about him?

Free of his arm, she sank down on the pew against the back wall.

"Pardon me, but are you unwell?" A young man was standing over her, bending down to look into her face. He was quite handsome, probably near her own age, with dark hair and eyes and a look of concern on his face.

"I am well." She smiled up at him. David wouldn't want her to appear weak.

"There is nothing wrong with her." David was suddenly beside the young man. "Henry Gilchrist. How are you?" David's voice was as bland and unemotional as ever in his greeting.

"Very well. I noticed your wife looking a bit ill. Is she all right, do you think? Should she get some air?"

"I am well," Penelope assured him. "I only needed to sit for a moment." Had this Henry Gilchrist noticed that her eyes were puffy and slightly red? Hopefully he wouldn't guess that it was from crying half the night.

She stood quickly, making her vision go dim. She refused to heed it. Besides, if she allowed them to see any weakness, David might humiliate her by showing that he did not care at all and simply walking away and ignoring her.

She smiled in spite of her blurred vision.

"See, Gilchrist?" David chuckled. "You're like an old woman, worried every lady is about to swoon."

Mr. Gilchrist did not appear to be amused. Instead of replying to David, he bowed to Penelope. "I am glad you are well. May I escort you to your place?"

His manner was so polite, his eyes so kind, she got lost in them for a moment. And even though her husband was right beside her, he was no longer paying any heed to them, so she allowed Mr. Gilchrist to walk her down the aisle to her husband's family's pew. When they reached it, David was no longer nearby, but she could hear him talking, rather loudly, to someone at the door of the church.

"Are you sure you're well, Lady Hampstead?"

"I am very well. Thank you for your kindness."

She studied his face. Was he truly so concerned? David would never pay so much attention to her. To another man's wife, yes. But not to her.

Mr. Gilchrist's expression—how would she describe

it? Kind but unsure. There was no undue interest, no lasciviousness or untoward manner. He finally nodded, as though assured that she was well, and moved away.

She saw other couples come in and sit down together. As usual, David would stay away from her until the last moment before he had to be seated, while he talked and even laughed with the other parishioners—the wealthy, important ones, that is.

Her friend—actually more of an acquaintance—Maud Crumbly and her husband Thomas, were sitting two rows in front of her.

Maud was a gossipy, snide person who seemed to take pleasure in other people's pain, but there was her husband, leaning close to her, whispering something in her ear. She turned toward him and he gave her a tender smile. They sat close, their shoulders touching.

When had David ever looked at her like that, or sat so close to her? Not since their wedding day. Apparently that had only been for show.

She watched other married couples enter the church and sit down. Were they happy? Were the husbands faithful? Were the wives kind? She noticed Mr. Gilchrist, the man who had been so solicitous, sitting alone. Was he not married? Not that it mattered.

In spite of what David had said, she had no intention of taking a lover. Such behavior was beneath a lady's dignity, her grandmother had said. Besides that, she had too much fear of God's judgment to do such a thing.

She wanted her husband, but he didn't want her, and it was a pain that stabbed deep inside her chest. There was no remedy for it. She was trapped in a loveless marriage.

Would Mr. Gilchrist be kind to his wife? She had

seen David behave very kindly toward ladies he barely knew, and yet he seemed to resent having to take the time even to hand her into their carriage. Usually he let the servant do it.

What would it be like to have a husband who cherished her? Did not the Bible say something about that, admonishing men to love their wives? But in spite of faithfully attending church, David didn't care any more about what God said than he cared about her.

~ ~ ~

Penelope awoke. Something, a sound perhaps, had awakened her.

Her room was dark, with only the faintest light from the streetlamps shone through the edges of her window.

A loud thump came from David's bedroom, which was next to hers. A man was talking, but the voice didn't sound like her husband's. David had spent the night at home, had he not? Yes, she had heard him getting ready for bed as she lay awake.

"Give it to me!" Another loud thump, then another, as if heavy things were falling to the floor. Then there was a crash like glass shattering. Penelope's heart pounded so hard she could barely breathe.

She threw back the covers and pulled on her wrapper. She held it closed at the waist and slipped on her shoes. Then she stood still in the dark room, listening to silence.

CHAPTER TWO

Was there was some kind of danger in David's room? Had he fallen?

Penelope should go and help him, not stand there like a ninny.

She hurried to the door to the hall, since David kept the door between them locked. Outside in the hall, all was dark and quiet. She walked to David's door and tried the knob, expecting it to be locked as well, but to her surprise, it opened.

The back of her neck tingled as she stared into the dark room. "David?" she whispered. No answer. Why hadn't she brought a candle? She couldn't make out any movement in the dark, but then she heard rustling.

"David?" she said, loudly this time. But still there was no answer. Something was wrong.

"Harwell! Sims!" she cried. "Come quickly!"

She stepped further into the room. "David! Are you here?" Her heart was pounding so hard it made it difficult to speak.

Harwell's mumbling voice and footsteps were coming down the hall behind her. She stepped farther into the room, bumping into a table. Her eyes were becoming more adjusted to the dim light.

Another rustling sound, and she saw something move at the back of the room.

Penelope stopped. "Who's there?"

It was a figure. He seemed to be looking though

David's wardrobe against the wall.

"David? Is that you?"

The man stayed hunched inside the wardrobe, his arms moving, as if he was tossing things on the floor.

"My lady, whatever is the matter?" Harwell was in his dressing gown as he came up beside her. Thankfully he was holding a lamp, which illuminated the scene.

Without looking up, the man who was going through David's wardrobe rushed toward the window beside the head of her husband's bed. He climbed up to the window sill.

"You, there!" Harwell shouted. "Get down."

The man suddenly went out the window and disappeared.

Had he jumped from three floors up? Harwell hurried toward the window, but stopped before he reached it.

"What's amiss?" The housekeeper, Mrs. Sims, entered the room.

"Fetch a doctor," Harwell said in a gruff voice, dropping to one knee. "Quickly."

Penelope rushed forward and saw that Harwell was kneeling beside David.

Her husband's eyes were staring straight up and his chest was covered in blood, while in his hand he clutched a knife.

She felt rooted to the spot. "O God." Her voice was barely audible as the air rushed out of her.

David was dead.

~ ~ ~

Penelope's grandmother came from Bath to London the next day. But for once, Penelope was grateful for her grandmother's way of taking charge, as she met with the funeral furnisher and made all the arrangements for the funeral procession and services, everything that must be purchased and everyone who must be hired, all the way down to the featherman who would dress the horses that would draw the carriages in the funeral procession with black-dyed ostrich feather headdresses.

So many rituals and traditions, and they must all be adhered to, for her husband had been an earl. It was expected.

Penelope was a widow now, and as such, she must sit in her black dress and look sad.

That was not difficult to do. After seeing David's murdered body on the floor of his room, she was numb all over, shocked in her mind as well as her body.

Whenever she went to bed the next two nights, she lay there reliving what had happened, the sounds of someone with her husband in the next room, the man rifling through her husband's wardrobe, the look on her dead husband's face.

She couldn't stop imagining what had occurred, how the person might have gone about stabbing her husband, how David had grabbed a knife and tried to fight back.

What was the murderer's motive? Was he simply a thief looking for money and valuables?

The constable said David looked as if he'd been dead an hour or two. But she'd heard a man's voice only moments before she went in and found her husband on the floor. He could not have been talking to a dead man. Had someone else been in the room?

The constable must have been mistaken.

Now, as she sat in the drawing room trying to drink her tea, she shuddered. Though it was a very cool autumn day, there was no fire in this room where David's body lay in its black velvet-covered coffin. The housekeeper Sims had admonished her that it needed to stay cool, as his body would be there for several days before the funeral and might start to stink.

Few people had come to keep vigil with her as she sat with the body, which was another of the traditions that could not be neglected. Almost no one came to condole with her. After all, Penelope had grown up in Shropshire, having rarely been in London before her marriage. As she had been educated at home, she hadn't made school friends like many other girls, and she had few cousins or other family members.

David's own extended family was cold and uncommunicative, he had no siblings either, and his parents were deceased. As she and David had never had children, the heir was a cousin she had never met, a Mr. Eustace Hammond.

But at least Grandmother was here to take care of the details of the funeral and burial. Penelope had never even been allowed to attend a funeral, as ladies nearly always avoided the actual procession and funeral services, and her parents died when she was too young to remember any particulars.

Her mind was so incapable of rational thought, her hands too shaky and fidgety to do any sort of needlework, she simply stared at the black cloth covering the walls and windows and ruminated on the past as she awaited visitors that didn't come.

The servant announced, "Mr. Henry Gilchrist."

Wasn't that the young man who was so solicitous toward her at church on Sunday? Penelope sat up straighter.

Henry Gilchrist entered the room and bowed. His

brown hair was nicely coifed, and his clothing was the latest in fashion, but his manner marked him as no dandy. He was tall and rather broad-shouldered, his boots slightly scuffed. His face was tanned by the sun, and his eyes were focused intently on her.

Where else would they be focused? There was no one else in the room, unless you included her dead husband in the coffin along the opposite wall. But those eyes and their intense gaze made her heart flutter.

"Lady Hampstead." Mr. Gilchrist bowed to her. "Please allow me to extend my condolences to you on the loss of your husband."

He seated himself opposite her. She did her best to rouse her sluggish thoughts to find something to say, finally coming up with, "Did you know my husband well, Mr. Gilchrist?"

He blinked, as though surprised. "Yes. Did he not tell you that we were on a committee together?"

"He did not." Would he realize that her husband rarely told her anything, that her husband didn't love or even care about her? Her cheeks warmed.

"It was a rather secret committee, after all," he said, as if sensing her embarrassment. "Having to do with conflicts . . . with France, actually."

"Oh?"

"Had you no idea your husband was working on a committee of that nature?"

Penelope stared back at him. He was so handsome, with a sincere, concerned look in his eyes. David never looked at her that way. Her breath shallowed. She almost felt as if she was being unfaithful to her husband.

What was wrong with her?

A picture of David lying on the floor, covered in

blood, flashed across her mind. She could never seem to get that image of him to leave her alone. She even saw it in her dreams. And now it accused her of indecency and infidelity, of feeling an attraction to a man who was not her husband.

But in reality, she no longer had a husband.

Mr. Gilchrist had asked her a question.

"Forgive me, what did you say?"

"I asked if you knew your husband was working on a committee of that nature."

"Of what nature?"

"Pertaining to a possible conflict with France."

"Oh, yes. I mean to say, no, I had no idea. Lord Hampstead, my husband, rarely spoke about his business as a member of the House of Lords. Are you also a member of the House of Lords?"

As soon as she asked the question, she knew she had misspoken. Of course he was not in the House of Lords. He had no title.

His smile was kind. "I am a Member of Parliament, but in the House of Commons."

"Yes, of course. Very good." Most of the members of the House of Commons were just as wealthy, if not more so, than their titled counterparts in the House of Lords. But not having a title was a source of irritation for some, as it had always been for Grandmother. She'd been determined to marry Penelope off to a viscount or earl, anyone with a title.

Penelope hadn't cared about titles. She wanted love. But when had she ever gotten what she wanted?

She sighed, the tears rising into her eyes. She must stop pitying herself. It did no good and would only cause her embarrassment.

At least Grandmother was not here. She'd shame Penelope if she even suspected she might be tearing up.

"I believe I heard that Lord Hampstead's estate is entailed upon a cousin."

"Yes." Which was probably the real reason Grandmother looked even more sour than usual. She'd even remarked, "If only you'd had an heir. Did you even try?"

Why would Grandmother blame her? She wasn't the one who slept elsewhere most nights. No, she was home, the perfect wife, wasting her life on a man who cared nothing for her.

"Pardon me if I seem to be prying, but the events on the night of your husband's death must have been very shocking. Do you not have friends or family to sit with you?"

"My grandmother is here. I believe she is away on a small matter of business." Probably shopping to relieve the dullness of sitting here endlessly awaiting fellow mourners that hardly ever came.

"I suppose you will move back to Shropshire when the funeral is over, with your grandparents?"

"Why, yes." How did he know so much about her?

"Will you miss London?"

Miss London? "What is there to miss?" She smiled to soften her words, but truly, at the moment she felt as if she hated the city. Only evil had befallen her here, pain and sadness.

Mr. Gilchrist smiled. "I see you take my view of the city."

"I do not mean to be severe. Of course, there are many people who love London and appreciate its parties and shops and concerts and theaters, but I . . . have not been very happy here."

"I am sorry to hear it."

She should not have said that. He would think she was complaining about her husband and her marriage. She was fighting back tears again already. She blinked frantically and looked away.

"I prefer more open spaces myself," Mr. Gilchrist went on, "places for riding where I'm not likely to run someone over if I let my horse have his own gait." He had a look of good-naturedness on his face. "But there are certainly more occasions here to meet with friends and see interesting theatricals."

"You enjoy theatricals, Mr. Gilchrist?"

"I do, if the play is well-written."

"I have only been to one or two plays in the last five years, and I confess, I was not very impressed."

"Perhaps they were the wrong plays."

"Perhaps so." Penelope felt her tense facial muscles relax. When was the last time she smiled? "I used to like plays, and I like concerts, though I rarely attend."

"Rarely? Does—Did—Lord Hampstead not enjoy concerts or the theater?"

"Not especially." Or if he did, he attended with his paramour instead of his wife. Honestly, she did not know what David enjoyed, whether concerts or theater or lectures. She knew little more about him than that he disliked broiled fish. He once dismissed their cook after she served broiled fish as the main course at dinner.

"Mr. Gilchrist, have you ever lost someone, a close family member or friend?"

"I lost my brother two years ago."

"Oh, I'm so sorry." Penelope placed a hand over her chest, her eyes widening. "Please accept my condolences. It must be very painful to lose a sibling, and he must have been very young. I don't have any siblings of my own but I imagine you must have been very attached, as siblings are often each other's closest friends. Forgive me for chattering on so." He would think she was completely daft.

"There is nothing to forgive." Mr. Gilchrist was shaking his head. "Losing my brother has been the most devastating event in my life. And we were very close friends. But I understand that losing a husband can be even more devastating, as it changes the course of a lady's life. We lost my father a year before my brother, and it has been very difficult for my mother. But she and my sister comfort themselves with many parties and shopping trips to London."

She laughed at him referring to his mother and sister's shopping trips as "comfort."

"Forgive me, Mr. Gilchrist. I do not know what came over me." She glanced at her husband's coffin and a pang of guilt assailed her. One of the servants would tell Grandmother, who would no doubt berate her for laughing in the presence of her husband's deceased body! Even Penelope was appalled.

Truly, she did not mean to disrespect the dead. She had not been happy in her marriage, but neither did she wish her husband dead. And she must be careful or people would realize the truth—that she was shocked and horrified over the way he had died, sorry that he had experienced violence and pain at his death, sorry that there was now no hope of their marriage becoming more joyful, and shocked at becoming a widow at twenty-three years of age. But rather than feeling great sorrow over losing her husband, she felt a sense of relief deep in her heart that the struggle to make her husband love her was over.

And she was more afraid than sad—afraid of what

would become of her now.

She would have to go back to living with her overbearing grandmother, who would force her to socialize in her attempt to introduce her to her next husband. And the thought of being married again, if it was anything like her first marriage, filled her with dread.

She could not change her feelings, she could only admit them. And in her defense, David had done little in their five years of marriage besides hurt her.

"I am not sorry for making you laugh." His brows went up slightly as he inclined his head toward her. "Anyone could see from your face when I walked in that you are suffering, and relieving suffering is a good thing."

She lifted her brows and smiled. "It is true that I have not laughed in a very long time."

"Then you needed some levity. And this custom of shutting a person away with their loved one's dead body . . . It does not seem conducive to sanity, much less good health."

"But we have no control over the customs of the day, I suppose." Penelope felt the levity drain right out of her again. "I am a widow now and must behave as such. No more laughter, Mr. Gilchrist. It is forbidden."

But the expression on his face somehow had her smile returning.

"I would never endanger your reputation, my lady." He placed a hand over his heart, and though his words were serious, his expression was much too serious—mock serious.

"That is good, Mr. Gilchrist, for I fear I shall have little more than my reputation now."

He frowned. "A travesty, this entailing a man's estate on a distant relative. A widow and her children should be entitled to whatever a man leaves her."

"Well, I have no children, and the law would not agree with you on this, Mr. Gilchrist."

He frowned again. "Your husband's heir will be disappointed, I would imagine."

"Disappointed? Why?"

Mr. Gilchrist sat very still. Finally, he answered, "Forgive me for bringing it up, but . . . your husband had taken on quite a bit of debt."

"Debt? I do not think so." Penelope would have heard rumors if her husband was in debt, wouldn't she? "How did he acquire this debt?"

Mr. Gilchrist opened his mouth, then squirmed a bit in his chair. "Perhaps I should not have spoken of it. I assumed you knew."

"Knew what?"

"Of your husband's gaming debts."

"I did not know he gambled at all." Penelope stared at the wall. How had she not known this? But perhaps his true paramour was not a woman but a gaming table. It made more sense. David had always had a certain cold recklessness, a focused determination that might drive him to gamble until he'd either won . . . or lost utterly.

"I had no idea about any gaming debts. Is this a well-known fact?"

"I'm afraid it is. I'm sorry to be the one to tell you. I did not mean to bring another shock to you."

"It is all right. I am not terribly shocked. And it little affects me, as he did not leave me his estate. I do not believe he left me anything. Will his heir, Mr. Hammond, receive anything?" Many a wealthy man had gambled away everything they owned.

"I believe the house here in London is still safe, but

his estate in Hampstead . . . it was only a matter of time before he would have to vacate the premises."

This was a shock. How could anyone be so foolish as to gamble away something so valuable for . . . what? A few hours of some sort of excitement at the gaming tables?

"I am sorry, again, that I'm the bearer of bad tidings. That was very unkind of me."

"But it is the truth. I don't fault you for telling me." What kind of man she had married! "To be honest, Mr. Gilchrist, I hardly knew my husband. He was virtually a stranger to me, even after five years." Her voice went hoarse as she spoke the latter few words. Why had she told him that? She cleared her throat.

"I am sorry."

Though Mr. Gilchrist so often looked kind and compassionate, when she glanced up at him, she caught him with a shrewd, narrowed look in his eyes.

Perhaps she should not be so open with this man. After all, she knew nothing of him or his character. Was she being as naïve and foolish as when she'd believed her husband would fall in love with her kindness and affection for him?

CHAPTER THREE

Henry Gilchrist eyed Lady Hampstead. Was she telling him the truth? If she was, if she truly did not know anything about her husband's activities, then he might be wasting his time. However, she could be hiding the plans, waiting to sell them and take the money. After all, she admitted that her husband left her nothing.

Also, her mother had been French. Did she feel more loyalty to her mother's country than to England?

She had such a sweet face, such an expression of innocence. But he didn't want to trust his own judgement when it came to women and their expressions of goodness. He'd certainly been wrong before. And this Lady Hampstead—Penelope was her Christian name—was very pretty, with her brownish-blonde hair and blue eyes, her thick eyelashes and perfect mouth. She must know what a beauty she was.

He'd seen her once when that slug Hampstead had just married her. She'd been only about eighteen years old and looked like a child, but now . . . She'd grown more beautiful as she'd matured, and yet Hampstead had not seemed to appreciate her enough to even go home to her at night. Not a clever man. And now he'd gotten himself murdered.

Could it be that Lady Hampstead realized her good fortune at losing a worthless husband, more than she was letting on? She certainly did not seem bitter at losing access to his fortune, nor did she seem to be bothered by the loss of the prestige of his title. Truthfully, and in spite of the fact that he'd trusted in a lady's false innocence before, he could easily imagine that Lady Hampstead was simply an ill-used and neglected wife who had been unexpectedly relieved of her duty to a man who was not even faithful to her. A beautiful ill-used and neglected wife at that.

But perhaps he was as foolish as ever.

She was staring back at him, her expression almost fearful. He must stay focused or *she* would become suspicious of *him*. And he needed her to trust him.

"You say your husband was virtually a stranger, but there must be some reason he was murdered. Do you know any reason why anyone might want to do him harm?"

"No, not at all." Her blue eyes were wide as she stared at the wall behind him, as if lost in thought. "I cannot imagine."

"Did he have any meetings here in the house with anyone, secret meetings?"

"No. He always met his friends at his club."

"Did he have any particular hiding places? Forgive me for asking so many questions, but it is in reference to the committee we were on."

"Is that why he was murdered? Something to do with this committee? And with France, did you say?"

"It is a possibility. And yes, the conflict with France is at the center of our committee's purposes."

"I'm afraid I know nothing of it." The beautiful Lady Hampstead shook her head. "Nothing at all."

He needed to search her husband's room where he died, just in case something had been missed on the night he died. She would probably say no, but it couldn't hurt to ask, could it?

"Forgive me for asking this of you—I know it is presumptuous, as we are so little acquainted—but the committee Lord Hampstead and I were on has asked me to investigate his murder. I wonder if you would allow me to search his rooms for evidence of who might have attacked him. I know it is presumptuous."

"Not at all. Of course you may, since you are investigating the murder." Her expression was clouded over, but she did not seem suspicious of his motives, nor afraid of what he might find.

Perhaps she did know nothing of Hampstead's nefarious dealings and the plans he had stolen.

"Will you show me the room?"

"Of course." She stood, her black skirts rustling as she moved, and led him to the stairs.

They encountered a maidservant, who gave them a curious look, but ducked into another room to avoid them. Which made him wonder—could Hampstead have had an accomplice, perhaps one of the servants?

Certainly it was likely his paramour, Camille Dupre, was involved. But that was not something he could ask his widow, not on such short acquaintance.

"This is David's—Lord Hampstead's bedroom." Lady Hampstead opened the door and led the way inside.

It was a typical gentleman's bedroom, with dark furniture, sparsely decorated.

"Did he keep the window locked?" Henry walked toward the only window in the room.

"I am not sure. But I believe his manservant, Bristol, would have kept it locked."

"And the intruder left by way of this window?"

"Yes, I saw him leave."

"And the man's description?"

"He was of medium to slender build and normal height. I did not see his face. He kept his back to me."

"Never even turned his head when you cried out?"

"No. He simply went to the window, climbed out, and was gone."

"And this is where you found him?" Henry indicated where Hampstead's blood had been spilled on the wood floor, a dark stain that had obviously been scrubbed but was still faintly visible.

"Yes," Lady Hampstead said, her voice soft and faint. "He was already gone when we—the butler Harwell and I—found him on the floor."

"Can you speculate on what the murderer was looking for? I believe the room was in disarray when you found him."

"I don't know. The servants and I could not tell if anything was missing."

"And the constable said your husband was holding a knife, I believe?"

"Yes." The lady looked a bit pale.

"Did the knife have any blood on the blade? Forgive me. I know these questions must be painful to answer."

"No, no, it is all right. I did not look . . . but now that I think on it, there wasn't any blood, because I remember thinking that David—Lord Hampstead—had grabbed a knife to defend himself but had not been able to." Her voice grew faint with the last couple of words, a haunted look in her eyes.

"I am sorry to cause you to relive it."

"It was a horrible shock," she said softly. "But I do want whoever did such a terrible thing to be caught and locked up in prison where they cannot hurt anyone else."

"Thank you for your help." He looked into her eyes, those lovely blue eyes, and his heart did a strange little hiccup. "I am much obliged."

If she was everything she seemed—innocent, gentle, and kindhearted—then he might have to be more careful about guarding his heart. But that was just the problem he always seemed to have—believing women were everything they seemed. For, as he had learned in the most painful of ways, not all women were honest and sincere.

Henry had seen Lord Hampstead's body; he'd actually been one of the committee members who had gone through all of the earl's clothing, searching for any indication of where he might have hidden the plans. So he did not need to ask the lady about that, thankfully.

"And now I need your permission to go through your husband's possessions. I am sorry—"

"Of course, of course, whatever you need to do."

"You are welcome to stay and observe, or you may send in a servant to watch me and make sure I don't pilfer anything."

"I am sure you would never do anything . . . I have no fears of that nature. You may look wherever you like."

"I am most grateful." He nodded to her before beginning.

Henry went to the wardrobe, and as he was standing in the open piece of furniture, he heard a gasp behind him.

Lady Hampstead was standing there with her hand over her mouth. She looked away when he turned to stare at her.

"What is the matter?"

"It is nothing. It is only that . . . when you were

standing there, it came flooding back to me—the shock of the strange man going through my husband's belongings, while his body was lying—" She kept her hand over her mouth and squeezed her eyes shut.

"I'm so sorry."

She looked so fragile standing there. He longed to comfort her, to tell her that all would be well. The poor woman. To say she had had a shock was an understatement. But he couldn't very well comfort her, to take her in his arms. That would be much too familiar and forward.

"Perhaps it would be easier for you if you were not here, watching. Send a manservant, if you like."

"No, no. I am well, and I have nothing better to do." She let out a little nervous burst of air. "I have to face it. If not now, then I will only be haunted by it later, by the memories of that night."

He gave her what he hoped was a sympathetic look. "As you wish." Then went on searching.

He was highly aware of her presence in the room, even while he kept a sharp eye out, paying especially close attention to every scrap of paper he came across, which so far had all turned out to be laundry lists left by a servant, letters about his gambling debts, or written schedules for when Parliament was sitting.

It seemed the only thing Lord Hampstead was serious about was his duties as a Member of Parliament, and that was probably only due to his being paid by France to spy for them.

When he had gone through everything in the wardrobe—old papers and clothing items piled in the bottom—he went on to a small bedside table containing a drawer. Inside he found more papers, including a tiny, neatly folded letter.

"Dearest David, my love,

My heart and my body are yours. Come to me tonight. Do not forget me. I will never forget you.

Yours forever in body and spirit,

C."

Lady Hampstead's name was Penelope, with a P and not a C. A letter from one of his paramours, possibly Camille Dupre.

Henry slipped the letter into his pocket. After all, it might be helpful if he found the writer of the letter. Certainly Lady Hampstead did not need to see the proof of her husband's infidelity.

He turned his head, hoping the lady had not seen him take the letter. Indeed, she was sitting in a leather armchair, staring at the wall as if in a daze.

Henry searched a trunk next. He took out all of the man's clothing, one piece at a time, and checked all the pockets. Nothing important besides proof of more of his gaming debts.

He was in the middle of searching a second wardrobe when he heard an imperious voice say, "What is this? Who are you?"

"Grandmother," Lady Hampstead began, "this is Henry Gilchrist. Mr. Gilchrist, this is my grandmother, Beatrice Whitewood. He is—"

"I do not know what you are about, young man, but my granddaughter is in mourning and this room was the scene of her husband's murder, and it is highly improper for you to be here with her."

"Forgive me, I—"

"He is investigating Lord Hampstead's murder, as Mr. Gilchrist was on a government committee with my husband and has reason to believe that his murder may have been connected with that."

The older woman stared, quite wild-eyed, at Henry, her head held so high, leaning back, that he wondered she could see him at all. But then she turned toward Penelope Hammond.

"What is the meaning of you being in here? Send a servant to watch him. You are to be in the drawing room receiving mourners."

"There are no mourners, and I can go down to the drawing room should any arrive."

The old woman stared fiercely at Lady Hampstead without even the blink of an eyelash or the twitch of a jaw muscle. Finally, she uttered one syllable. "Go."

Lady Hampstead stood and walked slowly past Mrs. Whitewood. In the doorway, she glanced over her shoulder at him, then was gone.

"Young man, I hope you have a letter of recommendation from this committee you speak of. I am not as naïve as my granddaughter. How do I know you are not the very man who murdered my grandson-in-law, come back to rob him of whatever you think he has?"

"Madam, I assure you that I am no robber. I am a Member of Parliament and—"

"Do you have proof of what you say?"

"I can produce my family crest." Henry might not have a title but his family was an old one with a large holding of land in Hertfordshire. He reached in his pocket and produced a letter he had sealed that morning.

Mrs. Whitewood seemed reluctant to take the letter, but finally did. She dug out a pair of spectacles from a tiny purse that dangled from her wrist, put them on, and peered down at the wax seal. Then she handed it back to him.

"You may be a gentleman, but that does not prove that you have the expressed authority of the government to search our home."

It wasn't her home, or even her granddaughter's home anymore, now that her husband was dead.

"If a letter is what you require, madam, I shall return with it as soon as possible."

"You could forge a letter." Her faded eyes were sharp. She quickly asked another question. "How do you know my granddaughter?"

"We attend the same parish church. I often met with her and her husband, may he rest in peace, on a Sunday."

She stared a long time, and finally said, "It is highly irregular, but I shall allow you to search. I shall have a manservant come and observe. I daresay there are items of value in the room that Lord Hampstead's heir would not wish to be taken." She rang the bell.

Henry had the distinct urge to roll his eyes at her insinuation that he might steal something. But he refrained and waited politely with Mrs. Whitewood for the servant to appear. When he did, Henry carried on with his search, but even with the manservant there, the old woman continued to stand behind him and watch over his shoulder, making observations here and there.

"Oh, that is a handsome watch. I should imagine his cousin Eustace will enjoy it, if it keeps good time."

"His cousin Eustace" was Lord Hampstead's heir, and he would inherit whatever was left after the creditors took what was owed to them. To have this woman, who had no claim on anything in the room, watching him so begrudgingly made his hackles rise, but he did his best to ignore her.

Henry looked for the better part of an hour, even checking for loose floor boards, but try as he might, he could find nothing in the room that would point him toward the plans he and the rest of the committee members were sure Hampstead had stolen.

As he left the room with no more than the short letter from his paramour, Henry went in search of Penelope Hammond, to take his leave of her. And as ever, Mrs. Whitewood was right behind him.

He found the new widow in the drawing room, alone, a book in her lap as she stared out a window with the same dazed look she'd had before. But when she turned to see him walking in, her face split into a smile so bright it made his heart skip a beat.

"Thank you for coming," she said. "I mean to say, I am glad you are investigating, trying to find the evil man —or men—who did this."

"Do you have reason to believe there was more than one?"

Her expression turned serious. "I heard a man's voice and a sound like something falling to the floor. That is what caused me to leave my room and open Lord Hampstead's door. But according to the constable, my husband had been dead for at least an hour. Who was the man speaking to if not another villain such as himself? He was not yelling, only speaking in a normal tone."

"That makes sense, yes." Henry knew that there had been more than one man in the room. The men who had killed her husband had been the mercenaries that he and his fellow committee members hired. But he had no intention of telling her that.

The mercenaries had been instructed to find the papers Lord Hampstead had stolen. They were even given permission to break into his house and question Hampstead. However, they'd not been given permission to kill him. Their excuse had been that he'd gotten belligerent and pulled a knife on them.

"Did no one see anyone leaving? Besides the man who left out the window?"

"No." She shook her head and a small strand of her dark blonde hair slipped from her coiffure and dangled by her cheek.

Could any woman as pretty—or as poor—as Lady Hampstead be without guile and caprice?

The words of his mother came to him: "You are too young to be so cynical."

No doubt he was cynical. But he had good reason. Besides, it seemed very coincidental that Lady Hampstead's husband was in league with the French and yet she knew nothing of it, especially since she herself was half French.

The man's paramour was also French. Obviously he had a preference for French women.

"If you think of anything else from that night, or find any sort of evidence, anything of a suspicious nature, please send for me." He handed her his calling card. "I am here while Parliament is sitting, and while we are investigating this matter."

"Thank you." She glanced at the card and smiled up at him.

It was just possible that she was simply a neglected wife whose husband was a traitor. She might be half French, but so were many people living in London. And if she'd lived on English soil her whole life, with her English father's people, she might not have any more loyalty to France than the next person.

But there was still the possibility that she knew more than she let on, that she was allied with the French spies, and that was the belief of everyone on the committee. Especially since she was now penniless.

"I must take my leave of you now, Lady Hampstead," he said, still calling her by the title that was no longer legally hers to hold, but he did not wish to be the first person to leave it off. "I greatly appreciate your help and cooperation." He bowed to her, then turned to her grandmother. "Mrs. Whitewood. I bid you both a good day."

He'd done his best, having gained more access than he'd thought he would, but as expected, he'd found nothing.

They were not finished with Lady Hampstead—Mrs. Hammond now that she was no longer an earl's wife—as the committee would continue to see her as an object of suspicion until they found the plans her husband had stolen.

His path and Penelope Hammond's would cross again soon.

CHAPTER FOUR

Penelope picked up her book, but instead of reading what was on the page, her grandmother continued to speak of Mr. Henry Gilchrist's prospects, while Penelope's thoughts went to his gentlemanlike manner and his handsome face.

"Who is this Henry Gilchrist? Who is his father and grandfather? Is he married?"

"He is not married, and I believe his family estate is in Hertfordshire."

"His father must have been William Gilchrist. They are very rich. What else do you know of this young man?"

"Nothing. He's a Member of the House of Commons."

"He must be rich, then. Too bad he doesn't have a title. But you could do worse. You must flirt with him when he returns."

"Why would he return?"

"You will say you found something suspicious among your husband's belongings."

Her cheeks heated. She did not want to do any such thing. How shameful to flirt with another man when her husband had only been dead two days.

"We could invite him to dinner."

"I am still mourning. It would be improper." And her grandmother never did anything that was improper —or at least she never let Penelope do anything improper.

"Well, I shall think of something. And you should

be thinking too." Grandmother shook her finger at Penelope. "When the funeral is over, Eustace Hammond will come here and throw you out. You'll have to come home with me, and your cousin Wilfred is the heir to your grandfather's and my fortune. You have no family on your mother's side, which were all French anyway and mostly dead. You will be penniless and alone when your grandfather and I are gone."

Penelope the penniless.

"But I have it in mind for you to marry Eustace Hammond," her grandmother went on, as serious as ever. "Who better to marry than your husband's heir? He is young and unmarried, and you may keep your title as Lady Hampstead. And he has his own estate in Kent. There. Is that not a lovely outcome for you? You are still as pretty as you ever were, so there is no reason you cannot secure him."

Penelope stared down at her book. If only she could jump right into the pages and be someone else in some other world.

She wanted to say, "When I was eighteen, you told me I would never have to worry about anything if I just married Lord Hampstead. And now you're trying to get me to sell myself again to someone I don't know, whose character I don't know. I won't be so foolish again."

Though her grandmother never said it in such explicit terms, she and everyone else, it seemed, believed that wealth was the only thing that mattered when choosing a husband. But Penelope now knew that that was not true.

She had developed a new philosophy on the subject, and that was that there were only two things that truly mattered when choosing a husband. The first was that man's character, and the second was his love for her.

Never again. She would never again marry a man for money and status. A man who was good and kind and loved her, that's who she wanted—if she ever married again.

Her grandmother was right about one thing—she had no family. Horrible enough to have to go live with her grandmother again, with her coldness and rudeness and controlling nature. But when her grandmother died, where would she live? How could she sustain herself?

"If only you'd had an heir." Her grandmother sighed.

If her husband had loved her, perhaps she would have had an heir. But he was elsewhere most nights.

Useless to tell her grandmother that. Penelope had told her already and she had made excuses for him, saying, "That is common these days. Men only take a wife for procreation." Or she would say, "Perhaps you should make yourself more available to him," as if it was her fault that he was staying away from her, forgetting about her, not loving her.

That was the worst thing of all, knowing that her husband hadn't loved her. Had Penelope ever been loved? Even her grandparents didn't love her, not really.

God loved her, according to the Holy Writ, but God had given human beings marriage and families to love them, hadn't He? He'd said, "It is not good for man to be alone."

Well, she was alone, so she had to harden herself. She had to realize that she didn't need anyone to love her. She would love herself. She would find an occupation, something to take care of herself. She'd always been good at painting. Perhaps she could paint portraits or landscapes on commission. Then she could be proud that she hadn't needed a husband to depend on. She was Penelope Whitewood Hammond—no longer the wife of an earl, no longer a titled lady, no longer Lady Hampstead.

She would not allow her grandmother to coerce her into marrying another man she did not know. She'd met Eustace Hammond, and he was not a man who was likely to appeal to her.

As for Mr. Henry Gilchrist, he could hardly be interested in her, a widow with nothing to offer. He was young and handsome and wealthy and no doubt had many marriageable women to choose from. He would hardly look twice at an unloved, penniless widow.

~ ~ ~

"I didn't find anything," Henry told the members of the committee.

"Where did you look?"

"All through his bedroom, through everything."

"Everything? All his furniture? Did you look behind tapestries and paintings on the wall?" another member asked.

"Did you check for loose wallpaper and floor boards?" asked a third.

"Yes, yes. I found nothing."

"The mercenaries stole the contents of his locker at his club but there was nothing of interest there either."

"They are planning to search his house again. Perhaps it's in another room, not his bedroom."

"I don't think that's a good idea." Henry leaned forward. "The widow is still there. Tell them to wait until after the funeral, after she has moved out."

"Why?" The questions began, one on top of the other, as the committee members leaned toward him, almost as one body.

"Why should they wait? They should question the widow before she leaves."

"She's half French on her mother's side."

"Before she finds the plans and sells them herself, to those damnable Frenchies."

"She probably has them. Best search *her* bedroom!"

Henry cleared his throat. "She doesn't seem to know anything of her husband's dealings. I don't want you endangering her." Henry glared into eyes that were staring hard at him, beginning to regard him with suspicious expressions.

"What makes you say that?"

"Huh. What makes you think this piece of baggage doesn't know where he hid those plans?"

"She's turned Gilchrist's head, this pretty widow."

"Hardly." Henry let his most cynical thoughts show on his face. "I am no more trusting than any of you. But I did have a long talk with her. She seemed naïve in the extreme, without suspicion. She and her grandmother let me search Hampstead's room. But I'm telling you, her husband hardly had anything to do with her. She knew nothing. She didn't even know he was in debt."

Why was he defending her so adamantly? He hadn't planned to. Was he so sure of her innocence?

They all stared at him, then the chairman said, "We can't trust her. We have to let the mercenaries do what they want—break into the house again and question the widow."

"The last time those men broke into the house to search it and question its owner, Lord Hampstead ended up murdered, stabbed through the heart." Henry felt his blood begin to boil, heat rising into his forehead. "Hampstead may have been a traitor, but do you want the murder of his innocent young widow on your conscience?"

"Do you not know what will happen if we don't get those plans back?"

"The Frenchies have plans of their own, you know!" one excitable member said, waving his arms. "They will invade England. Kill our wives and children in their beds."

The gentlemen started to talk among themselves, their voices rising.

He leaned back and observed the eight other men in the committee. None of them were particularly good or godly men. Most were unfaithful to their wives. A few had gaming debts like Hampstead's, which, like Hampstead, could possibly make them vulnerable to bribes and offers from French spies. If Henry were in charge, he would have picked a much different set of gentlemen to be on this committee.

Although . . . finding ten morally upright Members of Parliament would not have been easy. Still, he could have picked a better set than these. His friend Viscount Withinghall would have been an excellent choice.

He waited as they continued to shout and argue.

The man in charge, the elderly Lord Ingleburt, cleared his throat and all talking ceased. Then he began to speak.

"Now, as Henry Gilchrist has visited the widow and seems to have her trust, I say we let Henry visit her again tomorrow, ingratiate himself to her even more, and get her to talk to him about where her husband might have kept his valuables, hiding places, maybe even the names of his paramours."

Henry was supposed to ask Lady Hampstead which women her husband was spending his nights with? He cringed. But he would, if it kept her from being questioned—more like attacked—by those unrestrained mercenaries who had killed her husband.

"Yes, give me a chance to get more information out of her." Henry tried to infuse his voice and expression with more eagerness and confidence than he felt. "I'll get more out of her than those mercenaries, who will only frighten her."

Or if she was feisty enough to fight back, they would have no qualms against murdering her.

"You have one day, Gilchrist," Ingleburt said. "Then we are letting the mercenaries have at her."

"One day is not enough. I need more time than that."

"We cannot give you more. We cannot risk the Frenchies getting to her or finding the plans themselves."

"The Frenchies also wouldn't hesitate to kill her, if that's what you're afraid of," another member said. "Unless she's one of them."

Now they all knew that he was concerned for Penelope Hammond's life. But at least Henry had a conscience and a modicum of compassion for a woman who might be innocent. Besides, he was right. The French spies would kill her.

"I will do my best, but if I'm making progress with her, you need to give me more time."

"I can't promise you that." Ingleburt's wrinkled face stared back at him, unflinching.

Henry had to get more information from Penelope Hammond. She was unprotected and in danger, and if he could not get her to cooperate with him in her naïveté, then perhaps he would have to impress on her just how much danger she was in.

CHAPTER FIVE

Penelope was trying to concentrate on her book—it was a novel, so it was much more likely to be successful in holding her attention than a book of essays or sermons. But it was also by the authoress Mrs. Radcliffe, and therefore was rather sensational. Her use of ghosts and fantastical situations had Penelope putting the book down and sighing. She would have liked the story more if it had been more believable.

Penelope was installed, once again, in the room with her husband's body to receive fellow mourners, who so far had been few and far between.

It was still quite early, so she was startled to have the servant announce, "Miss Camille Dupre."

She felt her heart lift at the name of the young woman she had met at a recent ball. The pretty brunette entered the room a moment later with a swish of silk skirts.

"Oh, my poor friend!" Camille said in her French accent. She came and clasped her hands, a look of profound concern on her face. "You must be so heartbroken, shocked, and frightened! Whatever shall you do now?"

"Thank you. You are very kind for coming." Penelope was gratified by her friend's great concern. Certainly no one else had expressed so much concern for her.

"Of course I would come to you in this terrible time! You are my friend." Camille patted her hand and sat very close beside her. "You must have been so frightened! Are you able to sleep at all?"

"I am not sleeping very well."

"Are you afraid those evil men who murdered your husband will come for you? Why did they do it? It is unfathomable."

"I think it had to do with a committee that my husband is on, as a Member of Parliament." *Was* on. She kept forgetting to refer to her husband in the past tense.

"A committee?" Camille leaned back, pressing her palm against her chest. "What committee is that? Could this committee want to murder him?"

That was a question she'd been pondering ever since Henry Gilchrist had left her the day before, and she intended to ask him as soon as she saw him again. Indeed, she'd decided, if he did not visit her again she would go in search of him, or summon him, even though it would only encourage her grandmother's thoughts of him as a marriage prospect. But Penelope had thought of so many things to ask him.

"I don't know. I was not privy to my husband's business, either at Parliament or his gambling, as I'm just learning about his considerable debts."

"Oh, my poor dear." Camille patted Penelope's hand again, making a moue with her mouth. "But, you have no idea what kind of committee it was? How did you find out about this committee?"

Camille was peering at her so intently. The concern and sympathy seemed to have vanished and there was a strange, cold light in her eyes.

Penelope's heart began to beat irregularly, the way it had after Henry Gilchrist left and she started to wonder if she had been too open and honest with him. Why had he been so eager to search her husband's room? He never told her what he was looking for. But obviously, since the murderer was searching his room as well, they were looking for the same thing.

What was it Henry Gilchrist had said? That it was a "rather secret committee" and that it was "pertaining to a possible conflict with France." Camille was originally from France, and she still had a French accent. Could it be unsafe to tell her about it? She looked so eager that it made the hairs on the back of Penelope's neck stand up.

She'd been so naïve in her marriage to David. She'd been naïve to think he would start to love her after they were married and would not be unfaithful to her. And now, was she being even more naïve? She'd let a man who was a virtual stranger search through her husband's things, and her grandmother had not objected solely because that man was rich and unmarried. And now Camille, a woman whose acquaintance she'd made only recently, whom she knew very little about, was questioning her as if she was suspected in the murder.

She needed to choose her words carefully.

"I know nothing of this committee. Someone mentioned it to me, that Lord Hampstead had been on a committee, but . . . it must have been someone who came to mourn him."

"Do you not wonder what kind of committee could have gotten your poor husband murdered? I should wonder, if it were my husband."

"I don't know what good it can do me now." Penelope stared down at her lap. "He's gone and I'm a penniless widow who must go and live with my grandmother in Shropshire."

"Yes, yes, but are you not afraid that the murderers will come back for you?"

"For me? Why would they?" But it was indeed something she had thought about. In fact, she'd spent more time thinking about that last night than sleeping.

"I don't know. But if this committee had him murdered... there must have been a reason."

Penelope didn't have to try too hard to look frightened. "But what could the reason have been? I cannot imagine why they would have murdered my husband, and there seems to be no possible reason to murder me. I knew nothing about David's business dealings, nothing about his work on this committee, nor anything else he did as a Member of Parliament. It is all a mystery to me."

"You poor dear." Camille's concerned look came back, but Penelope was too suspicious now to trust it.

Grandmother came bustling into the room, breathing hard.

"Grandmother, this is Miss Camille Dupre, and this is my grandmother, Mrs. Whitewood."

The two exchanged a brief greeting before Grandmother said, "Lord Hampstead's cousin and heir, Eustace Hammond, is arriving tonight."

Why had her grandmother rushed to tell her this news? Her cheeks were quite pink in her breathless haste.

Grandmother was so uncommunicative as to be almost impolite, and indeed, Camille had also grown much less talkative with her grandmother in the room. But after a few minutes of no one saying very much, Camille turned to address her grandmother.

"Penelope seems to have no idea why anyone would have murdered her husband, but I am quite concerned for my poor friend, staying in the same house where he was killed. I don't suppose you have any ideas about what could have been the murderers' motive? I am so very afraid for Penelope."

"The constable was here. He did not tell us we were in any danger. It was a robbery, and Lord Hampstead interrupted them." Grandmother did her usual looking down her nose at Camille, as she did when she did not care to speak to someone, or when she was displeased.

"Of course. A robbery." Camille eyed Penelope with a raised eyebrow and a wink. "What would you say, madam, to some kind of conspiracy having to do with Lord Hampstead's work on a committee as a Member of Parliament?"

"I would say you have no idea what you are talking about." Grandmother pursed her lips, as she did when she had just been very rude.

Penelope felt her cheeks burn with embarrassment. She gave a slight shake of her head to Camille in apology, but Camille did not seem to notice.

"Perhaps I do not, but most robbers do not risk murdering a man of Lord Hampstead's stature."

Grandmother said nothing.

The servant appeared. "Mr. Henry Gilchrist," he announced.

Penelope's heart fluttered. Was it because of all the questions she had thought to ask him?

Camille jumped out of her seat. "I should be going. It was so good to see you again, Penelope. Send for me if you need anything at all." She pressed a calling card into Penelope's hand as she hurried from the room, nearly bumping into Henry Gilchrist on her way out the door.

Henry Gilchrist turned, watching Camille leave for a moment, before bowing to Penelope and her grandmother.

At least Grandmother would be glad to see Henry

Gilchrist, as she had hopes of him as a suitor for Penelope. But strangely enough, though Grandmother smiled, she did no more than acknowledge him.

Ah, yes. Grandmother must be thinking of David's cousin, Eustace. After all, Eustace would inherit David's town house and his title. He'd be a better husband than Henry Gilchrist, in her grandmother's eyes. After all, to Grandmother and Society, the only things that mattered in a husband were wealth and social standing.

But Grandmother was not foolish enough to offend someone as wealthy as Henry Gilchrist just because she hoped a better suitor would find her granddaughter.

Penelope had her own ulterior motives. Henry Gilchrist had used her to get access and information, and now he was back. Another woman in her position might think that it was because he was interested in her as a marriage prospect, but she was realistic enough to think he probably was after more information from her.

Now it was Penelope's turn to find out what Henry Gilchrist knew.

~ ~ ~

Henry watched Camille Dupre leave the room—rather quickly and nervously, and she was careful not to look him in the eye.

Camille Dupre was suspected of being a French spy. There was no evidence against her, but her name had been mentioned once or twice in the committee meetings as both a spy and as one of Hampstead's paramours.

If Camille were the man's paramour, and if she was a spy . . .

"Mr. Gilchrist. Thank you for calling on us." Penelope Whitewood Hammond smiled at him.

Her smile was different, less naïve and trusting

than the day before. Why did Henry get the impression that she was trying to be charming, as almost every unmarried—and some married—women behaved toward him?

He'd expected the same quiet, shy, unsuspicious and unassuming young woman he'd encountered the day before, who let him have access to search any room without even questioning his motives. And the grandmother, though hostile when she found him searching Lord Hampstead's room, had been quite charming when he left, assuring him he was welcome to visit any time.

Now, the grandmother was less friendly and Miss Penelope Hammond was charming but cautious. And her smile was utterly disarming.

"Was that Miss Camille Dupre?" he asked, remembering the shock of seeing the suspected French spy.

"Do you know her? She is my friend whom I met at a ball a week ago. It was kind of her to come and sit with me for half an hour during such a trying time."

"You must have a lot of friends calling on you now, during this time."

"Not many, I'm afraid. I don't know a lot of people."

"Penelope was tutored at home, where she received the best education, supervised by myself and her grandfather." Mrs. Whitewood looked down her imperious nose, the usual mixture of disdain and arrogance in her expression. It was a common expression among her social set.

"I see." He also knew that Penelope Hammond had few family members. She was very nearly alone. Be that as it may, associating with Camille Dupre was not safe. She needed to pick better friends.

That is, unless she and Camille were in some kind

of alliance.

If Penelope Hammond had discovered the plans, could she be trying to sell them to the French? After all, she was poor now.

"Mr. Gilchrist, please excuse me, as I have some business to attend to." Mrs. Whitewood stood and left the room, leaving him alone with Penelope Hammond.

"I hope you are well, Mrs. Hammond."

"Yes, I am very well. And you?"

"I am well."

"Mr. Gilchrist, I have been wondering a lot about the committee you told me that you and my husband were both members of. And even more, I have been wondering why, exactly, my husband was killed. Furthermore, what were you, specifically, searching for in his room yesterday?"

This was not the trusting Penelope of the day before. Perhaps Camille had told her that if she found the plans, the French would pay her for them.

He did his best to put on his most artless and trusting face and pretend not to suspect anything.

"Those are good questions, and I'm not surprised you are wondering those things."

"I was still in shock yesterday, as I am sure you understand. The murder of my husband was not something I ever would have imagined happening."

"Of course. It must have been a great shock."

She looked as if she was waiting for him to go on. He had to tell her something. He had to either lie . . . or tell the truth. If he told her the committee didn't know exactly why he was killed, that would be a lie.

"The truth is, Mrs. Hammond . . ." He sighed. This would not be easy, if she was honest and did not know anything and was not a traitor to her country. And if she was a traitor, he had to be careful as well not to let her know his suspicions.

"You may tell me the truth, even if it puts my husband in an unfavorable light." She said the words softly, her face and body very still, as if she was bracing for something ugly.

"The truth is, your late husband had stolen some very important and secret plans from the committee, vital to the wellbeing of our country and its soldiers who are bravely fighting to keep our country protected from the French."

Her eyes went a bit wider, and her cheeks a bit paler.

"Some men who are not known for their gentility were hired by our committee to retrieve those plans before your husband could sell them to the French."

"Sell them? To pay his gaming debts?" she whispered.

"Yes. Exactly."

"And he was killed by . . . ?"

"I am sorry to say, by those men we hired tried to make him tell them where he had hidden the plans. In their ruthless efforts . . ."

"They killed him." She sat very still, staring at the floor.

"I am very sorry to be the one to tell you. And you knew none of this?"

"No." She gazed into his eyes. "I was not even aware of his gambling debts. I knew he had a paramour—at least one—but I didn't know of his debts, or his involvement with this committee, or anything about any plans to protect the country." She kept her voice low.

"I am truly sorry."

She was silent for a moment, staring again at the floor, and then said, "As I said, I knew he had at least one paramour. Ours was not a particularly affectionate marriage. My husband ignored me and I rarely saw him or spoke to him."

Her expression was one of sad resignation, but also a hint of pride. She wanted him to know that he should not pity her, that she was not mourning a loving husband or happy marriage. But there was real sadness behind her eyes.

Perhaps what she was mourning was not her husband's death, but the unhappy and unfulfilling marriage to a man who had made her feel unloved.

His heart squeezed painfully in his chest.

Of course, his cynical side immediately warned him that she might only be manipulating his emotions. He needed to keep his guard up and analyze her reactions.

"And you have not found the plans? Is that why you're here?" There was a pragmatic look in her eyes.

"We have not found them, and the men who were looking for the plans—"

"The men the committee hired?"

"Yes. They are wanting to come back here and look some more."

"I will let them in. They can look all they like."

"That could be good, if you are willing. But they also wanted to question you, and I objected to that, since..."

"Since they killed my husband when they questioned him?"

"Well, yes."

"I appreciate your concern. But I would not resist

them or refuse to answer their questions, as my husband must have done. The only problem is that I truly know nothing." She turned her hands palm up in her lap.

"They might ask you if your husband has taken any trips to other homes he owns in the last week."

"He has not, not that I know of."

"Or if he had some other places he might hide things besides this house."

"He goes to his club a lot. He spends more time there than anywhere else, if what he told me was the truth."

"You said he was unfaithful. Do you know any of his paramours?"

She shook her head. "I don't know any names."

"Did you know . . . there is a rumor that the woman who was here, Camille Dupre, is one of his paramours."

Her expression changed and she gasped. "Oh. No, I did not." The blood drained from her face as her lips turned ashen.

His stomach tightened into a knot. Perhaps he shouldn't have told her. But one thing he was certain of—Mrs. Hammond had not known that her friend Camille was her husband's lover. She could not have faked that reaction.

CHAPTER SIX

Penelope felt sick. David and Camille?

How Camille must be laughing at her for being gullible and senseless. When she thought of how much she liked Camille, the two afternoons they'd spent together, talking and shopping, how Penelope had confided in Camille, had even told her how sad she was in her marriage . . . And all the while Camille was laughing at her, triumphing over her, as she was the one getting Penelope's husband's attention, the attention Penelope so desperately craved.

But she had to keep a cool head. Mr. Gilchrist was sitting in front of her, watching her as she felt herself sinking into despair and humiliation.

Penelope cleared her throat and forced her shoulders back and her head up. She refused to bear the shame that belonged only to her husband and Miss Camille Dupre.

"Thank you for telling me that."

"I am so sorry. Perhaps I should not have—"

"No, I'm glad you told me. I needed to know." She cleared her throat again as she imagined how Camille was probably laughing at her at this very moment.

"I just wanted you to be on your guard with her. We suspected that she was a French spy and that Lord Hampstead might be using her to arrange a price for the plans he stole."

"I see." Her husband was using Camille and she was

using him. And if Mr. Gilchrist had not come when he did, Camille probably would have found a way to use Penelope to find the plans.

"The fact that she was here, talking with you, virtually proves that the French don't have the plans either. It seems as if Lord Hampstead was the only person who knew where he hid the plans, and he is gone."

"Yes."

She would let her heart go numb. She would not show emotion. She would become as cold and unfeeling as David had been, as cold and unfeeling as Camille.

No. She did not wish to be like her husband. Or this Camille, who could pretend to be her friend, all the while she was betraying her with Penelope's own husband, not to mention betraying Penelope's country.

Even though she did not wish to be cold and heartless like Camille and David, for now she could pretend. She could hide her feelings so that she could think clearly, be clever, and possibly even save her country's secret plans from falling into enemy hands.

"Tell me what I can do to help you and the committee."

Mr. Gilchrist's blue eyes were kind and gentle as he began telling her how much he appreciated her help and cooperation. She barely heard his words as she remembered him gazing into her eyes this same way at church this past Sunday when she'd stumbled, her eyes dimmed by sadness, and he'd taken her arm and helped her to her seat. How different he was from David, who had ignored and dismissed her.

She felt a strange feeling now as she had then—and she wanted more of that feeling.

She must concentrate on this moment of helping

him find the plans. She had promised herself to be cold and numb to her feelings, had she not? No more gazing into Henry Gilchrist's eyes. He was just a man she knew very little about.

Just like David on the day she married him.

"If you could think of any special hiding places he might have had," Mr. Gilchrist was saying.

"I will try."

"In the meantime, we could try searching the house, with your permission."

"Of course. I'll help."

They stood up just as Grandmother entered the room.

"Where are you going?" Her usual half-angry, no-nonsense tone was in her voice.

"There is something that David hid in the house that the Members of Parliament need, and I'm going to help Mr. Gilchrist look for it."

Grandmother's jaw clenched and her eyes narrowed. "Your husband's cousin will be here this evening and he will not wish his house to be searched."

"That is his misfortune, but I have lived here with David for five years now and I have a right to search where I like." Penelope walked past her grandmother without even looking at her.

She never spoke thusly to her grandmother, and she'd no doubt pay for it later, but it felt good to curb her emotions, including fear, and just do whatever she felt was right. And it was right to search the house for those plans that David stole.

What kind of monster had she been married to? She'd thought he only wronged her, Penelope, and therefore she hadn't been able to completely condemn him.

After all, she'd never been taught that she was worthy of respectful treatment, never was told to stand up for herself or to expect her husband to treat her well.

Now that she knew her husband had not only wronged her, but had wronged his fellow Members of Parliament, and was even betraying his own country, she felt free to eject him from her heart.

She did not even want to think about him anymore.

Penelope and Mr. Gilchrist started in the library where the gentlemen withdrew after dinner parties—of which there had been very few—to smoke, while the ladies went to the drawing room.

They searched through all the furnishings. Mr. Gilchrist even turned over chairs and tables to check for false bottoms where something might be hidden. They searched David's desk very carefully, pulling out the drawers and inspecting them thoroughly. They took the paintings and portraits off the walls and inspected the backs, as well as the wallpaper for cracks where someone might slip in a piece of paper. But they found nothing unusual at all.

"Look here, you must be finished with this by the time the new Lord Hampstead arrives." Grandmother looked worried and angry at the same time, a look that she often wore when Penelope was younger and her grandmother was fretting about who Penelope might marry and speculating about whether or not Penelope was pretty and accomplished enough for each suitor she thought of.

"We will do our best," Mr. Gilchrist said. And when Grandmother wasn't looking, he gave Penelope a wink.

She almost laughed.

"Perhaps we can hide from Eustace and continue

searching." Penelope's back was turned to her grandmother and she met Mr. Gilchrist's eye and smiled. He twisted his mouth, as though trying not to smile.

"No, no, that will not do at all. Mr. Hammond will wish to inspect the house."

"He surely will not inspect the house the very first moment he arrives, with its previous owner not even in the grave yet, his body still in the drawing room."

"We shall see. But I would not be surprised."

They continued searching the library, and Mr. Gilchrist attempted to pull the bookcase away from the wall, but it would not budge. Next, she helped him pull all the books from the shelves, and he even flipped through the pages looking for loose pieces of paper hidden inside.

"I will tell the men that they cannot come and question you without me being there with you. I hope I shall be able to prevent them from behaving too badly."

"That is very kind of you."

David never would have been so kind, at least not to her. What had she done that was so wrong, that had kept him from loving her? What made him look for other women like Camille? Why was Penelope not enough for him?

But she knew where these thoughts would lead her —down a dark, terrible path that she'd gone down before. Besides, it was just possible that David was the one to blame, not her. Obviously he was not a man of strong moral character, and perhaps there was something about illicit relations with ladies of the night, women who accepted money for their favors. Perhaps that was the only kind of woman David felt comfortable giving his affections to.

"If there's anything I can do . . . I want to help."

Henry Gilchrist stopped in the middle of searching through the drawers of a small desk and stared into her eyes. "Thank you. The way you have cooperated and allowed me to search the house is more than we ever expected or hoped."

"Is there anything else I might do?" An idea had been coming to her. "If Camille is a spy, then perhaps I could use my friendship with her to help me find out something."

"Perhaps." Mr. Gilchrist's brows drew together as if he was pondering this. "However, I doubt she would tell you anything very pertinent. And she might get suspicious that you know too much. Probably best to pretend you know nothing of Hampstead's affair with her or her involvement with France. When you see her again, carry on as if you're not suspicious of her. In fact, it might be best to avoid her, as she is involved with some dangerous men."

Penelope certainly had no experience with such things as deception and espionage. He was probably right to advise her thusly. But it bothered her to wonder if Mr. Gilchrist thought her incompetent. Hadn't her grandmother always made her feel incompetent? And her husband as well? What must it be like to be respected and entrusted with a task as Mr. Gilchrist had been?

They continued to search, going through everything in the room.

"What if I invited Camille on an outing, and when it was over, I followed her?"

Mr. Gilchrist suddenly straightened from where he had been looking under a small table.

"Perhaps. That could lead us to the French spies." His eyes were bright and his face had a far-off look. "We could also give the French a false plan. We could write it up ourselves and pass it off to them as the real thing."

"That is an excellent idea. But how would we present it to them?"

"You could say you found it in your husband's things . . . But that would not explain why your husband would want you to give it to a strange woman."

"I know. I could show it to Camille, as my friend, and tell her that I found it but I have no idea what it is. Then she would no doubt come up with a reason to take it from me."

"I think that might work. But you must be sure and give it to her. If you don't, the Frenchmen she works for will come back for it, and they could harm you in the process."

"I am sure I can think of some excuse for giving it to her."

"Very good." His eyes were still bright and a wide smile was spreading over his face as he looked at her. "You are quite good at this business, Mrs. Hammond, if I may say so."

"Why, thank you." She smiled. Was she truly flirting with Mr. Gilchrist, only days after her husband's death? She should feel ashamed, perhaps. But she didn't.

"He's here." Grandmother's voice hissed from the doorway of the room.

"Who?"

"Eustace Hammond!" Her grandmother glared at Penelope for forgetting about Eustace, the man on whom Grandmother, obviously, had pinned her hopes for Penelope to marry well again.

"Tell him I am indisposed, overwrought with grief." Truly, Penelope must have lost her mind, for she nearly laughed out loud after making the false statement.

"I will do no such thing. You will come downstairs at once and greet him. Mr. Gilchrist, I am sorry, but you will have to leave now. And I would be much obliged if you informed Mr. Eustace Hammond that you are an old friend of the departed Lord Hampstead and were only here to pay last respects to him and his widow."

"Grandmother! I don't think he needs to tell a lie."

"Nevertheless . . ." Before either of them could protest, Grandmother simply walked away, hurrying down the hall.

"I am so sorry for my grandmother's impoliteness. She is accustomed to getting her way."

"It is all right. Perhaps we are going about this the wrong way, and the plans are not hidden but in plain sight somewhere. Or perhaps he even sent them through the post to someone from whom your husband meant to retrieve them."

"I can't imagine who." Her husband had had very few living relatives and she knew of no close friends.

"It could be anyone, even someone whom he told not to open the letter." He glanced around the room, which was now in disarray. "Or we could just be overlooking it."

Penelope's stomach twisted at what her grandmother would say to her about the messy room if Eustace were to see it.

She should stop calling him Eustace in her head and start thinking of him as Lord Hampstead, lest she have a slip of the tongue and call him Eustace to his face.

"If you wish to leave me in here for a few moments, I can try to straighten the room a bit." Mr. Gilchrist picked up some books he had left on the floor and put them back on the shelf.

"No, no. Please don't bother."

But he continued picking up the books and putting them back on the shelves, and she joined him. Soon the room was in much better order.

"Let us go and face the new master of the house, shall we?" He smiled and gave her his arm.

Truly, his smile was much too appealing, his eyes warm and friendly, his jawline masculine and covered in short stubble. Her heart actually did a strange double beat as she took his offered arm and they walked downstairs.

Eustace—the new Lord Hampstead—was standing in the drawing room looking down at David in the coffin.

CHAPTER SEVEN

Eustace Hammond and Grandmother stood together, her head leaning toward him.

"He looks very young, does he not? Just as he did the last time I saw him," Grandmother was saying in a hushed, funeral voice. "He has very little gray in his hair."

"Hm, yes, the Hammonds always did age well." Mr. Hammond looked up. "Ah, Lady Hampstead—or Mrs. Hammond, I should say."

Eustace—or Lord Hampstead, she should say—took a step toward Penelope with his hands outstretched.

"You poor dear," he said, squeezing her hands and holding them between his. "I am so sorry you had to endure such a frightening and tragic thing. There, there."

But his face did not seem to match his words. He was smiling and looking past her at Mr. Gilchrist.

"Lord Hampstead," Grandmother said, already calling Eustace the name they had only days before called her grandson-in-law. "Allow me to present Mr. Henry Gilchrist, a Member of Parliament and the late Lord Hampstead's friend and colleague. Mr. Gilchrist, this is the new Earl of Hampstead."

"How do you do?" they each greeted the other.

Thankfully, Eustace did not look at Mr. Gilchrist with any rivalry, and Mr. Gilchrist was the utmost in gentlemanlike politeness.

Eustace Hammond, the new Lord Hampstead, was a large man, tall like David, with a bit more weight in his upper body, his shoulders surprisingly rounded for a man of only thirty years. He was not as polished as one might expect from a titled man of society, but Penelope had heard from her late husband that Eustace's mother was a hypochondriac who kept her only son on a very short tether, fearing all manner of terrible events befalling her precious boy should he venture from home. Penelope had only met him once and that was at his family home, where his mother had refused to leave her room to greet them, saying she was unwell.

Mr. Gilchrist said, "Allow me to express my condolences on the loss of your cousin, Lord Hampstead. Very tragic circumstances."

"Indeed," Eustace agreed, raising his brows. "Most distressing circumstances. A murder. Such a thing is unheard of in our family. My mother did not want me to spend a single night in the house until the murderers were caught. But I told her that I would take every precaution and have the manservants stay up and keep watch all night."

Penelope wanted to tell him, "You will do no such thing. When would they sleep if they stayed up all night?" But she held her tongue. This might be his house now, but she would do what she could to ensure he did not mistreat the servants.

She said, "You might hire a few former soldiers, perhaps, to guard the house."

"That is a very good idea." Eustace tapped his chin, his brows drawing together. "Although I intend to be a stickler for economy. 'Economy,' Mother always says, 'is the mark of a true gentleman, for he will never lose his home if he sets his mind on economy.'"

It was not lost on her that Eustace was essentially criticizing her husband, who was losing his country house due to gaming debts, and right in front of his corpse.

"Economy, the mark of a gentleman. Yes." Mr. Gilchrist widened his eyes.

Penelope nearly laughed out loud at the obvious facetiousness of Mr. Gilchrist's words. She wanted to add, "Then the poorest souls in England must be the most gentlemanly." But again, she held her tongue.

Eustace began talking about his impressions of the house. "It is a good location, very near the park, but the front façade makes it look quite a bit smaller than it is. The house should have had a bolder design. I do like the choice of situating the sitting room where it is, facing the south, with the dining room on the north side so the evening sun cannot heat the air just before one sits down to dine. I do detest being overheated while eating."

Grandmother was nodding in agreement to everything he said, while Mr. Gilchrist had a look of slight shock, just before covering his mouth with his fist and clearing his throat.

"Forgive me, but I must take my leave of you," Mr. Gilchrist said. "It was my pleasure to meet you."

"The pleasure was all mine," Eustace said, smiling and giving Mr. Gilchrist a slight bow.

"I will walk Mr. Gilchrist to the door," Penelope said. After all, they had not said when the interview with the mercenaries would take place, and she could not very well have that conversation in front of Grandmother and Eustace.

"That is not necessary," Grandmother said. "The servant can show him—"

"Lady Hampstead—forgive me, I mean Mrs. Hammond—wanted to point out the place where her late husband always laid his Parliament papers when he came home from his duties there, in case there was something there that needed to be returned to the other Members."

Of course, there was no such place or papers.

"Very good, then," Eustace said, immediately taking up his discussion with Grandmother about the house and what he liked and disliked about it.

Grandmother sent Penelope a sharp look from beneath hawklike brows before giving her full attention to Eustace again.

Penelope and Henry hurried out. Once they were alone in the corridor, he whispered, "I shall return tomorrow night with the men who wish to question you, if you think you can get your grandmother and the new lord out of the house."

"Yes. Grandmother has a friend who has invited us all to dine tomorrow night. I can say I don't feel well and beg to stay home."

"Perfect. We will arrive at ten in the evening."

"That will give my grandmother and Eustace enough time to be gone and your men enough time to question me before they come home."

"Good." They arrived at the door, where Mr. Gilchrist retrieved his walking stick and hat. "Thank you again, Mrs. Hammond. Your help is valued and appreciated."

"You're very welcome, Mr. Gilchrist." Her voice sounded a bit breathless, even to her ears. Would Mr. Gilchrist guess how the handsomeness of his features and the kindness in his eyes stole her breath?

He bent over her hand, gave it a brief kiss, and was gone. And she dwelled far too long on how his lips felt on her skin.

~ ~ ~

Henry was hard-pressed to convince the committee members to allow him to accompany the mercenaries to Mrs. Hammond's home to question her, but they finally, reluctantly, agreed.

Henry met with the men in a back alley not far from Penelope Hammond's home.

They were a rough crew, with markings on their arms and hands from their time at sea or in prison, and bloodshot eyes staring out of weather-beaten faces. They gave Henry sullen looks, some even glaring, as they obviously did not appreciate his interference.

"You may question her, but you are not to touch her, understand?"

One man spat on the ground. No one spoke.

"Do you understand?" he repeated in an even, slow, firm tone.

"We understand." A skinny man with rotten teeth gave a rather sinister smile. He seemed to be the unofficial leader.

"Thank you. Now, we shall proceed. I shall go first, knocking at the back door where the lady will be waiting for us."

Henry led them through the alleyways as far as he could. They followed at a distance once he was on the open streets.

He knocked on the back door, his teeth clenching in anticipation of having to stay tough with the men to keep them from harassing Penelope Hammond in too rough a manner. He had even brought a pistol, hidden inside his coat.

He waited, but there was no answer to his knock.

He knocked again. Finally, a servant came to the door in his nightshirt.

"Is the lady home?" Henry asked.

"The lady is not at home. She's at a dinner party." He closed the door in Henry's face.

That was strange. He was sure they had agreed on tonight.

The men were all behind him, lurking in the shadows of the mews. No doubt they'd be furious he'd wasted their time.

He heard a slight noise from around the front of the house.

"It's the lady," a man said in a rough whisper.

Henry hurried around the side of the house just in time to see Penelope Hammond in the light of the street lamps and two other figures following very closely behind her. One looked like Camille Dupre, and the other was a man.

Henry ran down the alley and peered around the front of the neighboring house.

Mrs. Hammond was climbing into a closed carriage, and the man and woman were helping her inside rather roughly, almost shoving her. They leapt in after her and closed the carriage door. The horses set out at a brisk pace.

"What is this?" the men were asking.

"I believe the lady has been taken."

"Who took her?" a man demanded.

"The French." Henry hurried down the street, his mind on where he'd left his horse. But he'd surely lose the carriage with Mrs. Hammond inside if he had to stop at the livery.

The street was nearly deserted, but when the carriage turned, Henry followed it, running as quietly as he could, trying not to draw attention.

He heard the mercenaries behind him, drawing down curses on his head, Mrs. Hammond's head, and the Frenchies' heads. Most of them seemed to be still following, though growing farther behind every moment.

There were more and more carriages on the street as they went. Many carriages were making their way to and from a certain house up ahead. No doubt there was a fashionable gathering there.

The carriage carrying Mrs. Hammond was forced to stop in the crowded street, and Henry was able to catch his breath, while the mercenaries caught up to him.

"She has betrayed us," one man said between huffs, as he was breathing very hard.

"Why would she do that?" Henry asked. "She wouldn't betray us when she knew we were coming. They've taken her."

He clenched his fists in frustration as heat rose to his forehead. If they harmed her . . . But what if she had betrayed them? What if she found the plans after he left and decided to sell them to the French? He didn't believe she would, but he couldn't pretend it wasn't a possibility.

Whether she was innocent or not, he could not let that carriage out of his sight.

CHAPTER EIGHT

Penelope's heart beat painfully hard. She was scrunched in between two big, burly men, with Camille sitting across from her. What was it she'd said? "I am sorry, Penelope. They made me do it."

Now Camille was looking demure, her lips pouty, as she sat unmoving, and as snug as Penelope was, between two brutish men. No one had spoken since they'd entered the carriage.

As planned, Penelope had been waiting for Henry Gilchrist at the back door a few minutes before ten o'clock. But then someone knocked at the front door.

A servant came and told her that Camille Dupre was asking to see her.

"I cannot see her now," Penelope told the servant. "Tell her to come back tomorrow."

But somehow Camille had gained entrance anyway, as she hurried down the corridor toward Penelope before the servant could go back and tell her.

"Thank you for seeing me," Camille said breathlessly, taking hold of Penelope's arm.

Penelope dismissed the servant, and as soon as she was gone, Camille sank to her knees in front of Penelope.

"Some bad men are forcing me to ask you where your husband's secret papers are. If you will just tell me where they are, they won't harm us."

"Secret papers?" Penelope's stomach sank to her toes. "I don't know where any secret papers are."

Camille's face looked desperate, then sinister. "Lord Hampstead told me himself that he would give you the papers, in case something happened to him. Tell me, Penelope! If you don't, they will kill us." She hissed the last word, and Penelope was put in mind of a snake about to strike.

"I cannot tell you because I don't know. He never gave me any papers. Who are these men? Why would they kill us?"

"You do not know how cruel, how evil they are. They are the ones who killed your husband, and if we don't give them what they want . . . please, just give me the papers."

"I don't have the papers. If you know where they are, go and get them."

"You do know. Your husband told you where they were."

"He never told me anything."

"Penelope, please! I beg you!" Camille's voice was strident, though quiet, and her eyes were wild, almost angry, as she seized Penelope's hands in a hard grip.

"Why do you think he told me where they were?"

"He . . ."

"Did he tell you he told me?"

"Yes, he told me that he would tell you."

"He did not tell me." She wanted to ask Camille why her husband would be telling her, Camille, anything.

She opened her mouth to accuse Camille of being her husband's paramour, when a man suddenly came out of the shadowy corridor toward them, a large man Penelope had never seen before.

"No, please, no." Camille sounded hysterical, but she did not seem surprised to see the man coming, and she was purposely overreacting. Because, even though she seemed hysterical, her voice stayed quiet, as if afraid of alerting the servants.

Penelope was *not* afraid of alerting the servants. But when she reached for the bell pull, the strange man lunged at her, grabbing her arm in one hand, preventing her from pulling the cord, and he grabbed her face in the other, covering her mouth.

"Don't scream," Camille said, no longer hysterical. "It will go better for us if you don't."

She would have screamed if she could, but the man's huge hand prevented her. She could hardly breathe.

The large man had dragged her out of the room, down the stairs to the front vestibule, and whispered in her ear, "Don't make a sound or I'll stab you through the heart." He let go of her face and pulled out a knife, holding it up to her face in front of her eyes. "You will walk to the black carriage. If you try to run or scream, I'll kill you."

He pressed something in the small of her back—it felt more like his fist than the point of his knife—and opened the front door.

"Walk," he commanded.

"I'm walking." Penelope's heart was in her throat, but she somehow managed to stay calm. Perhaps it was Camille's hysterics earlier that made Penelope calm. Whatever the reason, her mind was clear and she was thinking, *Henry Gilchrist is nearby. He will surely see me. He will follow and help me. And in the meantime, I will look for a way of escape.*

She walked calmly and slowly, knowing the man with the knife could easily overpower her and kill her. She just had to bide her time, keep her eyes open, and stay clearheaded.

They forced her into a black, unmarked, closed carriage, practically shoving her inside. That was the moment her face grew hot. How dare these people treat her this way?

Inside were three more men, and Penelope imagined clawing their eyes out. All her life she'd been bullied by her grandmother, then her husband, who alternated between bullying and ignoring her. Now these strangers wanted to bully her? Well, they had not paid for the right.

But what could she do? At the moment, nothing. So she sat unmoving, not making a sound, but she glanced all around, looking for a way of escape.

That was when the carriage suddenly stopped.

Penelope guessed that they were in Mayfair, on a fashionable street where many wealthy people lived and gave lots of parties. She could hear the sound of carriage wheels, horses' hooves, and the voices of men and women. Was this her chance to run?

She looked carefully at the men seated around her to see if they had any weapons in their hands. No doubt they had weapons—guns or knives or both—as the beefy man who'd abducted her had held a knife on her. But even he had put his weapon away: The men's hands were empty.

The only problem was that she was not next to a door. She was seated between two men. If she lunged for the door, they could easily grab her.

Perhaps they would let her go when they realized she knew nothing, that she had no idea where her husband had hidden the secret plans—or secret papers, as they'd called them—and she'd better call them that too or they would think she knew more than she was telling.

But that was naïve. They would not let her go. Why would they? She could identify them to the authorities. No, they would kill her, once they were finished questioning her.

Suddenly, the carriage door was flung open. Henry Gilchrist was standing there.

Her heart leapt with gladness, but just as quickly sank. He would get himself killed!

"Would you be so kind as to help us?" Mr. Gilchrist said in his gentlemanly voice. "My carriage overturned and—"

"No. Get back," the beefy man with the knife said.

"I only need a hand or two. It will only take a moment, while you're waiting on these carriages that are blocking the way."

The big man grunted, then took his time stepping out of the carriage. She noticed the other men in the carriage reached a hand inside their coats, their eyes shifting and their bodies tense.

As soon as the man got out of the carriage, the door closed and Penelope heard some muted grunts, shuffling sounds, and more scuffling.

The other men lunged toward the door.

The door opened and Penelope slipped across the seat toward it. When she did, two hands grabbed her around the waist and hauled her out.

Yells erupted as men swarmed around the carriage.

Henry Gilchrist let go of her waist and took hold of her hand without looking back. "Run."

She ran, letting go of Mr. Gilchrist's hand and holding up her skirts. She ran harder than she'd ever run before.

He took her straight toward the crowd of people

entering a home with their formal evening clothes on. Behind them, yells, then a scream and a gunshot rang out. But she did not look behind them.

Henry Gilchrist weaved in and out of the people, grabbing her hand again when they had to slow down. He went around and behind the carriages waiting to let their occupants disembark. They ran down the street away from all the people. Finally, he slowed and looked over his shoulder.

"I don't think they're following us."

That was when she noticed he was holding a gun in his hand.

"Why?" Penelope was breathing so hard, she could only manage one syllable.

"Why would they not be following us?"

"Yes."

"Because the mercenaries were with me and they will have made sure they didn't follow us."

"Oh." She wanted to ask if they would kill the men with Camille, and what they would do with Camille, but she wouldn't use her breath for that. Besides, it was probably best she didn't know.

"Let's go," she said, thinking of those frightening men. "But where are we going?"

"Someplace safe. Come."

Henry Gilchrist let go of her hand and shoved the gun inside his coat. He turned down a side street, plunging them into the darkness of a narrow alley. Thankfully, no one was around. Or at least, she didn't hear anyone. It was too dark to be certain. She took hold of Mr. Gilchrist's arm, so thankful for its warm strength, the hardness of the muscles under her hand.

They walked to the end of that street, which came

out onto a larger one. Penelope tried to recognize it but it was too dark. Soon he took her down another dark alleyway, then another. Finally, they arrived at the back of a large townhouse. He walked up to the back door and took out a key.

"This is my home," he said as he unlocked the door and led her inside.

He took a moment to light a lamp, then waved her to a chair. It was the first moment she'd felt safe since Camille and the burly stranger came into her house.

Henry Gilchrist pulled a chair up in front of her and sat down, staring intently into her eyes.

"Did they harm you?"

"No, but I think they were French spies."

"They were." He leaned even closer. "Your face looks flushed. Let me get you a glass of wine."

"Thank you." She didn't wonder her face was flushed. She'd never run that fast or that far in her life. Mr. Gilchrist wasn't flushed, but his normally perfect hair —a dark chestnut brown—fell over his forehead and was otherwise a bit mussed. Somehow it made him more handsome than she'd ever seen him.

He poured her a glass of dark liquid and she took a sip.

"Can you tell me what happened?"

The look in his eyes was kind and attentive. Was this how David looked at Camille? Somehow Penelope couldn't imagine David looking at anyone like that.

Penelope took another sip of her wine and told Henry Gilchrist everything that happened, every detail she could remember. He listened without speaking, only nodding or changing his expression a few times.

"Thank goodness you are unharmed," he said. "And

now, I'm afraid we must go back to your home. The men who want to question you will be meeting us back there. Do you think you can bear it, after everything that happened tonight?"

"I think I can." She wanted to be brave, to not make him think she was weak, but her hand trembled, betraying her, as she reached for the glass of wine and took another sip.

"Stay here while I have the coach made ready. You will be safe." He touched her shoulder, as if to reassure her, then walked out, locking the door behind him.

Penelope sipped the wine. A few minutes later, when she heard the scrape of the key in the lock, her heart was beating normally again.

"The carriage is ready." Mr. Gilchrist held out his hand to her and she took it. His hand sent a warm, tingly sensation up her arm, while his eyes conveyed strength and compassion. What would it be like to have a husband like him, so masculine and alive, attentive and kind?

But that was not something she should be dwelling on, now or later.

Soon they were making their way back down the streets of London, sitting across from each other inside his carriage. He took the gun out of his coat and held it in his lap.

"We should be safe now, but just in case."

She could barely see his face in the dark carriage, and she imagined him looking capable and yet at ease.

What would she have done without him, if he had not arrived when he did? Or if she had never heard from him why her husband was killed? Camille showing up tonight with that scary man would have frightened her completely out of her wits. As it was, she was able to stay relatively calm. In fact, she couldn't help feeling a bit proud of herself.

Not that she would ever want to go through that experience again.

The carriage stopped.

"Wait a moment." Mr. Gilchrist opened the carriage door and got out.

She waited, listening, but heard nothing. Her heart beat hard against her chest. Could the French spies have killed all of Henry Gilchrist's men? She thought she'd seen a lot more men with him than the four with Camille. *Please, God, let them not be dead.*

Finally, the carriage door opened and Henry Gilchrist got inside and the carriage moved on.

"What happened to Camille and those men?"

"The mercenaries killed one of the spies, but the rest got away in their carriage, including Camille Dupre."

Soon after, the carriage stopped again. Henry Gilchrist got out first, then he helped her down.

Her house was across the street. As they crossed toward her front door, Mr. Gilchrist kept his arm around her, walking very close, as though shielding her from view. They went right up to the front door and he opened it, ushering her inside. The door was not locked.

The dark shadows along the vestibule moved. They were not alone.

"Gilchrist?" a voice said.

"Here, with Mrs. Hammond. Let's go into the drawing room."

For some reason, she shuddered at the thought of being near David's body. She'd been near it for days, hadn't she? But she also didn't want the servants to hear or know what was happening, and the drawing room was closest.

Mr. Gilchrist lit a lamp and one of the men, who seemed to appear out of nowhere, struck a match and lit some candles. Soon, she was sitting down and they were all staring at her.

CHAPTER NINE

There were seven of them, all rough-looking and dressed like laborers.

A tall, thin one with leathery skin took a step toward her.

"First . . ." Mr. Gilchrist held up his hand and stepped between the man and Penelope. "You can ask what you like but you are not to harm her or even touch her."

"You made that clear yesterday." The thin man frowned and crossed his arms over his chest.

"Very well. Proceed."

"Show us the contents of your pockets." The man suddenly leaned down, shoving his face so close to hers that she could smell his body odor.

"I don't have any pockets." Raw fear snaked through her veins. Would these foul men put their hands on her? They could easily overpower Henry Gilchrist, as he was only one man.

"You were going somewhere with those Frenchies. Where were you going? To get the plans your husband stole?"

"No. I don't know where we were going, and I don't know where the plans are." Her heart trembled in her chest at the man's threatening manner.

"Step back," Mr. Gilchrist said, putting his hand out, thrusting it between the man and Penelope. "There's no need to crowd her."

The man slowly took a step back. Penelope felt as if the air cleared and she could breathe better. She might have thanked Mr. Gilchrist, but the atmosphere in the room was so tense, she didn't dare.

"What is your name, madam?"

"My name?"

"You heard me."

"My name is Penelope Whitewood Hammond, widow of the late Lord Hampstead."

"And how do you know Camille Dupre?"

"I met her at a ball three weeks ago. She endeared herself to me, and we have gone on two shopping excursions since. She also came to my home after my husband's murder to sit with me. The only other time I've seen her was tonight when she came and must have let in the man who forced me, at the point of his knife, to get into the carriage with three other men."

"And what did she and the men say to you?"

Penelope went through the whole story again, remembering a few little details that she had forgotten when she told the story to Henry Gilchrist. She told them everything.

"Now tell us what you know about your husband's dealings, his work with the secret Parliament committee, the secret plans that he stole, and his relationship with Camille Dupre."

"I didn't know anything about Lord Hampstead's affairs with Parliamentary committees or with Camille Dupre, and I certainly never knew he stole any secret plans. He never told me any of that. He never told me much of anything. What I know I learned from Mr. Gilchrist."

"You did not know your husband spent time alone

with Camille Dupre on the nights of . . ." He pulled a small piece of paper from his pocket. ". . . the tenth of March, the twenty-first of March, the twenty-fourth of March, the first of April, the fourth of April, and the seventh of April?"

With every date the man read, Penelope's heart sank more, her face burning hotter, every date another example of her husband's indifference, his betrayal and rejection of her. There could be no greater proof of his having no love for her.

"I did not know." Her voice sounded pathetic to her own ears.

"Where did you think your husband was?"

Henry Gilchrist shifted his feet, staring intently at Penelope, as he looked uncomfortable with this line of questioning.

Penelope swallowed, fighting back tears, as the pain of her husband's infidelity, and indeed, the last conversation that passed between them, stabbed her like a knife in her chest. How could he have treated her so, when she had done nothing but try to love him, when she had pinned all her hopes on him, when she'd wanted nothing from him except his love?

How humiliating, to have to fight back these tears, to look so vulnerable in front of these rough men and Mr. Gilchrist. But try as she might, she could not drive them away, and they were staring at her harder and harder the longer it took to answer the question. Better to answer and get on to the next question, even if the tears fell and her voice cracked.

"I thought he was—" The pain was so fresh! As if the betrayal had happened today, she had to force in a breath to keep going. When she did, a tear dripped from each eye. "At his club."

"You thought he was at his club?"

"Yes." Her chin trembled uncontrollably, so she pressed her hand against her mouth to stop it.

The pain was like a knife. She wished she could sink through the floor, but the pain was stronger than the embarrassment. The salt drops continued to fall.

"Give her a moment." Mr. Gilchrist was pressing a handkerchief into her hand. "Give her some room to breathe." He waved the rough men back, and they reluctantly took a step or two away from her.

Penelope gratefully pressed the lavender-smelling cloth to her eyes, praying the tears would dry up. But thinking about Mr. Gilchrist's compassion somehow made it more difficult. Why was he so kind to her, when everyone else in her life had not been? Her grandmother, her grandfather, her husband, no one had loved her. Even now she was so alone. Perhaps that was why Mr. Gilchrist's kindness meant so much.

She took deep breaths, trying to distract her thoughts away from anything that might make her cry. She had to think of something else, of her horse, the dress she would wear tomorrow, the rector's sermon last Sunday.

Soon, she had her thoughts under control and the tears had dried.

"Forgive me. You may continue." She held her head up, trying to pretend complete serenity.

"Mrs. Hammond, are you saying that you knew nothing of your husband's paramours?"

"I had heard rumors that he had paramours, but I had no idea that Camille Dupre was one of them until Mr. Gilchrist told me, nor did I know any of the others."

"And you expect us to believe you knew nothing of his work on this secret committee? That he was in a committee?"

"I knew nothing of it."

"How did you think he was to pay his gambling debts?"

"I did not know he had gambling debts."

"Mrs. Hammond, how is that possible?" The thin man, with his beady eyes and lined face, looked as if he might laugh. "How could you know nothing of your husband's affairs?"

"Because my husband did not share any of his affairs with me."

"Were you not curious about your husband's activities?"

She could feel the tears welling up again, the pain stabbing her. *O God, if only I'd never married him, never been so miserable and so unloved.*

"I was curious. He hardly spoke to me." Her voice cracked and another tear leaked out of the corner of her eye.

"That's enough of that kind of question." Mr. Gilchrist glared fiercely at the thin man, his voice gruff. "Ask something else or be done."

"Keep your shirt on," the thin man said dryly. "I'm just getting to the earl's hiding places. Did he have hiding places, madam?"

"I never knew of any hiding places. I always assumed he kept anything he truly valued at his club. I believe he had a locked strongbox there."

"There was nothing of value in the locker. We've already looked."

"Mr. Gilchrist and I looked here in the house. And I

believe the men who murdered him—" She suddenly remembered that these were the men, these men standing in front of her, who had murdered her husband when they came into his room and tried to question him. He had not cooperated and they had murdered him.

Which one of them had stabbed David in the chest?

She shuddered, a chill running across her shoulders and down her back.

"Go on, madam." The thin man leaned toward her.

"The men who murdered him also looked in the house for these secret plans you are seeking."

"Strange, isn't it?" the thin man said, leaning his head to one side. "No one can find them. But you were his wife. And you said yourself that Camille Dupre thinks you have them, that your husband said he gave them to you."

"He didn't, as I already told you. I don't know why she said that. It isn't true."

"Tell me, Mrs. Hammond. Were you meeting with the French spies tonight to sell them the papers?"

"No. I did not meet with them. They seized me in my own home. I did not go with them voluntarily, and I have nothing I can sell them."

"That is just what you would say if you did intend to sell them to the French. Tell me about your French people, your French mother and her family."

"My mother was French but she came to England to marry my father and never returned. She died when I was five years old. My father died a year later. They both had consumption. I've never met any of my French relatives, as my mother herself was an orphan. I am English and I have no loyalty to France."

"But you would sell the plans to the French, would you not? You have no money now. Someone else inherited your late husband's estate."

"All I can tell you is the truth. I am no traitor to England. I am loyal to my God and to my country and my king. I have no love for France, and even if I knew where the secret plans were, I would not sell them to France."

"She's a good and loyal citizen, she is," one of the rough men in the back said. He flashed her a smile of missing and blackened teeth. But it was a sardonic smile, as if he was laughing at her.

"She doesn't know anything," Mr. Gilchrist said, leaning closer to the thin man. "But if you want to have a look around, you'd better do it before the new owner gets back from his dinner party."

"Very well. I can see we aren't getting anything from the lady. Lads," he said, turning toward the men who were standing behind him. "Go see what you can find. Look everywhere you haven't looked before. Perhaps he left it in plain sight and not in his private rooms."

"Please try not to wake the servants," Penelope asked. "I shall be hard-pressed as to how to explain the mess as it is."

But they went about their search as if she had not spoken.

Penelope followed the men around, putting things back where they belonged when the men laid them aside or otherwise rearranged things in their search. Mr. Gilchrist helped, but there were more of the mercenaries making a mess and only two of them to clean it up. After two hours of this, Penelope was exhausted.

"The new Earl of Hampstead and my grandmother will be returning very soon, so I think you should go." Penelope said this to the thin man as he ransacked the sideboard in the dining room.

"Very well, very well." The thin man actually went and herded the rest of the men up, and soon they were gone.

"I am sorry this has been a very difficult night for you," Mr. Gilchrist said. "But I will send a couple of men to watch your house tonight, until daylight. I hope that will help you feel safer."

How could she ever feel safe again? In her own home, the only home she'd known for the past five years, her husband had been murdered in the room next to hers, and she had been taken by a man with a knife. How could she ever feel safe here? But she didn't wish Mr. Gilchrist to know she was afraid.

"Thank you, Mr. Gilchrist. You have been very kind."

As she remembered how he'd rescued her from those men in the carriage, she wanted to say more. Indeed, she wished she could throw herself into Mr. Gilchrist's arms. But that would not be proper at all, and she would never embarrass herself by throwing herself at a man who likely had no thoughts about her except as a widow embroiled in a strange intrigue that was all of her late husband's making.

"I shall be watching out for you every way that I can. And if you do find the plans, send word to me at once."

"I will." She had to say more. Her feelings were like a weight, pressing against her chest. She followed him to the door.

"I am so grateful to you, Mr. Gilchrist, for the service you rendered me in the street, when you pulled me from that carriage."

"Of course. I'm glad I was able to be of service." He

stopped and stared into her eyes. "Remember, there will be men watching over your home tonight. You likely will not see them, but they are there."

"Thank you."

"Good night, Mrs. Hammond."

"Good night, Mr. Gilchrist."

As soon as he left, she started up the stairs, staring hard at the shadows around her. Would someone jump out at her?

She kept remembering the man who had held a knife on her, threatening her, kept seeing Camille and imagining her with David. What kind of woman could have trysts with a man and then befriend his wife?

How could Penelope have been so fooled in the woman? She'd thought her a good friend—a bit flighty, but loyal.

How wrong she had been! So very wrong. And how wrong she'd been to think that she could make her husband love her. She had not, could not. These were the same old thoughts, chasing themselves through her mind.

Just as Penelope had readied herself for bed, she heard noises below. Was it just the sound of the carriage bringing Grandmother and Eustace home, the sounds of them coming in and walking up the stairs?

If it's more murderers coming to kill me, let them come. I'm too tired to fight tonight.

She lay in her bed, pulling the covers up to her chin, as the tears seeped from her eyes.

"Penelope." Her grandmother's voice came from the other side of the door as she knocked and walked inside.

"Did you have a good time?" Penelope asked.

Grandmother began telling her all about the house and the food and the people who were at the dinner. "You should have been there, Penelope. There was an eligible man there, a widower, whose wife died of a fever two weeks ago. I would not have wanted you to flirt with him in front of Eustace Hammond." She said this last sentence in a hushed voice. "But it would have been good if you could have made his acquaintance, in case things do not progress to matrimony with Lord Hampstead."

Penelope didn't bother to tell her that she was tired and wanted to go to sleep. She just let her talk.

"Penelope, why aren't you saying anything? Don't you care about your future? You should have come with us."

"Forgive me." She didn't have the energy to argue or say anything more. She knew that her grandmother didn't care that she had begged off because she was sick. She hadn't even asked if she was well.

"Go to sleep now. There will be other dinners and other balls, I daresay. And you are so young and pretty. I have high hopes for you." Grandmother, with a burst of high spirits uncharacteristic of her, smiled and closed the door behind her.

Penelope was alone now. So very alone. She had prayed every night of her life, for as long as she could remember, but they were mostly rote prayers. Sometimes she did talk to God the way she would talk to a friend, probably because she was so alone every day. She often talked about David, and she had begged God, every night in her prayers, to make her husband love her.

God would never answer "Yes" to that prayer, not now.

But she had prayed that same prayer for so long,

she wasn't sure what to pray for now.

"God," she whispered, "I'm alone and afraid. Please help me." She remembered how kind Mr. Gilchrist had been, and how capable he was when he saved her from her kidnappers.

"God, did you send Henry Gilchrist to watch over me?" She wasn't sure if that was the sort of thing God did, as she didn't think He had ever sent her anyone before. She'd had very few friends, few relatives, and her grandmother had verbally cut her to the heart too many times to even be able to thank God for her. But she could thank God for Mr. Gilchrist.

"God, thank you that he came when he did, that he was able to get us both out of the street without coming to harm, and that he has sent men to watch over me and my grandmother tonight."

But was Mr. Gilchrist kind to her because he was a good person? Certainly, he had ulterior motives, other objectives that were influencing his behavior toward her. But as long as he was kind to her, she would be thankful for him.

"And please help me find those plans before anyone else gets to them."

CHAPTER TEN

The next day, Henry walked the relatively short way to Penelope Hammond's home.

He was no closer to finding the missing plans than he'd been before. And though he would like to believe that the kidnapping from the night before was proof that Mrs. Hammond was not a traitor and was not in league with the French, it actually did not. After all, he had not seen the knife that Penelope Hammond said was used to force her to go with Camille and the men who had taken her in their carriage. For all he knew, she might have gone with them willingly, then gone with Henry willingly in order to not draw suspicion.

At least, that is what the other men in the committee would say, and indeed, it was what the mercenary men were saying.

Henry approached the home of Penelope Hammond, who would soon be going back to the country when her husband's funeral was over. And the funeral was tomorrow.

He was admitted to the drawing room where Penelope Hammond and her grandmother and Eustace Hammond received him. They talked about the usual things people talked of—the weather, the state of the roads, and when Parliament was sitting. They began talking of the speed of the post, when Lord Hampstead suddenly said, "Oh!"

"What is it?" Mrs. Whitewood said.

"Speaking of the post made me remember something. I received a small parcel from my cousin, David." He looked at Henry and added, as if to explain, "The late Lord Hampstead."

"Yes?"

"He must have sent it a day or two before he was ... well, before he passed on to the next life." He looked uncomfortable, glancing at Penelope Hammond as if afraid she might dissolve in hysterics.

"Yes?" Penelope Hammond looked at him, confusion and interest mingling in her expression.

"It was addressed to me, with a note that said, 'Please give this to my wife Penelope, Lady Hampstead.' And inside was a sealed letter."

"A letter?" Penelope Hammond leaned toward him.

Could this letter actually be the plans? If it was, then that might explain why Hampstead told Camille that he was giving, or had given, the plans to his wife.

"I shall go and get it now, if you don't mind excusing me and waiting." He raised his brows at Penelope Hammond and then at Henry and Mrs. Whitewood.

"By all means," Penelope's grandmother was saying.

"Yes, please go," Penelope Hammond said.

Henry nodded to him.

"I shall return shortly." He stood but only took one step toward the door. "It was so singular, as you might imagine, to get a note from David, but then have it contain something for his wife. Why would he send a letter to Lady Hampstead ... to me? After all, he was here in London with his wife, and I was in Kent and ... It was all very strange, very strange indeed."

Everyone stared at him, obviously wishing he

would just go and get it, as he was the only one in the room who knew nothing of the secret plans David had stolen.

Finally, he said, "I shall retrieve the parcel for you." He turned and left the room at a brisk walk.

Henry's eye met Penelope Hammond's.

Mrs. Whitewood talked of the origins of her family's ancestral home, as well as her husband's country estate. She asked about Henry's family's estate and its origins. She never addressed him directly like this when Eustace Hammond was in the room. It was obvious that if Eustace did not marry her granddaughter, she'd be happy to accept Henry as the next best choice.

Were all mothers and grandmothers the same? Forever seeking the richest man for their female progeny? Perhaps it showed love and concern, but as cynical as Henry was, he suspected it was prestige and social standing they really cared about. And for themselves, not their offspring.

How would Henry ever marry, when he had such an adverse attitude? And yet, he didn't want to be the proverbial bachelor either, never marrying, always bumbling about, avoiding marriageable daughters and their mothers, finally succumbing when he was old, too doddering and simple to make a wise choice.

Truly, he was cynical enough to imagine his ridiculous prediction coming true.

Eustace Hammond finally came back into the room holding a folded and sealed letter. He held it out to Penelope Hammond.

"Thank you."

Before she could say more, he said, "I'm sure you will want to open it later, in private, given the circum--"

"I shall open it now."

Hampstead looked shocked but Penelope didn't seem to notice. She broke the wax seal and unfolded the paper.

Henry could already see it wasn't the plans. The paper was a different size and texture.

Penelope's face looked slightly confused as she stared at it. Then she began to read.

"My dear wife, please know that if anything should happen to me, you should inform my cousin Eustace Hammond that I want you to have the tall longcase clock in the dining room. I believe it is baroque, from the late 17th century. You told me once that you admired it. Consider it my gift to you."

She folded the letter again and laid it in her lap.

Henry wanted to ask if that was all it said, but such was probably improper, especially since she suddenly looked a bit pale.

"I don't know why you wanted to read the letter in front of everyone," her grandmother said, brushing invisible crumbs from her skirt.

"I do remember that clock. It is in excellent condition." Eustace was staring at the floor, half mumbling to himself. Then he looked up. "Of course, if my cousin wishes you to have it, I am not one to argue, though some might. I believe the clock has been in the house since before he or I were born. But it is yours, if you want it, Mrs. Hammond."

He looked as if he hoped she wouldn't want it.

Penelope Hammond took a breath and said, "Thank you."

Such a strange letter. It must mean something.

"I would like some tea," she said, and rang the

bell. Just then, a servant introduced two men, supposed friends of the late Lord Hampstead. Henry rejoiced, for it was the perfect distraction to give him a private moment to speak to the lady alone.

Now he would see if she tried to avoid him.

~ ~ ~

Penelope felt a bit lightheaded after reading her dead husband's last letter to her. Perhaps some tea would make her feel better.

Penelope only faintly recognized the two male visitors as men she'd seen her husband talking to at a ball. They appeared to have an acquaintance with Eustace as well, and blessedly, they soon were talking amongst themselves and ignoring her. Henry Gilchrist moved closer to her.

"Was that all the letter said?"

"You may read it for yourself." She stood and walked to her husband's casket. While their backs were toward the other guests, she discreetly handed him the letter.

Henry looked it over quickly. She'd read the entire contents of the letter, all except the closing, which was a brief *"Yours, David."*

"Had you ever mentioned that you admired the clock?"

"I had, once. I'm surprised he even remembered that."

"And there was nothing else significant about the clock?"

"Not that I know of. I don't even know where it came from. David never seemed to care about such things as family heirlooms or furnishings."

"The tea is here," Grandmother announced.

Penelope knew that was her cue to stop whispering to Mr. Gilchrist before Eustace noticed her paying him particular attention. But Eustace did not seem to have much interest in Penelope as a wife, and Grandmother was grasping for something that could never be, for Penelope had no interest in Eustace. He was too much like David, in the fact that he cared nothing for her and did not see her as anything special.

Though she might lose her picky attitude after a few months with her grandmother in Shropshire, she had higher hopes than to settle for a man who saw her as nothing special.

Still, as bad as her grandmother treated her sometimes, Penelope was learning not to take her opinions to heart or let them cut as deeply. She'd also learned not to covet her grandmother's good opinion. It was too impossible to obtain.

Being married to David had been worse, in many ways, than her grandmother's harshness. He'd ignored her, which was like a slow death. She would get her hopes up on the rare occasions that he didn't ignore her. But then he'd say something cruel. Or he'd give her a few crumbs of kindness, then disappear for days with no word of where he was or when he'd be back. When he came home, she would question him, and he'd tell her she was supposed to assume he was at his club when he wasn't at home.

Now she knew. Many of those nights he'd been with Camille Dupre.

Never again. Never again would she wait for a husband who refused to care about her. Either she wouldn't marry, or she would find a love match, someone who truly loved her. Anything less was a life worse than death.

Henry Gilchrist handed the letter back to her. She clutched it tightly, the last bit of attention her husband would ever give her. But he wasn't her husband now, and she could admit, at least to herself, that she was starting to feel glad of that fact.

She'd met women who didn't seem to mind when their husbands weren't attentive to them. In fact, they made little comments about being glad their husband went to his club, so that they could have the freedom to do as they pleased. But Penelope suspected that their husbands never neglected them the way David had neglected her.

And now to have this letter to bring back all the mystery of why David treated her the way he did. Why did he care if she had the clock? Why not let Eustace have it? It was of little consequence to her now that her husband was dead and she was having to remove all of her personal things from the house.

She noticed Mr. Gilchrist looked as if he wanted to say something to her. But Grandmother was staring at them with a severe look.

They all sat and Grandmother poured the tea. Penelope was feeling better already, even before she drank the first sip of her tea or ate the first bite of scone with lemon curd. She was fairly certain she could live off the way Mr. Gilchrist looked at her.

She kept her eyes demurely lowered, at least until Grandmother wasn't looking.

"You never were any good at flirting," her grandmother had said with disgust years before after she'd tried to push Penelope onto a rich young gentleman at a ball. Besides her flirting, she'd also criticized Penelope's dancing, her embroidery, and how inattentive she was in her studies.

It was no wonder Penelope never enjoyed any of those things. She'd always believed she was bad at them.

Painting was the one area where even Penelope's grandmother complimented her talent and skill, the one area where she excelled.

Another thing her grandmother criticized her for was reading, including her choice of novels over other more intellectual reading. Though her grandmother called her lazy, Penelope still refused to give up reading. She read voraciously, daily, though strangely enough, since David was killed, she had not been able to read more than half a page in a sitting, her mind wandered so.

When the other men had finished their tea and stood up to leave, Henry Gilchrist seemed reluctant to join them. But it would seem strange for him to stay, so he took his leave of them, saying he would be attending the funeral the following day.

Penelope's heart sank. What would tomorrow bring? She would not be allowed to attend the funeral services. Indeed, it wasn't even safe for her to do so, since funerals took place at night and the processions were often set upon by thieves. But she'd be at home, thinking about them lowering her husband's body into the ground, no doubt feeling fresh pain. Or would she even feel anything?

One thing was certain. Right or wrong, she was looking forward to seeing Mr. Gilchrist again.

CHAPTER ELEVEN

The next day was gray and overcast, and Penelope watched as Eustace Hammond left to join the funeral procession, riding in the blacked-out carriage with its all black horses with their elaborate ostrich feather headdresses. He'd be riding just behind the vehicle carrying the coffin. Penelope had not wanted to stand in front of the house and watch the coffin being loaded into the vehicle, but Grandmother insisted.

When will I be an adult and stop letting her force me to do things I don't want to do?

It was her question to God. She tried to imagine how He would answer her. Would He tell her she was already an adult and just needed to stop letting her grandmother rule her life? Or would He tell her she had to endure trials for a season? Somehow she imagined Him telling her to stand up to her grandmother. After all, God said to honor her father and mother, not to do every little thing her grandmother told her to do. And God said that each person would answer for their own actions in the last day, and therefore, Penelope needed to live her own life and make her own decisions.

When that was over, she sat in her room and imagined the funeral procession driving in the night, in the rain, all the way to the church with the paid mourners, bearers, pages, and others. Then after the funeral would be the committal service, when they would actually bury the body.

Her heart felt heavy, like a dress that had gotten soaked in a rainstorm. But at least she would no longer be ignored by a husband who spent the night with other women and told her to go take a lover. Now she would be free from that false kind of marriage, a situation as joyless as death.

Was it wrong to think like that? She was sad, but more because she didn't want to be alone, and she was frightened because she hadn't been able to find the secret plans her husband had stolen. Her husband's actions had put her very life in danger.

She imagined the church, with its peaceful churchyard shaded by large trees.

Eustace returned before she expected him. Grandmother was still up, so Penelope joined them downstairs as Eustace sipped a glass of sherry.

Few mourners attended the funeral, it seemed, from what he told them. The rector actually seemed to cut the service short, probably because it was raining, which caused Grandmother to express her displeasure.

Henry Gilchrist had been there. He and anyone else there with any sensibilities at all probably felt sorry for her. Henry Gilchrist probably felt the sorriest, after that mercenary read the dates of the nights her husband had spent in the company of Camille Dupre. Everyone pitied the wife of a philanderer. But they seldom respected her. And probably never would want to marry her. Would everyone eventually discover that her husband was a traitor to his country, as well as an insatiable gambler who lost most of his family fortune?

Even though he hadn't been much of a husband, she would feel embarrassed when the truth came out.

These were the thoughts going through her mind

as Eustace described her husband's funeral. Surely she was a terrible wife at this moment, but was she not justified, after all her husband had put her through? She'd never have treated anyone that way.

~ ~ ~

The next day, Henry Gilchrist came to call, along with several other people who came to offer condolences.

While Grandmother and Eustace were talking with a few old men who'd known David's father, Henry Gilchrist moved closer to her.

"I'm sure yesterday must have been a trying day for you."

"I'm well." She thought of saying, in jest, "It was not as bad as the night I was taken from my home at knifepoint," but she refrained, lest someone should hear her.

"Do you know of a day when I might come to speak with you when you will be alone?"

"Oh. I could send you word when I know when Grandmother and Eust—Lord Hampstead will be calling on people."

Normally, when a man asked to speak with a woman alone, he was hinting that he wanted to ask for her hand in marriage. Her fast heartbeat stole her breath.

"I think there could be something inside the clock."

"Oh." The clock? Her thoughts were jumbled and she wasn't sure what he meant.

But of course. The strange letter that David had sent to Eustace, in which he told her that she should get the six foot tall longcase clock. He must have suspected that he might be killed, and he must have hidden the plans inside the clock. But why would he tell her? Very strange.

She should have known Henry Gilchrist was not

asking for privacy so that he could make a declaration and ask her to marry him. Foolish, foolish girl. Wasn't that what Grandmother had called her many times? "You foolish girl." She'd always said it as if it was the worst insult in the world, with a contemptuous twist of her mouth, the worst thing a person could be.

I am not foolish, Penelope argued back. *I was responding to what Mr. Gilchrist said, to his attentions, and to my own hopes. And why should I not hope? I am only twenty-three.*

Grandmother called for her attention. "This gentleman knew your husband when he was just a boy."

Suddenly feeling quite weary, Penelope said nothing. Why should she care? Her husband was dead, and he never cared for her when he was alive.

Yes. That was the whole truth in its barest and most appropriate form.

She pretended to listen as the man regaled them with a story of David when he was a child, unwilling to ride on his father's horse with him, telling his father, "It's too high. You might let me fall."

The men all laughed. But Penelope saw nothing funny in it. Thankfully, Henry Gilchrist did not laugh. He only gazed back at her with those warm eyes, his perfect mouth frowning slightly in sympathy.

Was he really as perfect as he seemed? Perhaps he was only kind to her because she might be able to help him find the missing plans.

But already Eustace had been hinting about Penelope taking her things and leaving.

"And since my cousin insisted upon you having the baroque clock in the dining room," Eustace said with a rather unhappy look, "then you must take it as well.

Though I do not understand why he would have insisted on your taking it. I rather think he would have known it belonged with the house. But no matter. I am not petty enough to deny him his last request."

Penelope could not have cared less about the clock. She was on the brink of telling him so when their visitors announced their intention of leaving.

She was desperate to get away from Grandmother and Eustace. Her grandmother was much nicer to her when Eustace was in their company, but the fakeness in her voice, the pretense in everything she said to Eustace, grated on Penelope's nerves.

As soon as Mr. Gilchrist left, she closed herself in her room, took off her dress without asking for the servant's help, climbed into bed, and covered herself up to her chin.

How good it was to be alone in her bed with no one talking, no one clucking their tongue at her, no one remarking how young she was to be a widow, or how tragic her husband's death was, how sad, how she would see him again in heaven. For the love of all that was holy, she just wanted to be alone long enough to clear her head.

She would have to pack her things and be gone, the sooner the better. She'd brought precious little with her into the marriage—only her basic necessities, clothing and such—so she had very little to pack. Still, it was a chore that must be done. She did not wish to trespass upon Eustace's kindness, for she saw him as being rather lacking in that sentiment.

And yet, there was a heaviness in the thought of leaving London. She did have a few acquaintances, though she had no close friends. But if she was honest with herself, the real heaviness came in having to leave

Henry Gilchrist.

The words, "Foolish girl," popped into her head again before she could stop them.

Truly, she should be more prudent. After all, she had known the man so short a time. And it seemed rather disreputable for a woman to have so many thoughts about another man when her husband was hardly in the grave.

Forgive me, God.

And yet, her newfound sense of standing up for herself, to her thoughts if not yet to her grandmother, made her retort, *Was I even married? I may as well not have been, as little attention as my husband paid me.* She'd hardly felt married. And he was dead now. Today had proved it. His body was gone, he was dead, and the frightening thing was that her grandmother would have her remarried to someone—anyone with wealth, status, and a title—as quickly as she could make it happen.

O God, please don't let her marry me off to another man who doesn't love me.

But there again, God might say to her, *All you have to do is refuse. You are an adult. You must use your own will to make your own choices.*

It was true. She was not only a woman grown, she was a widow. But a widow completely dependent on her grandmother. She had no way to support herself, having no fortune at all. All she really owned was a clock.

The clock. Perhaps she should go downstairs and look through it. But she was so weary from the funeral, for she had cried, though she hardly knew why, all through the service. And then she'd had to stand about and receive the comments and conversation of every person who had attended the funeral. It had been so tedious, especially since it was so damp and she had gotten her feet wet before she even entered the church.

She had also not yet discovered if Grandmother and Eustace planned to go calling the next day, though she believed they would. Grandmother loved to return a call, and she would probably insist Eustace call on every person who had been at the funeral, and then she would offer to accompany him. But surely the widow of the deceased would not be expected to go with them. Penelope could feign a headache, or just sorrow, and beg off.

Should she send word to Henry Gilchrist that she would be alone the next day during calling hours? How would she do so without her grandmother discovering she was sending private notes to an unmarried gentleman?

Actually, now that she thought about it, her grandmother probably wouldn't care in the slightest. She'd think Penelope was taking initiative to get a husband and be glad, especially since Eustace still showed no interest in her.

Before Eustace had left for the funeral the previous day, her grandmother had cornered her in her room.

"Why do you offer Eustace no encouragement at all? He might show some interest in you if you did. But no, you give him no attention, no flirtations. You give more of your attention to Henry Gilchrist, so it is no wonder Eustace does not show any interest."

Penelope couldn't argue with her. She only said, "I am not very good at flirting." Hadn't her grandmother told her that more than once?

Eustace was the sort of petty character who would never realize he was being petty. He had been little in society and was not adept at conversation. And yet, she imagined he would marry for love, and he'd at least go home every night and treat his wife with general kindness and respect.

But she was glad he showed no interest in her.

Perhaps this would be the cause of her remaining alone and unhappy. She wanted something more. Perhaps there was nothing more. The man who seemed to be more—brave, handsome, willing to face down danger to rescue her from ruffians, of sterling character and kindness—did not exist, and she should settle for a Eustace, who, while not brave or handsome or willing to face down danger to protect her, might at least love her and give her a peaceful home.

No, Eustace still did not appeal.

The servant came in to help Penelope dress for dinner. Part of her wished to stay in her room and hide, but part of her just wanted to see a friendly face, hear a friendly voice.

Too bad she wouldn't get that at dinner.

But to avoid a scolding from her grandmother, she dressed and went down.

"You are not feeling the effects of this weather, are you?" Eustace asked, as soon as they sat down to dinner.

"I am not feeling any effects from the weather," she answered. "Thank you for asking. That is very kind. You are not feeling the effects of damp weather, are you, Mr. Hammond?"

His eyes seemed to fasten on her face in a way they never had before. He leaned toward her from where he was seated on the other side of the table from her.

"Thank you for asking. I did imagine I felt a bit of a tickle in my throat, but it seems to be gone now. But I do fear for you, Mrs. Hammond, as a lady can get quite chilled in such weather. Or so my mother always says."

"You are very kind. I suppose we must guard our health."

"Poor Mrs. Hammond." Eustace looked quite concerned. What had changed? It was as if he was noticing her for the first time. "My mother has a tonic that she takes at night if she has gotten her feet wet at any time during the day. I shall send you some."

"That is very kind."

Grandmother's eyes fairly glowed. "We thank you, Mr. Hammond. That is very good of you to share your mother's tonic with my poor Penelope. She is all alone now and must mind such things as her health. You are very kind, and I'm sure your mother's tonic will do her a world of good."

Penelope wanted to laugh. Most ladies' tonics were just laudanum and perhaps a bit of licorice or feverfew. She'd never liked taking them. But it pleased both Grandmother and Eustace to fancy that they were helping her.

Eustace was much more attentive for the rest of the evening. Penelope knew to discourage him would only enrage her grandmother, so she continued to speak pleasantly to him. He was rather obsessed with his own health and spoke at length of remedies he used for various ailments. Penelope had only to nod and make very brief comments to keep him talking. It was a welcome distraction from her morbid thoughts, and it kept her from having to say very much.

When dinner was over, Penelope excused herself to go to her room. She thought of making an excuse such as a headache, but she was too afraid Eustace would insist on another tonic, or remedy, and she just wanted to go to sleep.

"I shall send the tonic to your room, right away." Eustace hurried away, too excited to offer to walk her to her room, apparently.

Penelope passed the longcase clock on her way. She should search it for the plans. Were they inside the clock at this very moment? The urge to look inside was almost irresistible, but she didn't want to draw the attention from Grandmother or Eustace, so she went up to bed. Perhaps later, when everyone was asleep, she would come back down and search the clock.

Eustace did indeed send her the tonic. But the servant had been instructed to give her one dose and bring the bottle back to him. Penelope almost laughed. Was he afraid she would take too much of his mother's precious tonic?

When the servant turned her back, Penelope poured some of the dose back in the bottle, only taking about half a spoonful.

"Please tell Mr. Hammond thank you very much for the tonic."

The servant nodded and left, and Penelope gratefully crawled under the covers and sank into her soft bed. Would she be able to sleep, after the heaviness of her husband's funeral? No matter. She'd go downstairs later and search the clock.

Soon her eyelids grew quite heavy, her head feeling strange. How fortunate that she hadn't taken the full dose of the tonic, for it was already having its effect. At least, hopefully, she would sleep.

CHAPTER TWELVE

The sun was quite high when Penelope awakened the next morning. The servants would be up and about, so she couldn't depend upon searching the clock without being seen.

Ridiculous tonic! Why had she taken it? Why was she always doing what pleased others? Why did she base all her decisions on what other people told her, what they wanted instead of what she wanted? She'd married David because that was what her grandmother wanted. She'd spoken pleasantly to Eustace Hammond and agreed to take his mother's tonic even though that was not what she wanted.

But she couldn't imagine changing. How could she? Grandmother would scold her like she was an unruly child, would accuse her of being obstinate and who knew what else, and Penelope would avoid that at almost any cost.

Why did she care so much? All she knew was that her grandmother's disapproval seemed to prove what Penelope already feared, and that her marriage had reinforced—that she was unlovable.

Grandmother came into her room without knocking.

"Get up. We shall call on as many of the people who came to Lord Hampstead's funeral as we can get to today." She strode to Penelope's wardrobe. "And you must wear this dress, for it—"

"I can't go out today." She felt it to her toes. Traipse about London visiting people who were virtual strangers to her, just because they had come to her husband's funeral. The very thought was a dark cloud of dread.

"What?" Grandmother pretended she had not heard her. It was a tactic of hers when someone said something she didn't like.

"I'm not feeling well. I cannot go calling with you today."

"Penelope, you will. Eustace Hammond showed quite a bit of interest in you last night, and you must not let him forget what it was he saw in you. You must go calling with him. It is your opportunity to impress him. Now get up. Once you're moving about, you will feel better, I daresay."

"I cannot." She covered her face with her hands. "I'm not well. Believe me, Eustace Hammond will not like to see me today." She let the tears overflow that were just below the surface.

She crossed her arms over her chest. "This will not do. You will ruin everything. Come, now. Stop crying and get dressed."

"I cannot." She let herself cry. Her tears were real, but she was being a coward. If she was brave she would tell her grandmother in straightforward language that she felt sad and had no wish to make conversation with Eustace Hammond nor anyone else.

"Well, that foolish crying will not impress anyone. We cannot let Mr. Hammond see you blubbering like a baby. Very well. I shall tell him that due to yesterday's event, it is too soon for you to be seen in public. We shall delay calling on people for a day or two."

"Cannot you and Eustace go without me?"

Grandmother tapped her fingernails on the door of Penelope's wardrobe. "Perhaps it will make his heart grow fonder to be speaking of you and having others speak with such compassion of you, of the poor young widow who is now all alone. Yes, I see no reason not to go calling without you. Very well. I shall tell Lord Hampstead."

Grandmother hurried away and Penelope rejoiced at her escape.

From her window she watched the carriage carry her grandmother and Eustace down the street. They were gone.

She dressed and went downstairs, heading to the dining room. The clock was where it always was, but she'd never looked as closely at it as she did now. How did one go about looking inside one of these? Then she noticed a little knob for opening the front of the case, but when she pulled it, it didn't budge. Then she noticed a keyhole.

It would have been helpful if David had sent her the key.

She hurried back upstairs, going into David's room and rummaging around in his drawers, but she didn't find a key that looked small enough to fit the clock case. So she grabbed a letter opener on his desk. It was quite sharp. Perhaps she could use it to pry open the clock.

She hurried back down the stairs. But as she neared the bottom, a man stepped out of the shadows and pointed a gun at her.

Penelope's heart stopped. Was it one of the mercenaries who had questioned her two nights ago? No, he looked like one of the men in the carriage when Camille and her cohorts had kidnapped her. He was big and burly, with a prominent pink scar down the middle of his left cheek.

It was happening again!

If she ran back up the stairs, the man would just chase after her, and that seemed more terrifying. None of the male servants would risk their lives for her, and some were too old to be of much help.

Then she realized she still had the letter opener in her hand. She could use it as a weapon, but had the man seen it? She kept it hidden in the folds of her skirt, her hand down by her side.

She turned to look behind her. Another man was coming down toward her. He too had a gun in his hand.

"What do you want?" she asked. She would keep her wits about her and concentrate on trying to escape.

The two men just leered at her, each coming closer, closing her in.

"How did you get in here?"

"Shut up and come quietly," the man with the scar said.

"The servants will see you and get help."

"That's why you're coming with us." The man at the bottom of the steps pointed his gun, holding it up to his eye as if he was aiming for her head. "If you make any loud noise, you're dead. Understand?"

"Yes." She didn't have to pretend to be frightened; she was. But she would stay calm so she could think how to get away. As long as the guns were pointed at her, she had to cooperate.

They walked at a normal pace to the front door, down the two steps to the street, then climbed into a waiting carriage.

Penelope managed to keep the letter opener hidden, holding it against her thigh.

Inside the carriage was another large man, but

there were only three men total and Camille was not there.

The carriage traveled at a brisk pace down the street.

"Where are you taking me?" she asked. "What do you want?"

"We want the plans," the man with the scar said. "And if you don't give them to us, we will torture you until you tell us where they are, or until we're convinced you don't know." The man gave her a gloating grin.

Terror made her throat constrict. What would they do to her? If they tortured her, would she end up telling them she thought the plans were in the clock? And what if they weren't there? They'd probably kill her.

Penelope had never had a broken bone, never suffered more than a scraped knee when she was a child, or when her horse threw her, she'd had the breath knocked out of her. How would she handle torture, if they cut her or hit her?

"Why don't you tell us where the plans are and save us all the trouble of torturing you?" The man leaned toward her.

She had to tell them. There was no other way out. And perhaps the servants had seen them and would get help. Or perhaps Mr. Gilchrist's men, whom he had sent to watch over her house, would be nearby and come to her aid. It was better than letting them take her somewhere no one could find her.

"I don't know where the plans are." She looked the man in the eye. "But I do know where they might be."

"Keep talking."

"Apparently my husband sent a letter to his heir saying that he wanted me to have the longcase clock in the dining room. It seemed strange, so I think he may have hidden the plans in the clock."

"Tell the driver to go back."

One of the men beat on the roof of the carriage, then yelled for the driver to turn around.

Penelope almost told him that the case was locked and she didn't have the key. Instead, she bit her lip.

When the carriage stopped, the scarred man ordered, "You stay here with her." Pointing at the other man, he said, "You come with me."

The two men got out of the carriage and closed her inside with the third, who sat across from her and kept his hand on the gun in his lap, his eyes on her.

Penelope tried to think how she could get away. Could she take the gun away from him? Could she stab him with the letter opener before he could pull the trigger? Then, when he was shocked and in pain, she could snatch the gun away and run.

That would probably not work. After all, he could easily shoot her before she could stab him.

I just don't want to be pathetic, God. Let me be brave, willing to do what I have to. And please don't let those men find the papers inside the clock.

She had to escape and alert Henry Gilchrist. Otherwise, she'd look like a traitor. And she would not be squeamish about stabbing her kidnapper, if the opportunity presented itself.

If he happened to get distracted and look away, she would do it. After all, he would not think twice about killing her. And many lives could depend upon her being brave.

They had not been sitting there long when she heard a thump, then another thud, like something heavy falling to the ground.

The man across from her glared at her. "Did you hear that?"

"What?"

Suddenly, the carriage jolted forward, knocking her captor forward. He cried out, then opened the carriage door to look out. When he did, Penelope clenched her teeth and stabbed him, sinking the letter opener in the back of his shoulder, and pushed him with all her might. He fell out of the open door, yelling in a high-pitched voice.

A man on horseback came alongside the carriage and bent down, peering in at her.

"Stop the carriage!" he cried. The man on horseback was Henry Gilchrist.

The carriage gradually came to a stop. Mr. Gilchrist dismounted from his horse and lifted her out.

"Did you . . . ?"

"I stabbed him with my letter opener." Penelope took hold of Mr. Gilchrist's arm, as her knees were so weak she feared she might fall. "How did you . . . ?"

"My men and I saw what was happening. I sent most of them inside the house to apprehend those thieves, but one got away. Then we dispatched the driver and took off with the carriage, not knowing how many men were inside. We were planning to take the carriage someplace where we could safely rescue you, but it seems you were ahead of us."

"I wanted to be brave."

"You were. Very brave." There was a smile on his face she didn't think she'd ever seen before.

She swallowed and pressed a shaky hand to her forehead.

"Are you well?"

"Yes."

The driver of the carriage jumped down and started toward them.

"Thank you for your help," Penelope said.

The man glared back at her and said nothing.

"She stabbed him in the back. Look." Henry Gilchrist pointed down the street, where they could see the large man she'd stabbed lumbering off in the opposite direction, her letter opener still in his back.

The driver glanced at her and grunted. "I still say she's in with the French."

Penelope's mouth dropped open. How could he think that?

"Why would she stab her own man?" Henry Gilchrist asked the man.

The driver grumbled something under his breath. "Do ya want me to take the carriage back to the house?"

Mr. Gilchrist nodded. "We'll take the man we captured to prison in it."

The man gave Penelope one more keen look and climbed back in the driver's seat.

Mr. Gilchrist said, "Wait here a moment," then he went to speak to the driver.

Penelope took deep breaths, as she remembered the terrifying moments that had just taken place—realizing she was being kidnapped again, and then forcing herself to stab that man as he was leaning out the window.

"Come." Mr. Gilchrist was motioning her back over to the carriage. "I'll tie my horse on and we'll ride back in the carriage."

Mr. Gilchrist handed her inside and was soon climbing in and seating himself across from her.

"Thank you for saving me," she said.

"It looks as if you saved yourself."

She did, didn't she? Air rushed into her chest and she felt buoyed by Mr. Gilchrist's smile and admiring tone. Perhaps she was not just a foolish girl whose only worth was in marrying well.

"You did help, and I am thankful." Her hands had stopped shaking and she allowed herself a smile—a flirtatious one, perhaps—at the handsome Mr. Gilchrist.

Her life was changed, and she was changing too, becoming brave and able to face any situation. *Please, God, let it be so.*

CHAPTER THIRTEEN

Henry gazed back at the pretty young widow. Thank God she had managed to stab her captor. That would go a long way in convincing the rest of the committee and the mercenaries that she was not in league with the French.

He would have to guard his heart even more now.

He needed to focus on the task at hand rather than thinking about how pretty she was and start guarding his heart.

"Mrs. Hammond, do you remember me telling you of my idea to write fake plans and try to pass them off as the real ones?"

"I do."

"I think now is the time to put that plan into action. The French will not stop trying to obtain the plans. So it is better to let them think they have them, but to give them false ones."

"That sounds like a good idea."

"But it has obviously become too dangerous for you here. We believe there is a servant in your household who has been letting the French spies into your house."

"Oh." Mrs. Hammond's brows drew together. "I can hardly imagine. But that would make sense."

"That is another thing that made everyone suspicious of you. The Frenchmen were getting into your house far too easily. But we discovered one of your menservants letting them in today."

"Oh my." A traitor among her servants!

"My proposal is this. You will tell your grandmother and Lord Hampstead that you are going to stay with a friend in Hertfordshire. That friend will be my sister. I shall take you to my family estate where you will be safe."

He watched her reaction to this. Her face was so expressive, it was often easy to see what she was thinking and feeling, but although he couldn't quite decipher her thoughts, she at least didn't look horrified.

"Meanwhile, I shall write up some fake plans and leave them where the French spies can find them. Once they have the fake plans, we shall apprehend your traitorous servant and, hopefully, be rid of the French spies, and the real plans will be safe."

"Very well." Was she truly so trusting of him? She simply sat with her hands demurely folded in her lap.

"Good. I shall write to my sister that you are coming. And now . . ." The carriage had come to a stop. He glanced out at her house. All looked quiet. "We shall go inside and retrieve a few of your things. As soon as your grandmother comes home, you can inform her where you're going and—"

"She will not like it at all." Penelope Hammond grimaced, then chewed on the inside of her lip.

"You cannot fret about that. My family is an upstanding one, so she shouldn't have any sincere worries about propriety or your safety."

She nodded slowly, then her eyes suddenly went wide. "Shouldn't we search the clock for the plans?"

"Did you not . . . ?"

"I was just about to. The case was locked and I went to find the key, and when I couldn't find it, I picked up a letter opener. That's why I had it in my hand, to try to pick the lock, when the French spies came and kidnapped me again."

"Then let us do that forthwith." He jumped down and helped Mrs. Hammond out before hurrying into the house.

"I do hope the neighbors are not watching our house," Mrs. Hammond whispered. "They must be seeing quite an unusual lot of coming and going."

"Let us hope they are not gossips."

Just inside, they were met with the mercenaries, who were just tying up the French spy they had caught, his mouth gagged with a cloth.

"Take him out, quickly, to the carriage before Lord Hampstead returns."

The men seemed to enjoy their work, grinning as they hauled the man rather roughly to his feet.

"You know where to take him." Henry nodded to them, and they were soon gone.

Henry pulled out his small pocket knife as Mrs. Hammond led him to the dining room.

The old longcase clock was nearly six feet tall, almost as tall as he was. He pulled it away from the wall and opened the door on the back of the clock face. He held a candle to it, looking around inside, but there was no sign of any paper.

Next, they felt all around the clock for secret openings and false backs and bottoms. When they found nothing, Henry set to work with his knife to pick the lock on the front of the longcase clock.

He felt around inside the lock with his knife point. "I think I will need another tool. Do you have another letter opener? Or, better yet, an ice pick?"

"I shall try to find it." She hurried away and soon returned with the ice pick.

He used both tools in the opening simultaneously, wiggling and poking inside for so long, a bead of sweat tickled his temple. He wiped his forehead with the back of his hand, suddenly wondering if anyone would mind if he smashed the clock to get inside.

Finally, he heard the telltale click and the lock opened.

He opened the front of the clock's case. Mrs. Hammond handed him the candleholder and he held the flickering light inside the case.

"There, at the bottom," Mrs. Hammond said.

He saw it too. He reached in, lifting out a folded piece of paper. He knew before unfolding it that it was the plans her husband had stolen.

At last, after everything, they had recovered them.

~ ~ ~

Penelope wanted to cheer when she saw the paper, then the look on Mr. Gilchrist's face. They'd found them!

Henry Gilchrist quickly closed the clock's casing and stood up, shoving the plans into his inside coat pocket.

"We can't let anyone know we found the plans," he whispered.

"Why not?" Her heart sank. She'd thought this whole ordeal was over. They could turn them in and she'd never have to worry about her country being betrayed by her dead husband, never have to wonder if she was about to be kidnapped again, never have to stab a man with a letter opener again.

"We need to write up some fake plans and plant them somewhere the French can find them. That will prevent them from continuing to try to steal the real ones."

"Yes, of course." They'd talked about this. She nodded.

She had to be brave, to do her duty to her country, and to not be as pathetic as she had always been in the past.

The mercenaries' faces said the words without speaking them. They wanted to know what had happened and if he'd found the plans.

They all went into the sitting room, put their heads together, and she heard Henry Gilchrist whisper to them, "We can't let anyone know . . . have to keep this quiet."

She couldn't make out the rest of his words, so she said a silent prayer that his plan would work.

The men began to leave, and Henry Gilchrist came to her and said in a low voice, "We'll go upstairs and pack a few things for you. Take enough clothing and necessities for a fortnight. Come."

They did just that. Penelope first sent her maidservant away, telling her she did not need her help, then stuffed as many of her gowns and necessities into a small trunk as she could get. Lastly, Henry Gilchrist sat down to write out some fake plans meant to mislead the French, and she sat down and wrote to her grandmother.

Grandmother,

Forgive me for this short note, but I'm going to be staying with Jane Gilchrist for a fortnight in Hertfordshire. You may send my things home to Shropshire or leave them and I will get them when I return.

Your granddaughter,
Penelope

"We need to get out of here before your grandmother comes back," Mr. Gilchrist said, motioning with his hand.

Penelope was quite eager to do that very thing, for she didn't want to have to face her grandmother's questions. Who was this Jane Gilchrist? How did Penelope know her? Why was she leaving in such haste?

No, she wanted to make good her escape.

Penelope took her note and was on her way out of her room when she suddenly thought of something.

"Wait." She stopped and turned back to Mr. Gilchrist.

"What is it?"

"Will the French spies come after my grandmother? Will they try to make her tell them where the plans are, when they discover that I'm no longer here?"

"We'll make sure they find the fake plans first before that can happen. Don't worry."

He seemed confident, so she went on her way and left the note on her grandmother's dressing table. She just had to make certain to instruct the upstairs servant to tell her grandmother where to find the note.

When she arrived back in the study, Henry Gilchrist was just folding up the fake plans.

"You wrote those very quickly," she said.

"I only hope they believe they're real," he mumbled, hurrying to take her elbow.

"Go down to the carriage," he whispered so close to her that she felt his breath on her ear. "I'll join you in a moment."

She hurried outside, but not before looking over her shoulder and seeing a glimpse of him slipping into the dining room.

Henry Gilchrist's coachman handed her into the carriage. She didn't have to wait long before Mr. Gilchrist joined her inside, and they were off. Traveling together. Alone. All the way to Hertfordshire.

Seated across from her, Henry Gilchrist let out a long, slow breath.

"If nothing goes wrong, you shouldn't have to worry about these plans ever again."

"Well, that would be lovely." She smiled back at him. Truly, she might not miss getting kidnapped and the terror of strange men in her house who wouldn't mind killing her to get something they thought she had. But she would miss her interactions with Henry Gilchrist when they inevitably came to an end.

"What will you do with the plans?"

"I'm taking them this very moment to the committee chairman. He lives not far from here. Then I shall send a trusted man to go with you to Hertfordshire. But don't worry. I'll send a note by express to my sister and she will be expecting you. She's a good girl, very lively. You will like her."

Penelope did her best not to let her disappointment show on her face. But her stomach sank as she absorbed the fact that he wasn't traveling with her.

The carriage stopped in front of a very large house and Henry Gilchrist got out. "I'll only be a moment." He closed the door and she watched through the window as he went inside.

At least she would be away from her grandmother for two weeks. Hopefully she'd at least have some peace and quiet there at the Gilchrist family estate.

And perhaps she might finally have a real friend in Jane Gilchrist, Henry's sister.

CHAPTER FOURTEEN

"Lord Ingleburt will see you now."

Henry went inside the ornately decorated home and was shown into the library, a room where the walls were entirely covered in bookshelves of dark wood. And standing in the middle of the room was the chairman of their secret Parliamentary committee, Lord Ingleburt, a portly man in his early fifties.

"Gilchrist. Good to see you. Won't you have a drink?"

"No, thank you. I'm in rather a hurry. I—"

"Don't mind if I have one, then."

"Of course. I—"

"I wasn't expecting you to show up here," he said while pouring himself a drink from a glass decanter. "We always discuss matters in front of the entire committee. Did you need my help with something?"

"Yes, sir, in a manner of speaking. I—"

"You found the plans?" His eyes widened and a smile spread over his face.

"Yes, sir, I did."

"That half French Lady Hampstead had them all along, did she?"

"They were hidden . . . Let me explain. Are you certain no one can hear us in here?" Henry moved closer to Lord Ingleburt.

"No, no," he said in a hoarse whisper, taking a sip of his drink. "You may speak freely, but quietly, just in case."

Lord Ingleburt leaned closer to Henry.

"My plan was to have the mercenary, Travis," Henry said quietly, "mention to the traitorous manservant, Reed, that Lord Hampstead had hidden the plans in the longcase clock in the dining room, and they were just waiting for Mrs. Hammond to come home and unlock the clock case. Meanwhile, I wrote up some fake plans—I shall tell you what they said later—and left them inside the clock case."

Lord Ingleburt, who had been sipping his drink while Henry talked, suddenly started to cough and gag, pulling at his collar.

"Sir?"

Lord Ingleburt dropped his glass and it shattered on the floor. He grabbed for Henry's arm, still gagging and coughing. Henry tried to hold him up, but he pitched forward. Henry was only able to slow his fall.

Lord Ingleburt lay on the floor, unmoving.

Henry sank to his knees beside his fellow Member of Parliament. By all appearances, the man was dead.

Henry went to the decanter he'd seen Lord Ingleburt pour his drink from and sniffed it. It definitely didn't smell like brandy.

Had someone poisoned the man's brandy?

Henry hurried from the room and stopped the first servant he saw. "Lord Ingleburt has collapsed. Send for a physician, quickly."

The servant, a young woman, looked frightened and hurried away.

Henry went from room to room until he found another servant. "Take me to your butler."

"Yes, sir." The maidservant took him downstairs to the kitchen, then stopped in the doorway. "Mr. Dawes, this gentleman asked me to take him—"

"What is this?" Mr. Dawes looked none too pleased.

Henry brushed past the servant and strode to Mr. Dawes. "May we speak in private?"

Mr. Dawes, still looking annoyed, led Henry to a tiny office and closed the door.

"Sir, I am Henry Gilchrist, a Member of Parliament, and I believe your employer, Lord Ingleburt, has been poisoned."

Mr. Dawes's brows drew together and he leaned away from Henry ever so slightly, his only visible reaction.

"If you could question your staff and tell me every single person, from staff to household to visitors, who has entered this house in the last twenty-four hours . . . Your help is a matter of national importance. You must keep these matters quiet, and you must send me a list of these names, along with anything suspicious you have observed or learned."

Henry grabbed a pen from the desk that was in the room and began to write on a sheet of paper lying there. "I need you to send this list to me at this location, and do not speak of anything I have just told you with anyone except these men."

Henry wrote the direction to his country estate and the names of the four men from the committee whom he most trusted.

"Remember, the wellbeing of our country could depend on your discretion."

"Yes, Mr. Gilchrist. You may depend upon me."

"Good man. Now, I must go. Best not to mention that I was here, if you can avoid it."

"Go out the back door, if you prefer."

Mr. Dawes led Henry out the back way. Henry thanked him and hurried around the back side of the house to his carriage, which was unmarked and a relatively plain and common-looking vehicle. Inside he was thankful to see Mrs. Penelope Hammond sitting calmly, her hands lying placidly in her lap. But as soon as she saw his face, her mouth fell open.

"What is the matter?" she asked, as the carriage lurched forward.

Was she able to read his expression so well?

"I believe Lord Ingleburt, the committee chairman and the man I came to give the plans to, was murdered."

"Murdered?" Her eyes went wide and she covered her mouth with her hand.

"It's even more urgent now that I get you—and these plans—out of London."

The driver opened the tiny window between them. "Someone is following us," he said.

"Lose them."

Henry's blood quickened in his veins. He motioned to Penelope Hammond. "Forgive me, but there's something under your seat that I need."

She leapt up and moved to the seat opposite.

Henry lifted the seat and pulled out his gun. He checked to make sure it was loaded before moving aside the curtain that hung over the tiny window in the back of the carriage.

Penelope Hammond saw it all without fainting or screaming, much to her credit. The only evidence of alarm was a tenseness in her shoulders and the way she was sitting.

"Forgive me, but if I have to shoot, you'll need to get down on the floor. I am very sorry."

"Don't be sorry. Do what you need to do."

Her cheeks were pale but her voice was quite calm. He wasn't sure he'd ever admired a woman more.

The carriage was moving faster and the man on horseback kept pace. But as long as they were in London, he could do nothing.

Henry carefully moved the gun to the crook of his arm. "For now, you may move back to your place so you're riding facing forward. I can't shoot until we're out of town."

"I am well where I am. Is the man following us a French spy?"

"I believe so."

God, help me keep Mrs. Hammond and the plans safe.

~ ~ ~

Penelope stayed calm, more because there was nothing she could do to help their situation. If she'd been the one in charge of protecting them, she would have been more terrified.

Henry Gilchrist, however, looked as cool and confident as if he was on his way to a ball at the assembly rooms in London. Every so often he checked behind them, looking through the back window.

"Is he still there?" Penelope would ask.

"Still there."

"Could it be possible that he's a friend, just trying to catch up to you?"

"No, I recognize him as one of the spies. Besides, he could catch up to this carriage if he wished."

Penelope sat with her hands clasped in her lap and prayed while the carriage swayed and jolted underneath them.

Another murder. It brought back all the feelings of

the night she'd found David's lifeless body on the floor. Would she ever feel safe again? It seemed so unreal, like a dream, and yet he was gone, and she could never forget the image of the knife sticking out of his chest.

How could anyone be so cruel as to take another person's life?

She was not opposed to Henry Gilchrist defending them from the man pursuing them. Certainly those spies would kill Mr. Gilchrist, the coachman, and her to get the plans. If Henry killed the man following them it would be different, because it was self-defense.

Her heart beat harder against her chest as they started to leave London and all its people behind, trees going by her window now instead of buildings.

Mr. Gilchrist was still watching out the tiny window in the back.

"Is he still there?"

"Yes."

Penelope redoubled her praying efforts, silently but with her eyes open.

"He's coming," Mr. Gilchrist said. "Get down."

Penelope fell to her knees on the floor of the carriage while Mr. Gilchrist checked his gun, then moved to the door. He positioned himself to look through the larger window in the door. He stuck his head out, then pulled it back in.

A loud crack came from behind them.

Penelope wanted to ask if that was a gunshot, but she didn't want to distract Mr. Gilchrist.

He stuck the long barrel of the gun out of the window and fired. The sound was deafening.

Penelope covered her ears with her hands, watching Henry Gilchrist from where she knelt on the floor of the carriage. *God, please don't let anything happen to Mr. Gilchrist.*

Another shot rang out behind them at the same time the back window shattered and pelted her with glass. Henry Gilchrist was taking out another long-barreled gun from beneath the carriage seat.

"Are you all right?" Mr. Gilchrist asked.

"I am well." She brushed some pieces of glass from her hair, but she was not injured.

Could the bullets go through the carriage and hit them?

"He probably only had two pistols on him, and he can't reload while riding."

"How many guns do you have?"

"Two." Mr. Gilchrist took aim out the window again and shot. "Got him."

Mr. Gilchrist moved to look out the shattered back window. Penelope got up off the floor and joined him. A riderless horse was slowing down and stopping at the edge of the road.

"Where did he go?"

"He fell off his horse. I must have hit him."

"Thank goodness we're safe." She let out a breath, pressing her hand over her heart.

"There may be more coming after us. We can't let our guard down."

"Coming after us?"

"They must suspect we have the plans. That's why he tried to kill us. We just have to hope that he hasn't heard from the other spies that they found the plans—the plans I planted in the clock."

They both sat across from each other where they'd started the trip, only this time he had a gun laid across his lap and his hair was mussed from leaning out the window to shoot at their pursuer.

"What should we do?"

"We needed to get out of London. We'll be safer at my home in Hertfordshire. Meanwhile, the French will find the plans I left for them in your clock, and if we're fortunate, they'll think they're the real plans. The committee's men in London may be able to apprehend the rest of them. But if we're not fortunate . . . the spies may realize, after a time, that the plans are fake and come looking for us."

He sat staring at the carriage door, not moving, his brows slightly lowered.

"Is something wrong?" she asked. "You look worried."

"All will be well, I'm sure." He kept one hand on the gun. "I will need to make sure we have enough men to defend my home. I wouldn't want anything to happen to my mother or sister either. But all will be well." He raised his head and shoulders a fraction higher. "We will be able to defend ourselves very well out in the country."

But Penelope wasn't sure if he was only making light of the danger in an attempt to reassure her.

The driver suddenly turned and spoke through the little window between them.

"Well done, sir," he said. "Shall I slow down to save the horses?"

"Yes, thank you, Burke."

The carriage slowed, which helped her not to feel so jolted and bounced around.

"Thank you for saving us."

He smiled. "I'm glad I was able to. And I'm sorry you had to experience yet another shock."

"I am well. Who else should suffer besides the wife of the traitor who stole the plans to begin all this trouble?" She smiled to show she was in jest, but it wasn't a very good joke.

"None of this is your fault, so you must not blame yourself. A woman is not responsible for what her husband does."

She nodded. Intellectually, she knew he was right, but the shame of her husband's behavior lingered inside her like a black cloud. Why had she ever married him? It was foolish in the extreme.

"So what is our plan now?" she asked.

"We'll continue on to Hertfordshire. I want to make certain you arrive safely. Then . . . I have to get the plans back to London."

"You will be careful, won't you?" Her heart hiccupped inside her at the thought of him being shot.

"I will." He gave her such an endearing smile, his eyes locking on hers. "If we're fortunate, they've now found the fake plans and are convinced they're authentic and will not bother us again."

Yes, that was something to pray for.

They rode the rest of the day in companionable conversation. Henry Gilchrist had so many stories of "running wild about the countryside, getting into every scrape imaginable." His childhood sounded like the complete opposite of hers.

"My brother Benny and I once challenged each other to see whose horse could jump the most fences in one day. He was two years older, so I was very keen to beat him at something—he was forever winning every game we played." Henry Gilchrist smiled as he spoke.

"I was as reckless as any boy ever was, and my

gelding jumped one fence after another, but Benny was jumping just as many. Then, just as my horse was getting ready to jump another one, he stumbled. It was too late to pull up, but the horse couldn't get high enough. We both tumbled head first to the ground on the other side."

"Oh no! Were you hurt?"

"Oh yes. I broke my collar bone and my leg when the horse landed on me, and I dislocated my shoulder. I was in terrible pain for weeks." He looked as if he thought it was the funniest joke.

"That sounds terrible. How old were you?"

"Twelve. But it taught me to be a bit more cautious."

"What was your brother's reaction?"

"He cried. He thought I was dead." Henry Gilchrist did laugh then. "It's one of my favorite memories of my childhood."

Penelope shook her head. How could such a terrible thing be one of his favorite memories? Certainly men were different from women.

"Are you and your brother still such good friends?"

"No." He suddenly sobered. "No, he died two years ago."

She knew that. How could she forget? "I'm so very sorry."

"He was very sick for a fortnight and died. It was so shocking, for he was never sick. I was the sickly child, and he was the picture of health."

Mr. Gilchrist stared out the window with a sad, thoughtful gaze.

"I'm so very sorry. Did he have any children?"

"No. He was married, but no children."

"How sad for his wife."

"Don't feel too sorry for her. She remarried a few months after."

Penelope wasn't sure how to reply to that. She'd never known Mr. Gilchrist to be ungracious, but it was clear he did not himself feel any pity for his former sister-in-law. Was it only because she remarried quickly? Or was there some other reason for the acrimonious look on his face? Of course, she didn't know the full story, and it didn't seem wise to ask.

"But you have never had a sibling, have you?" He turned his attention back to her, his expression relaxing.

"No. I was an only child. My mother's family were mostly all deceased and . . . there was only me." She tried to smile and failed. Her childhood had been so much less eventful and happy than his. And even now, it hurt to think about it. Still, something made her want to tell him about it.

"My grandmother, whom you met, never approved of my mother. By all accounts, she was furious when my father married a French woman. And she always blamed my mother for my father's death, since she died of consumption, and he followed a year later.

"As it is, I know very little of my parents, especially my mother. And I always longed for a sister and a brother to play with and talk to."

"That does not sound like the happiest childhood. But you and my sister will become fast friends. She's very friendly and talkative and she will like you very much."

"What makes you so sure?"

"I know my sister. She hates inauthenticity, so . . . she will appreciate you."

Was he saying she was authentic? Penelope had never thought of herself that way, but it was true. She didn't like being fake, and there were ever so many fake people in the world.

"What did you do when you were a child, since you had so few playmates?" he asked.

"I read a lot of books and I learned all the things girls are supposed to learn—how to sew, how to embroider, how to paint, and how to sing and play the pianoforte."

"That is good, because my sister and mother are both terrible at playing and singing, and we all love music. It's a sad state of affairs."

Penelope couldn't help laughing.

"So you see, you'll be asked to play and sing a lot."

"I shall do my best."

"What was your favorite, of all the things you learned?"

"Painting landscapes and portraits was and is my favorite, but sewing and embroidery were too tedious for me. I do like to play and sing, but I worry that I'm not good enough, and that always takes away some of the enjoyment, especially in company."

"Well, prepare to change your thinking. My mother and sister will have you convinced that you are the best player and singer in England."

"But you haven't even heard me yet. I could be terrible."

"You won't be. And even if you are, you'll still be better than my mother and sister."

Penelope shook her head and covered her smile. But now she was dying of curiosity to meet his sister. She only hoped she was a congenial, forthcoming girl, because Penelope was also curious to know why Mr. Gilchrist was so bitter against his late brother's wife.

137

CHAPTER FIFTEEN

Henry said a silent prayer of thanks that he'd brought Penelope Hammond safely to his home as they emerged from the tree-lined avenue into full view of the house.

"Oh my. It's beautiful," she said, staring out the window in the twilight shadows.

His heart swelled at her words. Though he'd heard much more long-winded and eloquent praise, her opinion made a deeper impression on him.

Take care, said the warning in his head. Hadn't he promised never to let his heart grow fond so quickly and easily? He hardly knew anything about Penelope Hammond besides that she had a very lonely childhood, and her late husband was not a good man—nor a good husband.

He must admit, he'd seen her in many stressful situations, and he'd had many conversations with her. Perhaps he hadn't known her long, but what he did know made him want to care for her.

Again, that was his foolish heart talking. After he'd been so foolish with his sister-in-law, foolish enough to fall in love with a woman he hardly knew, a woman who was poor and had her heart set on money, not love, he'd sworn never to marry a poor woman, never to even think of falling in love with a poor woman, and he didn't intend to break that vow.

His sister Jane ran out of the house just as he was

helping Penelope Hammond out of the carriage.

"You're home!" she cried, throwing her arms around him. "What brings about this sudden but welcome visit?"

"My sister is very demonstrative," he said, trying to soften the blow of his sister's high spirits on the timid Penelope Hammond. Though he'd told himself he couldn't call her timid anymore after she stabbed that French spy in the back with a letter opener.

"Mrs. Hammond, this is my sister, Jane. Jane, this is Penelope Hammond, the former Lady Hampstead."

"Of course! We got the message that you were coming. I am so pleased to meet you." She clasped Mrs. Hammond's hand.

"I am very pleased to meet you, Miss Gilchrist."

"Please, call me Jane."

The way Jane was smiling, he was sure she already liked what she saw in Mrs. Hammond.

"I cannot stay," he told Jane. "I will be here long enough to give instructions to the men to be vigilant, and then I must go."

"Tell me what's amiss."

"I will, but you have to go find Mother so I can tell you both at the same time. I don't want to talk myself hoarse with telling the same story half a dozen times."

"Mrs. Hammond, have you ever heard anyone so rude as my brother?"

"I think he is only taking liberties because you're his sister."

"Well, I sincerely hope your brother doesn't treat you so rudely."

"I don't have a brother, but I'm sure if I did, he could not be as good to me as Mr. Gilchrist has been."

Jane stopped mid-stride and stared at Penelope Hammond. No doubt she was trying to discern if Mrs. Hammond was being sincere.

"I am sorry you have no brother. Forgive me, Mrs. Hammond." His sister slipped her arm through Mrs. Hammond's. "Come. You must be tired. We will get you into a room and a change of clothing before suppertime."

Already Penelope Hammond had passed Jane's inspection.

Once again, his mind and his heart had completely opposite reactions.

~ ~ ~

Penelope found herself seated at the dinner table with Henry Gilchrist's mother and sister.

"Henry won't be joining us," Jane Gilchrist said to Penelope as the first course was being served. "He's making sure the menservants and the groomsmen and a few of our tenants are armed and ready to patrol the property, just in case those ruffians try to come here."

"What a frightening time you've had," Mrs. Gilchrist said. "I do hope you have not had any ill effects to your health from all the shocks of the past week."

Had it only been a week since David had been murdered? It seemed much longer.

"I am holding up very well, I think. Thank you for your kindness, Mrs. Gilchrist."

"You are young, but many women would have had a breakdown in your circumstances."

"Please allow me to thank you, Mrs. Gilchrist, for allowing me to trespass on your hospitality, especially when you don't know me at all."

"My dear, it is my pleasure. We don't have enough company at the present time, Jane and I, and we are looking forward to making ourselves acquainted with you. Henry has told us a bit, but we want to know all about you."

"Thank you. You are very kind, and I am indebted to you. And I am very much looking forward to getting to know you and Miss Gilchrist better." Indeed, there was something about this lady, who was kind and pleasant-looking, and her lively, enthusiastic daughter wanting to get to know Penelope that made her feel warm and happy.

"Do you play?" Jane asked.

"I do, but—"

"And sing?"

"Yes, but not exceptionally well, so please don't get your hopes up too high."

"Oh, I can hardly wait to finish dinner so we can hear you," Jane said, her smile stretching her face.

"Jane, darling, you will frighten Mrs. Hammond with your high spirits and strange ways."

"Mama, I hardly think I could frighten Penelope Hammond with my 'high spirits and strange ways.' She stabbed a man three times her size with a letter opener!"

"Heavens," Mrs. Gilchrist said, placing her hand over her heart.

"Jane will have you thinking I am a violent criminal," Penelope said. "That is a long story and probably not appropriate for the dinner table."

"Oh no, we would love to hear you tell the story, wouldn't we, Mama?" Jane cast an eager gaze at her mother.

"It does sound very interesting," Mrs. Gilchrist said. "We would love to hear it if you are willing to tell it."

"Of course." Penelope told the story of her second kidnapping by the French spies, finding herself actually enjoying the telling of what, at the time, had been harrowing in the extreme. She even found humor in the descriptions of the kidnappers and how she felt after she stabbed him.

"You are very brave. Isn't she brave, Mother?"

"Very brave."

"Henry said you were meek and timid, but he obviously misjudged you."

Meek and timid? Was that how Henry Gilchrist saw her?

Her stomach churned and her cheeks burned. Was she as pathetic in his eyes and she was in her grandmother's—and her own?

"Jane, you are far too outspoken," Mrs. Gilchrist said with a frown. "Mrs. Hammond, you must forgive her. Henry only meant that you were a mild-mannered young woman, not high minded and difficult like most young women of society these days, nor high-strung like Jane."

"Oh, he meant nothing unflattering at all. Forgive me, Mrs. Hammond, if I offended you." Jane looked truly contrite, her voice softer than she'd ever heard it.

"No, no, of course not." She smiled but her cheeks were still heated.

She longed to be confident and mature in her manner, like Mrs. Gilchrist, and high-spirited and cheerful, like Jane. But she was not like either of those women. She'd lived such a sheltered, and—it humiliated her to admit it, even to herself—a neglected and ill-used existence with few friends and little-to-no affection.

Obviously, these two women had known plenty of family, friends, and affection, though they had also known great tragedy in the death of their son and brother, then their husband and father.

"I am normally rather timid, I suppose," Penelope said, finding it hard to look the two women in the eye, "but I was trying to be brave, to defend and rescue myself. I did have a lot of help from Mr. Gilchrist."

"He helped rescue you from the kidnappers, did he not?"

"Yes, two times, in fact."

"There were two kidnappings?"

"There were."

"Was it very romantic? Like a novel by Mrs. Radcliffe?"

"Jane!" Mrs. Gilchrist exclaimed. "Of course it was not romantic. What strange notions you have. Forgive her, please, Mrs. Hammond."

The truth was, Penelope had thought it rather romantic, the way he had so valiantly come to aid her and had made sure she was safe. But if he only saw her as meek and timid . . . Obviously he had not seen it the way she had.

"Mrs. Hammond, did you go to school somewhere, or were you taught at home?" Mrs. Gilchrist asked, preventing her from having to answer Jane's question about whether her interactions with Henry Gilchrist had been romantic.

"I was tutored at home."

A discussion about music and favorite compositions followed, and the dinner ended pleasantly before the three women retired from the dining room to the music room.

"Please do favor us with a song, Penelope."

Even though it was unusually familiar of Jane Gilchrist to call her Penelope, her heart lifted inexplicably at Henry Gilchrist's sister saying her Christian name. David had only called her by her Christian name a handful of times. Even her grandmother rarely said her name.

"Yes, we love music," Mrs. Gilchrist said, "and we're eager to hear you."

"Do you have a request?"

"Choose your favorite."

Penelope sat down at the pianoforte, and Jane Gilchrist hurried over to her.

"If you don't see anything you like in the music here, there's more." She found more sheets of music and offered them to her.

Penelope found one of her favorites. It had been a while since she'd played anything, so she studied the music for a moment before beginning.

As soon as she began to play, Henry Gilchrist came into the room and sat down.

She felt a rush of relief that she'd chosen a piece that did not have accompanying lyrics. She was more reticent about displaying her voice than her playing.

When she finished playing, Jane clapped her hands and said, "Brava! That was beautiful."

Penelope felt herself blushing. She stood up and started to move away from the instrument, but Jane's protests stopped her.

"Won't you sing something for us now?" Mrs. Gilchrist said. "That was so lovely, we would love to hear another."

"If you're not too tired," Henry Gilchrist said. "Don't insist, Mother. She has had a trying time and may be wishing to rest."

Jane and her mother exchanged a look, but Penelope could not read it.

"I don't mind playing another," Penelope said. "Mr.

Gilchrist is very kind, but I'm not too tired. I'm enjoying the company."

"She's enjoying our company," Jane said, addressing her brother.

So Penelope chose another song and, ignoring her fear, sang and played.

Many compliments ensued, which she was certain were exaggerated. But they did make her believe that they were enjoying the music.

"She is certain to be tired," Henry Gilchrist said quietly to his mother and sister. "Let her stop, if she wishes to."

"You may stop if you wish to," Jane said, "but only because my brother is so concerned for you." She gave a sly grin to Henry Gilchrist.

He only frowned back at her.

"I shall play for you tomorrow, if you wish," Penelope said, seating herself next to Jane Gilchrist, who patted the settee beside her.

"We will look forward to hearing you tomorrow," Mrs. Gilchrist said with a smile.

They sat and talked, with Jane asking her brother for details about what had been happening, how he saved Penelope from kidnappers, just to hear his version of the stories, and what her brother thought about Penelope stabbing the man in the back.

Henry patiently answered his sister's questions and even seemed to enjoy telling the stories.

"Henry, I don't want you to go back to London tomorrow. It's too dangerous."

"I have to, Mother, to make certain the plans don't fall into the wrong hands. I promise I'll be careful."

"I just cannot believe they would allow a Member

of Parliament to put himself in so much danger. They should have soldiers to do such things."

"I know, Mother. Just have faith that all will be well."

He was a kind son and a patient brother. Those were two very important qualities, kindness and patience. But her grandmother would not be thinking about such qualities in a prospective husband for Penelope. No, she would be thinking about how large this house was and how he had inherited it from his father, how wealthy his estate was, and how old and unblemished his family name was. Those were things that mattered to Grandmother, and indeed, all of society.

Penelope couldn't be the only person who understood that character was infinitely more significant when choosing a husband or wife.

God, please help me choose wisely.

CHAPTER SIXTEEN

Henry left the next morning for London, leaving several men in charge of protecting Mrs. Penelope Hammond and his mother and sister. The French spies would certainly like nothing more than to kidnap his family members in order to force him to give them the plans.

The look his sister and mother had given each other when he was trying to keep them from fatiguing Mrs. Hammond was not lost on him. He knew they would be matching him to her, but he would not allow them to marry him off to poor Mrs. Hammond. Even though she was beautiful and had a talent for singing and playing.

When this was all over, she'd be far away in Shropshire with her grandmother. He only had to wait a fortnight for her visit at his home to be over. Then she'd be out of his sight, and therefore out of his mind.

He just had to make sure he didn't let her into his heart. He knew from experience, it was much harder to get a woman out of his heart once she was there.

On arriving in London, he skirted around the main streets and headed for the home of one of the other members of the committee that seemed the most trustworthy. They must all have heard by now of Lord Ingleburt's death.

Instead of going inside, he only delivered a note that read:

Call a meeting of the committee. I have the item everyone wants. Gilchrist.

Then he went to his own home, going in the back way and keeping his hat pulled low over his eyes.

After speaking with his servants and learning that the constable had been there looking for him, wanting to ask him questions, he realized he should have gone to the constable as soon as he arrived. But could he trust this constable?

Best to talk to the committee first.

Only an hour later, a note came announcing a meeting of the committee at the Palace of Westminster.

Henry went to the meeting with great caution, having two of his menservants follow him on horseback, for the protection of the plans.

Finally, when he had arrived at the meeting, which was conspicuously missing two of its members—the two that had been murdered—Henry breathed a sigh of relief.

"Gentlemen, I have the papers that have been stolen and now recovered from Lord Hampstead's home. Here is my proposal. Let all of eight of us memorize these plans so that we can then burn them."

"Won't that put us in danger?" one of the members asked.

"You are already in danger," Henry informed him. "Whether you like it or not, there are ruthless men who would kill you for this knowledge. Nevertheless, it is easier to steal a piece of paper than to steal the contents of your head. So let us memorize this information and then burn it."

Henry had already spent time memorizing the plans, so he handed the paper over to the others to memorize.

When most of them were satisfied they knew the information backward and forward, Henry told them about how the chairman, Lord Ingleburt, had died before his eyes, and he was fairly certain he was poisoned.

"The constable was looking for you," one of the members said.

"They think you may have killed him," another said, "since you ran away from his house and were the only person there when he died."

"I had the plans on me. I didn't want the murderers, who couldn't have been far away, to find me and steal the plans again."

Most of the members seemed to understand, but a few gave him suspicious side glances.

When all the members had memorized the plans, Henry used a candle to set the paper ablaze, watching it burn and making sure even the ashes were thrown into the fireplace and mixed in with the other ashes.

"When General Wellington comes into town, any one of us can write down the plans for him, force him memorize them, then burn them again."

A small chuckle went through the room at the thought of "forcing" General Wellington to do anything. But they all nodded.

"It is my hope that the French spies will take the fake plans and leave England. But in the event they don't, I also charged our merry band of mercenaries with following them, making sure they know where they are at all times, and capturing them, if possible."

The committee members nodded.

"We need a new committee chairman," one man said. "I say we appoint Henry Gilchrist."

Several "ayes" were heard, and it was decided.

He only hoped the same thing that happened to the last chairman didn't happen to him.

"Now, gentlemen, my suggestion is that we all leave London immediately and go back to the country. Scattered as we shall be, we should be safer. Are we agreed?"

They all nodded and murmured their agreement.

"Godspeed, and see that you don't get murdered by any nefarious Frenchmen."

No one chuckled in amusement at his bad joke. There were several nervous glances instead.

Henry would endeavor to do the same, and keep his family and Penelope Hammond safe as well.

~ ~ ~

Penelope walked arm in arm with Miss Jane Gilchrist through the shrubs and trees and flowers behind their grand home.

"This is such a pleasant garden. Who is responsible for the design?"

"Mother and Father. Mother had certain things she wanted, and Father had things he wanted, so they designed it together, with some input from the gardeners."

"That sounds lovely, a husband and wife working together." It was a wonderful, though foreign, concept for Penelope.

"My father was a good man. He was raised by a mother who was deeply religious, convinced that the only way to get to Heaven was to love the poor as Jesus did, so my father was much more inclined to listen to servants, to treat his tenants well, and to have little to do with the wealth and arrogance of Society people. He impressed this on Henry and me, and I believe that is why Henry decided to try for a seat in the House of Commons.

"He thought he could do some good for the common people there. But I think he's been a bit disappointed with how much he's been able to accomplish there. Or I should say, how little he's been able to accomplish."

"It is a very noble goal, at least."

"Yes." Jane smiled. "Henry is noble. But he was cruelly thwarted in love, and Mother and I have been afraid he would never recover, that he will never marry."

"Oh?" Penelope silently begged Jane to go on. She suddenly wanted to know, more than anything, what had happened to so upset Henry Gilchrist and turn him against marriage.

"Yes. There was a girl. She was from a noble family, the ward of a duke, but penniless and without an inheritance, who endeared herself to Henry when he was only twenty years old. There was such an attachment that Father allowed Henry to ask the girl to marry him. Only one month before they were supposed to marry, the girl avowed that her affection and attachment had all been transferred to our oldest brother, Thomas.

"The engagement was broken and Thomas swore he was in love with the girl. When Mother and Father protested the marriage, they eloped to Scotland. Within two years, Thomas had died of a fever. They had no children."

Jane's hazel eyes looked sad as she studied a leaf she picked off a tree.

"I'm very sorry. That must have been very difficult for everyone."

"I think Henry felt it the most. He and Thomas had always been inseparable, such good friends, but when Thomas married Henry's love, he swore never to speak to Thomas again. He did not keep that promise, but things were never the same, always so cold, when they had formerly been the best of friends. It was heartbreaking, but we hoped they could mend their relationship in time.

"That never happened, of course. And I know

Henry suffered a deep sorrow over his brother's death, more so because they had been at odds."

"Oh, how very sad," Penelope said. Poor Henry Gilchrist. What a blow, to have his love marry his brother. But worse to lose a brother when he hadn't forgiven him.

"That is why he has not married. He's afraid to trust. That's what Mother and I believe."

"And your father?"

"He died a year ago from a sudden attack of the heart."

"So many difficult things in such a short time. I'm so sorry, Jane."

"Well, there is nothing to be gained from fretting and sighing, so let us go riding. I want to show you a beautiful spot where a thousand wildflowers grow next to a pretty little stream."

Penelope rarely went riding, but she didn't want to curb Jane's enthusiasm or disappoint her, so they hurried to the stable and were soon trotting over the countryside with a groom following them—one of the stipulations Henry had put into place before he left.

By late afternoon, Penelope was happy to return to her room for a short nap before supper. She'd never had such an enjoyable day, full of riding and walking and talking, but best of all, friendship with Jane Gilchrist, who had already become the most amiable person Penelope had ever met.

~ ~ ~

"Henry's home!"

Penelope looked up from her dressing table as Jane burst into her room. In spite of herself, her heart jumped inside her at the news. Strange that she was so excited to see Henry Gilchrist again. He'd only been gone two days.

"Mother is beside herself with joy. Now Henry can join us at the big party the Bedfords are having at their country house tomorrow night. I'm sorry for bursting in your room like a stampede of cattle, as Father used to say about me."

"I don't mind. I'm dressed, as you see."

Jane laughed, pressing a hand to her chest. "Forgive me. But we weren't expecting Henry back so soon. He said he left at dawn. He must have been very anxious to come home."

"Perhaps he didn't want to miss the party."

"At the Bedfords? I doubt that was the reason. He isn't a great lover of parties."

Jane strode over to where all Penelope's dresses were hanging and looked through them.

"Which dress will you wear? I do like this one." Jane pulled out a pale green gown with lavender embroidery.

"And you?"

"I have a pink muslin I'll probably wear. I like putting pink ribbons in my hair."

"Oh yes, I can imagine you'll look very pretty in pink."

Jane Gilchrist had lovely dark brown hair and skin that was darker than most, probably from spending so much time outdoors riding her horse and "running amok," as she described her rambles in the woods.

Jane brought the dress over to Penelope and held it up to her chin.

"Yes, I think the green suits you very well. Your hair has such a lovely light brown, dark blonde color. And I have some ribbons that will exactly match this color green."

"Are you sure I should be going to this party? I am

newly widowed, after all."

"Of course. Why should you not?"

"Some might say it isn't proper for a woman whose husband has just died."

"I don't know anyone who says such things. Besides, from what you've told me, it was almost as if you weren't married anyway."

Had Penelope said enough to make Jane think that? She hadn't realized she'd been so forthcoming. But it was easy to talk to Jane.

"It is true that I don't know what a mutually happy marriage looks like. I know only what it's like to be shunned and ignored."

There she was, being too honest and open again.

"Well, if you let me help you, I dare say you shall fare much better the second time around." Jane gave her that sly, secretive grin she sometimes wore.

"Help me?"

"Yes! I helped my cousin Veronica find a husband, and now she is very happily married with two children in only two years!"

"Oh my."

"Don't worry. I shall find you a man who is everything you could want—rich, faithful, affectionate, and handsome."

"I don't truly care about him being rich. And a man looks handsomer when he is kind."

"No, no. You must have a rich man, and he must be handsome. Besides, I only know rich men." Jane laughed, a short, quick laugh. "And no amount of kindness can make a homely man handsome."

Penelope shook her head and covered her smile. Jane could say some of the most scandalous things.

"You know it is true. And my excellent nanny used say that an ugly man was inevitably a mean man. And you are so beautiful, Penelope. I don't think you understand how sweet and appealing you are. And if I don't find you some good marriage prospects at this party then I will cease calling myself a matchmaker."

"But Jane, what about you? Won't you be looking for marriage prospects? You already told me you are one and twenty."

"One and twenty is hardly old enough to get married. I prefer to wait until I'm ready. And I don't want to leave my home yet. Mother needs my company since Father died, though she won't admit it."

"Well, there is no need to be so self-sacrificing."

Jane made a snorting sound.

"You are old enough to enjoy a few suitors, to dance and flirt and have a good time."

"Oh, I shall do all those things, don't worry." She winked at Penelope. "How old are you, anyway?"

"Twenty-three."

"So young." Jane seemed to study Penelope. "Though you are a widow, I shall find you someone who might actually come close to deserving you. It may not be easy, but I shall find him."

Penelope shook her head again and stood to accompany Jane downstairs. Perhaps she should try harder to dissuade Jane from matchmaking.

"Some people would say it's much too soon for me to be hunting a husband. I should just sit with the dowagers and sip my lemonade and eat scones."

"You shall dance and flirt and enjoy yourself, the same as me."

"You won't ruin my reputation, will you? If my

grandmother hears I've behaved unseemly . . ." Penelope's cheeks grew warm just thinking about it.

"Your reputation will not be ruined. I shall take all the blame if anyone disparages you, but I don't think they would dare." Jane glared as if she was looking at the disparager. "Come. We shall welcome Henry home."

"Henry doesn't like women who get married quickly after their husbands have died."

"What makes you say that?" Jane gave her a sidelong look.

"He mentioned that when he was telling me about his sister-in-law who has already remarried."

"Oh. Well, he has other reasons for disliking our sister-in-law, as I told you." Jane lowered her voice. "Truly, I never liked her. She was much too manipulative, with her sad story of growing up poor and being neglected by her guardian. She was always trying to make everyone feel sorry for her." Jane shuddered. "I can never abide such simpering and pretense to get my pity."

"Have I done that?" Penelope's stomach sank to her toes at the thought of Jane Gilchrist and her mother and—worst of all—Henry Gilchrist thinking she was manipulating them into pitying her.

"No, of course not. You could never seem manipulative. You're much too artless and sincere. And besides that, your story truly is sad, and yet you don't go on and on about it, with that sly look she used to have when she was checking to see if her words were having the desired effect. You know that kind of woman." Jane rolled her eyes.

Penelope didn't, not really, but she certainly did not want to be that kind of woman!

"Come. No gloomy thoughts. We're going to find

Henry."

They walked toward the stables, and there he was turning his horse over to the groomsman and talking with him.

"Back already!" Jane exclaimed, her arm through Penelope's as they made their way toward him.

Penelope's heart did a strange flip at the sight of him, dressed for riding, his hair windblown. He was so handsome he seemed to steal the breath out of her chest.

Foolish girl. Henry was too young, too handsome, perhaps even too bitterly disposed toward women to ever think of Penelope. Besides, it had not occurred to Jane that she and Henry might make a good match, so that sealed it. It would never happen between them. The sooner she accepted it, the better.

CHAPTER SEVENTEEN

Henry's heart lifted at seeing how his sister had taken to Penelope Hammond, just as he'd predicted. The two looked like great friends already, after only two days.

"Glad to see you two looking well," he said.

Jane threw her arms around him and he permitted her to kiss him on the cheek, as they had done since they were children.

"Penelope and I are excited about the ball tomorrow night at the Bedfords'. You must be our chaperone, Henry."

"You cannot go without me, that is for sure."

"Whatever do you mean?" She looked at Mrs. Hammond. "Whatever does he mean?"

"I mean that there are dangerous men who have twice kidnapped Mrs. Hammond and would gladly kill us all if it helped them get what they want."

"Why are you being so sensational? Those men are in London. They wouldn't follow us all the way out here. Besides, I thought you took care of that when you went back to London."

"I am doing my best, Jane, but there's no way to know that they won't come after us again."

"We have servants enough to defend us. Give them guns and we shall be safe."

Henry smiled at his sister's simplistic answers to the difficult questions he'd been dealing with for more than a week now.

"Yes, Jane. All will be well. And yes, I will accompany you to the ball, as long as there are no signs of danger between now and then."

"Very good." Jane's smile widened and she squeezed Penelope Hammond's arm.

"How is Mother?" he asked.

"She's well. We are both enjoying Penelope's playing and singing. It has considerably lifted Mother's spirits. I do hope we can keep Penelope here longer than a fortnight."

"That is completely up to Penelo—to Mrs. Hammond."

Jane laughed at his blunder of almost calling the young widow by her Christian name. He hoped she wouldn't comment on it. He didn't want Penelope Hammond—Mrs. Hammond—knowing he thought about her any more than was necessary, or thinking that he had feelings for her. Her situation in life reminded him too much of the woman who duped him into thinking she was a good and kind person and that she loved him, only to reject him in favor of the older brother who would inherit the estate.

But then, the irony was that she never was to enjoy the fruits of her machinations, as he died and left her with nothing, since they had no child.

Had Penelope Hammond also married her husband under similar circumstances? Her husband had no brother, but if she wanted her husband's estate, she could have flirted with his heir, Eustace Hammond.

Henry excused himself from Jane and Mrs. Hammond.

Truthfully, her personality was nothing like his sister-in-law's, and he liked Mrs. Hammond. She was quiet but brave, gentle but determined. She intrigued him.

A little too much.

But his fear of making the same mistake twice would keep him from getting too close.

~ ~ ~

Penelope played and sang a little more each night after the evening meal. Jane and her mother seemed to enjoy it so much, she couldn't refuse. Besides, she'd forgotten how much she enjoyed playing and singing, and it was even more enjoyable with such an appreciative, complimentary audience.

But with Henry Gilchrist present, she was a bit more nervous, a bit more careful not to make a mistake, a bit more conscious of how she looked and sounded.

Henry Gilchrist's presence at the dinner table had added a glow to his mother's face and a depth to their conversation that was lacking without him. He was kind and attentive whenever Penelope spoke, but it was clear he was keeping his distance from her.

All the better. She needed to check her feelings, which had grown in the two days when he was gone to London, with his mother and sister talking of him so often. Feelings for Henry Gilchrist would only lead to heartache when he chose someone else.

Still, it was difficult. Her heart was starved for affection and attention and the sight of a good man behaving as a good man should. She finally told herself that it was all right to think of him, to consider him the most amiable man of her acquaintance, but to remember that she would never marry him.

She played her first number, something she had rummaged through all of the Gilchrists' music to find, an old favorite. When she finished, her audience of three praised her much more than she deserved, and yet their praise was sincere, which made it all the more gratifying.

At least she had moved beyond blushing at their gush of compliments.

"Shall I play another?"

"Of course. Sing that one you sang last night," Mrs. Gilchrist said. "The one about the maiden with the golden hair."

Penelope found the one she meant and said a silent prayer that her voice wouldn't crack, before commencing to play and sing.

When she was finished, she glanced at Henry Gilchrist. He was smiling.

"Wasn't that beautiful?" Jane enthused. "Her voice is like an angel's. I wish I could sing so well."

"You could, if you practiced," Henry Gilchrist said.

Jane's mouth fell open as she stared at him. "I'm not sure if that was meant as a compliment for me, or . . . Penelope clearly has a God-given talent."

"Of course. She is a good singer."

"Good?" Jane scrunched her face at him.

"You know how Henry is, my dear," Mrs. Gilchrist said. "He's always told you to practice more, that you're too flighty to practice as you should. It is only a brother's severity toward his sister."

"Mother is right. I meant no disparagement toward Mrs. Hammond, Jane, if that is what you're suggesting," Henry said dryly. "Mrs. Hammond plays and sings very well, as you have told her many times, I'm sure."

"Yes she does, and yes I have. And why shouldn't I? It's true, and Mother and I enjoy her playing and singing very much." She folded her arms over her stomach. "I'll never understand your ill temperament and stinginess with compliments. You've allowed your disappointment with one woman to ruin you."

"Jane!" Mrs. Gilchrist looked shocked and distressed.

"Well, it's true, and we all know it," Jane muttered with brows drawn together and a slight protruding of her lower lip.

Henry frowned. "Do we need to do this tonight? You make our guest uncomfortable."

Penelope did feel a bit uncomfortable with the direction the conversation had taken, mostly because those around her were uncomfortable, but it was worse having him bring attention to her discomfort. At the same time, it was refreshing to hear family members talking to each other, discussing an issue instead of ignoring it, and never raising their voices or saying cruel things.

"I shall play something." Penelope started a new song. Perhaps by the time the song was finished, they would no longer be at odds with each other.

She lost herself in the song, a soothing Scottish melody that had been one of her favorites. When she was done, everyone clapped politely.

"Very lovely, as always," Mrs. Gilchrist said.

"I thought it showed incredible talent." Jane turned her smirk toward Henry.

"I quite enjoyed it too," Henry said, looking strangely amused.

And the tiff was over.

Penelope played one more song, then, sensing they would not be disappointed if she stopped, she came over and sat beside Jane.

"Mama," Jane said, "don't you think Penelope would look lovely with her hair done the way mine was last spring at the assembly rooms in London? With some ribbons and pearls and a curl hanging down on either side?"

"Oh yes, that will be lovely. Penelope is such a lovely girl."

"I mean for her to have several dance partners tomorrow night. Every good-looking man in the room must dance with her."

"Now, Jane, you know your matchmaking can get you into trouble."

"I don't know what you're speaking of."

Jane made a face that caused Penelope to laugh. She quickly stifled her laugh behind her hand.

"Truly, I would not want you to make any efforts toward that end. I have my reputation to think of, and if my grandmother were to hear that I made a spectacle of myself at a ball . . . I don't want to appear so forward. I'm still in mourning."

"Penelope is right," Mrs. Gilchrist said.

"Perhaps I should not even attend the ball. It is too soon."

"No one is so fastidious about such things. This is 1810, for goodness sake." Jane rolled her eyes.

"It is certainly all right for you to attend the ball, my dear," Mrs. Gilchrist said. "No one is suggesting that you shouldn't." Then she quieted her voice, speaking in a loud whisper. "I'm only trying to convince Jane to not target you with her high-spirited matchmaking at the ball."

Henry Gilchrist laughed. Until now he'd been silent in the conversation.

"Very well." Jane gave a grudging smile. "I shall not make her dance all the dances, but I shall discreetly introduce her to as many gentlemen as I see fit. And if she thinks she's being too free with her dances, she can refuse as many partners as she likes."

Penelope gave Jane a demure smile. "Thank you."

But even though he'd laughed at his mother's good-natured jest at Jane's expense, Henry Gilchrist was rather quiet and even looked a bit out of spirits for the rest of the evening. But perhaps he was only tired.

Penelope went to bed happy that night, as the ball the next evening was sure to be memorable, with Jane there. But she did have trouble sleeping, wondering whether Henry Gilchrist would ask her to dance.

~ ~ ~

Henry went over in his mind the conversation from the evening before. Why did it annoy him so much that his sister was so determined to get Mrs. Hammond several dance partners and introduce her to all the eligible men at the ball?

He dressed with care, but also thought about how to make certain his family and Mrs. Hammond were safe at the ball.

Mrs. Hammond was a widow, so she could do as she pleased. If she danced with every eligible man in the room, it was her reputation that would suffer. He should not concern himself with that.

Still, the more he thought about Jane's attitude about it, the more he yanked at his cravat. Finally, he had to call Johnson back in to re-tie it.

Henry made sure they traveled to the party in his own carriage, which had two guns under the seat. He also had given the coachman and one of the groomsmen, who came with them, their own pistols, just in case. He kept an eye out for anyone following them, trying to be ever vigilant.

Once they had arrived, he went and talked to the

groomsmen and servants of the guests as well as the Bedfords' servants, just to get familiar with each one. Finally, when he entered the ball, he was ready to be social.

CHAPTER EIGHTEEN

Penelope's head hurt from all the pins sticking in her scalp, holding up her elaborate hair. There were ribbons and seed pearls, as well as false hair pieces and tiny braids. She was almost sorry she had let Jane talk her into wearing her hair this way, but it had pleased her so much.

Jane, with her dark brown hair and sun-browned skin, set off perfectly by her pink gown, was the most beautiful woman at the ball. There were many other young women, and Jane quickly found one of them to introduce her to.

"Penelope, this is my friend Harriet Schofield. Harriet, this is Penelope Hammond, and I am determined you two shall be friends. And now, you must tell me the gossip, for you know I rarely go anywhere."

"That is not true." Harriet turned to Penelope. "Jane goes everywhere, and she's invited to all the balls and parties in three counties."

"I suppose that's true, very nearly." Jane smiled. "But I have turned down more invitations in the last year than I usually do, you must admit."

"That is true," Harriet said.

Of course, that was because of her father's death and not wanting to leave her mother alone.

"We shall have to have a good time, then, to make up for every party you've missed," Harriet said with a wink.

"So, Harriet, you must tell me, which gentleman is

your particular favorite these days? I shall spare him, but no others, for I mean to have Penelope dance with every eligible man here. She is in dire need of some suitors."

"Indeed, that is not true," Penelope said in a low voice. "I am newly widowed, and you will have Miss Schofield thinking I am an incorrigible flirt, and I am no such thing."

"No need to worry," Harriet said. "I know Jane and she is the incorrigible one, always matchmaking. She thinks she knows who everyone should marry."

Jane, without replying to Penelope's and Harriet's words, said, "Oh, there is Edward Bennington. I didn't know he was back from his trip to France. And there is Charles Vernick. I must introduce you to both. Come."

Jane took Penelope's arm and weaved her way through the crowd, but discreetly, looking as though she had no real aim in mind. She stopped twice to introduce Penelope to other young ladies and their mothers, so that when they reached the gentlemen in question, Jane pretended to be surprised to see them.

"Mr. Bennington and Mr. Vernick. How pleasant to see you both. I was not sure you would be here." She turned on her brightest smile, and the gentlemen's gazes were fastened on her face as if she was the only sight to see.

"Penelope, allow me to introduce Mr. Edward Bennington and Mr. Charles Vernick. Gentlemen, this is Mrs. Penelope Hammond, the former Lady Hampstead."

No doubt she said it that way so they would know she was a widow. And no doubt these gentlemen had heard about her husband's recent murder, as their brows went up at hearing her name.

They were both polite as they greeted her, making

the usual trite conversation about the state of the roads and the weather.

"Please allow me to express my condolences on your late husband's untimely death," Mr. Vernick said.

"Yes, it must have been a terrible shock," Mr. Bennington added.

"It was, and I thank you for your kind condolences." It was the answer she'd given so many times at the funeral.

While a slightly awkward silence ensued, a young man approached them.

"Bennington. Vernick. Good to see you." He pretended to suddenly realize that there were two ladies standing next to Bennington and Vernick. "Miss Jane Gilchrist. How good to see you looking so well. And I don't believe I am acquainted with your friend."

"Penelope, this is Mr. Arthur Heywood—his wife Rebecca is there in the lavender dress. Mr. Heywood, this is my friend, Mrs. Penelope Hammond."

"Hammond? Lord Hampstead's widow?"

"One and the same." Jane's manner was rather brusque and her expression more of a frown than anything else. But Penelope didn't like the man's manner very much, neither the way he looked at Jane and herself, nor the way his eyes lit up at the prospect of hearing something titillating about her husband's murder.

Mr. Heywood started staring at Penelope's dance card. "Perhaps I could—"

"Oh, I see someone you must meet." Jane grabbed Penelope's arm. "Excuse us, gentlemen." She smiled at Mr. Vernick and Mr. Bennington but not at Mr. Heywood.

"I do detest that man," Jane said under her breath near Penelope's ear. "He flirts with every married woman he sees and he even fought in a duel with some poor husband of a woman he was dallying with. Best to stay far away from him."

"You won't have to tell me twice." Penelope was done forever with philandering men, she hoped.

"It is unfortunate that I had to move away from Mr. Bennington and Mr. Vernick, for I intended for them to ask you to dance. But I did it because that odious Mr. Heywood was just about to ask for a dance, and I didn't want you to be seen with him."

"Thank you, Jane. I'm so grateful for the escape."

"Well, there are plenty more men besides them. Come."

"Oh, look, it's Susan Claymore." Jane waved to a lovely young woman with buttery blonde hair, which hung down in perfect ringlets. Her skin seemed strangely perfect, but as she came close, Penelope realized it was because she was wearing powder.

"Susan! How pretty you look."

"You are very sweet, Jane, for you know you and your friend are the loveliest creatures in this room."

Jane simply shook her head and said, "Susan, I want you to meet Mrs. Penelope Hammond, the wife of the late Lord Hampstead. Penelope, this is Lady Susan Claymore. Her father is Lord Windemere."

"Very pleased to meet you," Penelope said.

"Likewise, Mrs. Hammond. Jane, where is that brother of yours?" Lady Susan Claymore barely glanced at Penelope before gazing around the room.

"Oh, he is here, or will be shortly. He had some business to attend to. I'm sure he will save you a dance, do not worry."

"Oh, I never worry." Lady Susan laughed gaily.

Jane's laugh lasted barely a moment before she raised her brows. "Well, I shall let you look for him. I want to introduce Penelope around. Excuse us."

When they were away from Lady Susan and had found a glass of something fruity to drink, Jane said quietly, "Lady Susan has been trying to get Henry for a year now."

"Is he interested in her?"

"Perhaps. It's hard to tell with Henry."

"I'm surprised you don't try your matchmaking skills with your brother."

"He does not like it when I do. In fact, if he even thinks I might be trying, he gets so angry." She shook her head with a rueful expression. "It's not worth trying and always has the opposite effect. But he has shown a bit of interest in Lady Susan."

Penelope didn't wish to let Jane know that that news made her stomach sink. Certainly Lady Susan was beautiful, and even Penelope had heard of Lord Windemere's wealth. She could never compete with that.

Not that she even hoped to compete for Henry Gilchrist's attention. He was not interested in her, certainly.

"Oh, look. Someone else you must meet." Jane walked as if she were moving past a gentleman wearing a military uniform, then feigned surprise at seeing him.

"Mr. Westbrook. When did you return?"

"Miss Gilchrist. You are looking as beautiful as always. And who is your equally beautiful friend?"

"Aren't you the flatterer? Penelope, this is Mr. Thomas Westbrook, a lieutenant now, I believe. Lieutenant, this is Mrs. Penelope Hammond, the widow of Lord Hampstead."

"Ah. Mrs. Hammond, please accept my condolences. I was very shocked to hear of your husband's untimely death."

"Thank you, Lieutenant Westbrook. You are very kind."

They again made small talk as someone began to clear the floor. The musicians looked ready to play their first number, and couples began lining up for the first dance.

Mr. Westbrook took her hand, instantly bringing Henry Gilchrist to her mind, of how he held her hand when they were running from the French spies, the times he touched her arm or shoulder to reassure her.

How telling that a man's touch reminded her of Henry Gilchrist and not her husband.

Mr. Westbrook was reasonably good-looking, with his soldier's uniform giving him a dashing air. And though he seemed pleased to be there, there was a languid look in his eyes that said he was not particularly interested in her.

All the better. She would dance and enjoy herself. When was the last time she'd done so? She could not even remember.

The music and the dance began. The dance was a lively one. They took their turn in the round and Penelope found herself smiling, actually smiling. And Mr. Westbrook smiled back.

Jane had found a partner as well, but she spent more time smiling at Penelope than at her partner. Was Jane really so disinterested in suitors and getting married? It must be wonderful to be in a situation where she didn't have to worry about such things.

Was Penelope envying Jane? *Forgive me.* She would never wish to take anything away from her new friend, who had been so good to her.

As the dance ended and she thanked her partner, Henry Gilchrist caught her eye. He was staring at her from across the room.

Her heart leapt. Did he think she was being scandalous and flirtatious? But perhaps he was only watching out for her, making sure she was safe. He'd been so kind in that way.

Jane caught her arm. "You and Lieutenant Westbrook certainly make a handsome couple."

"I enjoyed myself immensely," she admitted.

"Come. I shall introduce you to more young men." Jane was so good at not looking as though she was begging for partners, looking unstudied as she approached the people she introduced Penelope to, that she didn't think anyone could accuse them of artful flirting.

She danced the next dance with Mr. Vernick, who came looking for her. And the next she danced with another new acquaintance, a Mr. Jacobson.

Afterward, Jane caught up with her.

Penelope whispered, "I should sit out this next one. People will start to gossip about me."

She lifted her head and Henry Gilchrist was standing in front of her.

"May I have the next dance?" he asked, holding out his hand to her.

How could she refuse Henry Gilchrist? "Yes, of course."

The couples were already lining up for the dance. Penelope glanced back at Jane and saw her smirking, her eyes like those of a cat when it licks its lips.

Strange that she should have such a thought.

She gazed into Henry Gilchrist's eyes. Why did he

look almost angry? To be sure, it wasn't the cold anger that she'd sometimes seen in her husband's eyes. It was a controlled, almost subtle anger.

She was probably imagining it.

Neither of them spoke. Finally, the music started and they began to move with the other dancers.

Penelope caught a glimpse of Lady Susan, who was standing near the refreshments, and she was watching them with a disgruntled frown. Why was Henry Gilchrist not dancing with her? She was one of, if not the most beautiful woman in the room.

"I see Jane is responsible for your hair tonight," he said while they waited for their turn.

"Are you displeased with my hair?"

"No. It's very pretty, but I've just never seen you with such an elaborate coiffure."

That seemed a strange thing for him to say. Why did he care about her hair?

"You seem to be enjoying yourself," he said.

"I am. Jane has introduced me to so many people. I only hope I can remember half their names."

"And you've danced a lot?"

"I've danced every dance. I believe this is the fifth one."

He made no comment to that.

"Are you enjoying yourself? Or are you only making sure nothing is amiss?"

"I've been doing my best to make sure there are no French spies about. But I would ask you not to go out of doors to get some air, or for any other reason, without me."

"Very well."

His countenance was more sober than usual, and

he was behaving rather strangely all around.

"Are you well, Mr. Gilchrist?"

"Perfectly well, I thank you."

"I wish to thank you for your service to me and to your country."

"I am only doing my duty."

"Of course."

He seemed determined not to accept her compliment, and he even moved stiffly in the dance.

"Do you enjoy dancing, Mr. Gilchrist?"

"It is a pleasant activity."

"More pleasant than shooting at pursuers?" She smiled to show she was trying to make a jest.

"Both have their place."

"Indeed." Far be it from her to try any further to rouse him from his strange mood. If he wished to be morose, then she wouldn't stop him.

The dance ended. She politely thanked him for the dance and they went their separate ways.

Penelope did as she had determined to do. She sat out the next dance, watching Henry Gilchrist dance with Lady Susan, while Jane danced with Mr. Westbrook.

Just before the next dance, Bennington sought Penelope out and asked her to dance. She danced the next dance with him, then with another gentleman she'd just met. She noticed Henry Gilchrist danced a second time with Lady Susan, but then she lost sight of him.

"I think I'm done for tonight," Penelope told Jane. "I'm not used to so much dancing, and I fear my reputation will suffer already for how many times I've danced."

"Very well. Sit and rest, but I intend to dance all night. It is my favorite activity."

Jane did dance with great grace and enthusiasm.

She was a joy to watch.

Penelope found herself sitting next to Mrs. Rebecca Heywood, whom she remembered as the wife of the philandering Mr. Heywood whom Jane had avoided when he started to ask Penelope to dance.

Rebecca was pleasant enough, but there was a deep sadness about her, reminding Penelope of herself when she was married.

"Your dress is very pretty," Rebecca remarked.

"Yours is beautiful. I love the blue and lavender and pink embroidery."

"Thank you." She smiled, but even her smile was sad. No doubt she knew of her husband's dalliances. Penelope's heart ached for her, her own pain still so sharp and recent.

"I'm very sorry for your recent loss," Rebecca said. "Please accept my condolences."

"Thank you. That is very kind." After a moment, Penelope added, "I suppose it must seem strange that I have been dancing so much so soon after my husband's death, but—"

"Oh no, you mustn't worry about that. You of all people have a right to throw off your sorrow and dance. I only say that because, well, when a spouse has died, you have no obligation at all anymore. Is that not what the Scriptures say?"

"Yes." And when your husband has been unfaithful, you also have no obligation to him anymore. But that was not a very popular sentiment. After all, divorce was unheard of amongst her acquaintances, very costly financially as well as socially, so much so that almost no one ever attempted it.

She talked pleasantly with Mrs. Heywood, whose

countenance brightened and inhibitions lifted more the longer they spoke. When they parted, Penelope watched Rebecca catch sight of her husband, who was leaning down to speak close to a woman. The woman smirked up at him, her hand on his arm.

Rebecca walked straight up to them and said something to her husband, then to the woman, as if she didn't know the two were flirting. But of course she knew. A woman always knows when her husband is interested in another woman.

Again, Penelope felt the pain inside her own chest and wished she could do something about all the injustice in the world, especially all the unfaithful husbands who had good and kind wives who didn't deserve to be betrayed.

When the evening was over, Penelope had to stifle a yawn several times in the carriage on the way home. She'd had a wonderful time, quite possibly the most enjoyable time of her life, and it was all because of Jane Gilchrist.

Jane chattered on to her mother, who sat opposite Jane, mostly relating all the gossip, all the people who had been at the ball, and who they'd danced with and who said what.

Henry Gilchrist sat opposite Penelope. He said very little, though she caught him looking at her quite often, but he seemed to still be in the same disgruntled mood he'd been in at the ball. Was he worried about the spies? If he was, he'd look more vigilant.

"Lord Dunderhoff said you were the prettiest girl in the room," Jane said to Penelope, "but he is old, nearly sixty, so I tried to steer him toward someone else who might have fewer options than you, Penelope."

Fewer options? Penelope had no options at all. She almost said so, but Jane had already started talking of something else.

Certainly Penelope was not interested in an old man. Nor anyone else who wasn't sincerely in love with her. She'd learned her lesson the first time.

She kept sneaking glances at Henry Gilchrist. Why was he so out of sorts? And why had he decided to dance with her? He'd tried to tell Jane that she shouldn't push her to dance so much, agreeing with Penelope that it was not good for her reputation. If he'd truly been worried about her reputation, he wouldn't have danced with her.

It was all so strange.

Well, they were still good friends, at least, or he wouldn't have asked her to dance. And that thought comforted her as she realized there wasn't a single other man at the ball that she could even imagine being married to. And none of them had shown particular interest in Penelope either. But that was no surprise, since she was newly widowed and her husband had been murdered.

She could see her future now, in the sitting room alone in Shropshire, her grandmother scolding and scowling, while Penelope pretended to listen. Then she'd excuse herself to her room, complaining of a headache, and read books. Until Grandmother burst into her room and gave her a contemptuous speech about how books, and especially novels, were not good for the minds of young ladies, and how she should be out husband hunting, although not in those exact terms.

At least she could write letters to Jane and look forward to occasional visits with Jane and her mother and Henry.

"Why are you sighing?" Jane asked. "Are you unhappy?"

"No, of course not. I enjoyed myself immensely."

"She's tired," Mrs. Gilchrist said. "Let her sleep the rest of the way home."

Again, she caught Henry Gilchrist staring at her, but he quickly looked away.

"Rest your head on my shoulder, Penelope," Jane said, and continued to talk to her mother of all the people she'd seen, telling of all the news she'd heard.

Penelope did as Jane instructed and closed her eyes. How pleasant to have kind friends. *Thank you, God.*

CHAPTER NINETEEN

Henry huffed out a breath as he urged his horse into a fast trot, then a gallop, through the woods and into an open meadow. He let his horse move as fast as he liked, and Henry let the wind flow through his hair, wishing it could clear his mind.

Jane had introduced Penelope to every eligible man at the ball, and she'd danced with most of them. Why had it bothered him so much?

That was the question that had been nagging at him, pecking at him like an incessant bird, reminding him every minute that Penelope was a free woman and could engage the affections of any man she chose.

Why should he care?

He'd made himself responsible for protecting her. Perhaps that was it. The French spies could come back at any time, realizing his fake plans that he'd written up in such a hurry were not the real plans. But was that really the reason?

He didn't want the whole country to know that she was staying at his house. That information could get back to the spies if they were looking for her.

But that wasn't the reason either.

She was a poor, penniless widow now, and as such, she was not to be trusted. She only wanted the richest man she could find. Her heart was set on making a good match, not falling in love. That's how all poor women were. He was better off with Lady Susan, an earl's daughter with a hefty dowry and a comfortable home. There was no reason for her to vie for the richest suitors. She could marry for love.

But her conversation had not pleased him last night. And she'd been dancing with that soldier, Westbrook. He hadn't liked that. That was why he'd asked Penelope to dance.

But he'd been trying to think of a reason to ask her to dance even before that. He'd wanted to feel her small, soft hand in his. He wanted to watch her eyes while they danced, to see the way they sparkled and the smile on her face, as she obviously enjoyed dancing. He wanted to be close to her again, as close as they'd been when he was helping her escape from the spies when they kidnapped her.

And he couldn't deny, at least to himself, that seeing her dancing with other men, holding their hand, even when it was only part of the dance, had made him almost angry.

Jane. This was all her fault.

He pushed his horse to go faster as they neared the fence that he and his brother Thomas had been jumping when his horse flipped over and Henry had broken his collarbone and his leg.

Poor Thomas. He'd been so angry with his brother, had held a grudge against him for marrying the woman Henry loved, even though he'd told him he did not. They'd barely spoken for a year when Thomas died.

But Henry was the fortunate one. He would have been miserable if he'd married a woman who didn't actually love him, who only married him because she thought he was the richest man she could get.

The horse slowed as they neared the trees where a

small stream flowed. They made their way to the water and Henry dismounted.

Henry heard voices and a noise like horses moving through the brush. And then he saw them—Jane and Penelope leading their horses to the stream on the opposite side.

He saw them first. Jane was talking and Penelope was listening, that subtle smile on her lips, the one she wore when she was truly listening. When her grandmother spoke she looked completely different, her eyes saying she was far away, trying not to absorb her grandmother's barbs and controlling orders.

Had they ended up in the same place by happenstance? When he was trying to get away from everyone and just be alone with his thoughts?

His horse wasn't finished drinking, and even though they hadn't seen him yet, it wasn't likely he could get away without seeming as if he was avoiding them. The groom that was following behind them had seen him, and he waved.

"Good morning, ladies," he said. "I'm surprised to see you both up and out of the house after the late night last night."

"Good morning," they both said. Then Jane answered, "We both slept well and wanted a leisurely ride this morning."

"Both of you? Or did you want a ride and you persuaded Mrs. Hammond to go with you?"

Jane let her mouth drop open in that dramatic way of hers. Then she looked at Penelope.

"My brother would have you thinking that I'm controlling you, persuading you to whatever I wish. I have you know, Penelope Hammond has a mind of her own, and she's not afraid to express herself with me. Isn't that right, Penelope?"

"Of course." But Penelope looked amused and a bit embarrassed. "I enjoy Jane's company, and when she asked me to go riding, I told her I would enjoy riding on your lovely grounds."

"Oh no, you don't have to explain yourself to him," Jane said. "We are not children, having to justify our actions to men. We are grown women, capable of making up our own minds."

"Indeed." Just as his first love had made up her own mind that she preferred his brother to him. Just as Penelope had made up her own mind to marry an earl, a man much older than she was, a man she admitted she hardly knew when she married him, and a man who obviously did not love her.

"Henry, forgive me for saying this, but you seem out of spirits lately. Are you sure you're well?"

"Perfectly well." He wouldn't let her bait him into some sort of confession that would make her feel triumphant.

"You certainly seem out of sorts. Was this how he behaved in London, when you were saving yourself from kidnappers and spies and dodging murderers?"

Penelope's eyes went wide. She opened her mouth but seemed not to know what to say. Finally, she said, "I wouldn't say that I saved myself from kidnappers. Mr. Gilchrist helped me or I probably would never have escaped."

"I'm glad to hear he was helpful." Jane smirked at him.

"Always making light of everything." His statement was rather unjust. His sister could be serious when the occasion arose. In fact, she'd been the shoulder his mother cried on most often in the sad and tragic deaths of her son and husband from the past two years. But he was not in the mood for her goading remarks.

"You should try it more often," she quipped. "It might do you good."

He was out of spirits, but he did not have to discuss his mood with Jane.

"And now, I believe I'm going into the trees to relieve myself. I drank too much tea this morning."

Before either of them could comment, his brazen sister headed away from them, deeper into the trees. The red-faced groom followed after her, but at a distance, leaving him alone with Penelope Hammond.

"Your sister is a great friend to me," Penelope said, "and it is true, I do tend to let myself be influenced by others. But I would have said no if I hadn't wished to go riding this morning."

Henry crossed the stream toward her, sloshing through the shallow water in his riding boots.

"You don't have to defend yourself." Did he sound rude? In the kind of mood he was in, he knew he could be rude.

Penelope smiled. "I know."

They stood in silence, she about four feet away, staring at the stream and holding her horse's reins loosely.

"It's very pretty here. I like the peacefulness, the sounds of the stream and the birds. I suppose the home where I grew up had birds too, but I was never allowed to go beyond the garden, and it was so formal. I find I like the wildness of this land better."

She wasn't looking at him. But her profile was so gentle, so beguilingly sweet, it made his chest ache.

He mentally shook off the feeling.

"I've heard America is like this everywhere, and even wilder—thick undergrowth, briar brambles, all manner of creatures, including wild cats and an abundance of deer and elk."

She smiled and raised her brows. "That sounds like an exciting place."

"We should—that is, I've been thinking of traveling there, someday, in the future." He cleared his throat. "Fields and meadows, streams and woods are more appealing to me than the formality of a planned garden."

"I agree. Wildflowers growing in a field are so much more beautiful than trimmed rose bushes."

They stood in silence a moment longer, then she said, "What were you thinking about when we intruded upon your reverie?"

What was he thinking about? Oh yes. "To be honest, I was thinking about my brother."

"It must have been so difficult when he died."

"Yes. All the more so because I had let something come between us. And I was holding a grudge and keeping my distance from him."

"I'm so sorry." She was quiet for a few moments, then said, "Jane told me a bit about it."

He could have guessed that. "I was just thinking that I was the fortunate one, since she didn't marry me but married my brother instead."

"Oh?"

"Because she couldn't have loved me if she could so quickly turn away from me and choose my brother."

"I see what you mean." Her face was scrunched, as if in deep thought. "I only wish my husband hadn't married me. He didn't love me and didn't intend to be a faithful husband. Truthfully, I don't understand why he did."

She shook her head, a tiny, almost imperceptible movement. "It was such a shock when he was murdered, but . . . there was nothing for me to mourn that I hadn't already been mourning."

It was his turn to say, "I'm so sorry." He took a step toward her, wishing he could comfort her.

"You might wonder why I married him. My grandmother had been trying to negotiate the marriage, unbeknownst to me. When he made his offer, I initially said no. But my grandmother was incensed, so angry that I finally gave in."

He was surprised to hear that she'd originally turned down Lord Hampstead's marriage proposal. Perhaps she wasn't like his sister-in-law. Perhaps she wasn't only trying to marry the richest man she could.

"I did love him," she went on, "because he was my husband, and I honestly thought he would grow to love me." She shook her head again. "He didn't."

How could any man be married to this lovely, gentle creature and not love her? It was hard for Henry to fathom.

"He was a fool. He never should have treated you that way. Some men don't know how fortunate they are, and some men are more beast than human. I'm sorry."

She finally looked up at him. "I shouldn't have told you all that. I don't know why I did. It's over now and in the past, and I shouldn't dwell on it. I . . . I generally can name several emotions I'm feeling at any given time, but so many things have happened in so short a time that it has left me wondering how I feel, so I keep wanting to talk about it. Poor Jane has had to listen to it all more than once, I'm afraid."

She laughed, a small sound that she quickly stifled.

Jealous. That's the emotion he'd been feeling the night before when he watched her dance with other men. She was his Penelope Hammond, the young widow who trusted him and looked to him for protection.

What a foolish, dangerous sentiment.

"You don't have to worry. Jane loves you and I'm sure she doesn't mind hearing whatever you have to say. And I don't mind either."

He was starting to sound daft. And maybe even in love.

Perhaps he should go to America, the sooner the better.

The only reason he hadn't was because his mother would be beside herself with worry. She'd imagine all sorts of terrible things happening to him in that wild land—death by the natives' tomahawks they'd heard so much about; death by those diseases, yellow fever and scarlet fever, that were so prevalent there; or death by wild panthers, wolves, or bears. There were many possibilities and she'd be thinking of them all.

"Listen to me, talking of myself when you were saying that you'd been thinking about your brother. I'm so sorry. Please, go on."

"All's well. I was just thinking of how I should have forgiven him for marrying the woman who was engaged to me, the woman I thought I loved."

Penelope was gazing up at him with such compassion in her eyes, again causing the now-familiar ache in his chest.

"I regret holding that against him. I should have forgiven him and let it go. Indeed, I still haven't forgiven her. And that's also wrong. After all, the Holy Scriptures say we must forgive those who trespass against us if we want God to forgive us."

"That is hard sometimes. I understand, and I'm sure God understands."

"But it's time I forgave them both. I've already suffered the loss of a year of my brother's friendship by not doing so sooner."

She nodded with a sympathetic look in her eyes.

"And you? Do you feel as if you've forgiven your husband for all the ways he wronged you?"

She sighed. "I've thought about that a lot. During the marriage I realized I needed to forgive him each time he was cold and unloving to me, and then when I heard of his infidelity. It took me months, even years, but I finally did feel as if I'd forgiven him. But then he'd do something else and I'd feel just as angry and hurt and betrayed as ever, and I wondered if I'd ever forgiven him at all. I've felt that way many times since he died. But I think I just have to keep saying the words, 'God, I forgive him,' and God will help me, eventually, to feel that I have."

"I think you're right. God knows our hearts. He knows that we're willing to forgive. 'The spirit is willing but the flesh is weak.'"

"Exactly." She smiled and lifted her hand.

He wasn't sure if she meant for him to take her hand, but he did, reveling in the softness of her skin, her smaller hand inside his.

Her smile went slack and her eyes locked on his. A spot on the side of her neck pulsed with her heartbeat, and his own heart seemed to be pounding at the same pace.

He stepped closer, then slipped his free hand around her shoulders and pulled her to his chest. She immediately drew her arms around him and held on, her cheek pressed against his chest.

How good it felt to hold her. And the way she tucked her head against him, he could tell she was enjoying it just as much. The words, *This is the woman I have provided for you,* seemed to flow fleetingly through his mind.

Not so, Lord, he silently said back to the voice, *for I have sworn never to marry a poor woman.*

What was he doing? This was not planned, but he should not be trying to comfort her.

The truth was, he wanted to kiss her. He wanted to continue holding her and . . . he wanted to kiss her.

Penelope took a step back and extricated herself just as he heard the crunch of something underfoot and the swish of a branch being pushed aside from the stand of trees.

Jane stepped out of the woods.

His heart beat a dozen beats per second. What was he thinking? What would he have done if Jane hadn't come back when she did? But he couldn't think about it now. Besides, it was only an embrace, just a simple, innocent embrace.

At least, that's what he would keep telling himself.

CHAPTER TWENTY

Penelope wanted to soak up every feeling she could from this moment. What did it mean? She only knew that it felt wonderful to be held in Henry's arms.

Just as she was wondering why Jane had not returned, she heard a noise from the direction and pulled herself out of the warmth and comfort of Henry's embrace.

Warmth and comfort she wasn't entitled to. Warmth and comfort she'd so seldom felt before, but warmth and comfort that she questioned. Could he feel about her the way she felt about him? It was all so confusing, for she knew he had feelings for Lady Susan, not her. He'd never shown any undue interest in Penelope before.

"Did you wonder what had become of me?" Jane asked. "There was a pretty bird and I followed it. I'd never seen one like it and I wanted to be able to describe it to you, and then it took me a few minutes to figure out how to get back here."

Henry cleared his throat, staring down at his feet. "What kind of bird was it?"

"It was one of those birds with a long neck and a long beak. I think it was trying to catch a fish. And it had dark blue, sparkly feathers."

"It sounds very pretty." Penelope tried to sound normal, but her voice sounded strained in her own ears. Had Jane seen her embracing Henry? What would she think of her? Would she think Penelope was trying to secure the affections of her brother? Would she be angry? Jane thought Henry was thinking of marrying Lady Susan. Certainly Lady Susan was a much better match for him than she was, a recent widow with nothing to offer.

"It sounds like a kingfisher. How big was it?" Henry still wasn't looking either of them in the eye, but at least his voice sounded normal.

Jane used her hands to show him the size of the bird. "I'm surprised you didn't come looking for me. I was gone a long time. What were you two doing?"

"Talking." Henry stared straight back at Jane.

Penelope tried to change the subject. "Do you think you could find the bird again? I'd love to see it."

"Henry, you can come with us and keep us from getting lost in the woods."

"These woods? They're not big enough to get lost in."

"Stop being so morose and come on an adventure with us. It's only for a little while."

They all took hold of their horses' reins and started following Jane.

"I am not morose, by the way." Henry was taking up the rear. "I think you just like saying words like morose."

"No, it's you, Henry. It's all you."

Henry snorted. But when Penelope looked back at him, he smiled and winked.

Her heart started beating wildly again. *O God, don't let me make a fool of myself if Henry is only teasing me.*

"Watch your head," Henry said. "If Jane lets go of that branch it could snap back and hit you."

"Thank you, I will."

Jane had hurried at such a pace that soon that was not a problem. Was she trying to leave her and her brother alone?

No, Jane intended for her brother to marry Lady Susan.

"There's a low-hanging branch ahead," he said.

"Thank you. I see it." Penelope brushed it aside and held it until he could grab it, so it wouldn't snap back on him.

He gazed into her eyes. "Jane is ever the adventurous one."

"And she always enjoys herself. Sometimes I think she's my opposite." Penelope's breath was shallowing again.

"Do you not usually enjoy yourself?"

"I'm usually trying too hard to please someone else. Or to make sure I'm not doing something wrong."

"Yes, I could see that about you."

"Am I so transparent?"

"No, but you are . . . conscientious."

"I guess that's one way to describe it."

He gave her such a look . . . It made her heart stop beating for a moment. No one had ever looked at her like that.

"Most women aren't as self-deprecating as you are."

She wasn't sure what to say in reply.

"You two are so slow. Come." Jane motioned them forward with her hand.

Perhaps Penelope was imagining that Henry was looking at her with tender emotion. Jane certainly didn't seem to notice anything out of the ordinary.

They tramped around the forest next to the stream but did not find the bird.

"We must have scared him off," Henry said.

"He was very pretty," Jane said. "If we could have

seen him catch a fish I'm sure it would have been amazing. Perhaps we'll see him tomorrow."

They rode home slowly while talking of birds and storms and adventures Jane had had in the country. Once back at the house, Henry helped Penelope down from her horse, leaving his hands on her sides longer than was necessary, staring down into her eyes. Then, without a word, he walked to the house.

"Does your brother seem to be behaving strangely?" Penelope asked.

"Why do you ask?" Jane's face lit up. "What did he do? What did he say?"

"I'm sure it's nothing. He's very kind to me. I'm sure it is only because he feels . . ."

"What? Feels what?"

"Feels an obligation because of what happened in London and how I was in so much danger. Or perhaps because he pities me, being a widow."

"That does sound like Henry. He is very responsible, and he is the most compassionate man I know. But what makes you say that? Did he do something or say something untoward?"

"No." Penelope wasn't sure how much to tell her new friend. She didn't seem very good at keeping secrets, and Penelope would be mortified if she told Jane what had happened and then Jane told Henry what she said.

Oh, Henry. His chest had felt so good and solid beneath her cheek, his arms so warm and protective. How would it feel to have someone like Henry Gilchrist to love her? What would it be like to be his wife?

Sheer heaven.

~ ~ ~

Henry splashed cold water on his face and grabbed

a towel.

Putting his arms around Mrs. Hammond, holding her against his chest, such things were not permissible. What must she think of him? She hadn't exactly complained. But he had a responsibility to be the courteous gentleman he was supposed to be.

What was he thinking?

Well, he'd been thinking about kissing her, that's what he was thinking.

He had to stay away from Penelope Hammond. She was too much of a temptation. But he had no intention of repeating the stupid mistake he'd made before—falling in love with a poor woman who was only thinking about money, not love.

Penelope did seem much different from his sister-in-law. But he'd trusted her too, and look what it got him —the loss of a relationship with his brother, whose life was cut short, so much shorter than anyone expected.

He finished getting dressed and headed out of his room. In the breakfast room he was greeted by his mother, sister, and Penelope.

"Are you well, Henry?" his mother said. "You look a bit flushed."

"Perfectly well."

"What are your plans for the day? We were thinking of taking the carriage to the sea and doing a bit of sightseeing."

Sightseeing? "You know you need to take at least two men, with guns, if you go anywhere."

"Is that still necessary?" his mother asked. "I thought you remedied that problem when you were in London. Nothing has happened, and you and Penelope have been here for days now."

"Exactly. It has only been a few days. I don't know if the problem is solved just yet." The French spies could realize the plans were fake, but he didn't even dare say that out loud. "It is better to be safe, don't you think, Mother?"

"Yes, I suppose so."

"Couldn't you come with us?" Jane gazed up at him with an imploring expression. "You could be one of the two men with guns." Her expression changed to one of mirth. She was ever thinking of the irony and levity in every situation.

"Perhaps tomorrow." Why did he say that? Truthfully, part of him wanted to go with them, but he knew it was not wise. He obviously couldn't control himself around Penelope.

"We can put it off until tomorrow." Jane's enthusiasm showed, as usual.

"It will be better to have a bit of time to plan," Mother said.

"Penelope has never been to the sea. Can you believe that?" Jane squeezed Penelope's arm.

That lady smiled. "I'm just enjoying the company, wherever we happen to be."

"You're so sweet, Penelope, but I want to show you my favorite places, and the seaside is so beautiful. It's unlike any other place you could go."

"I'm eager to see it, but I don't want to cause Mr. Gilchrist any undue problems."

He should tell them it was safer to stay home, that ruthless men were out there who would kill them if they thought they had something they wanted. But then he would be admitting that he might not be able to defend them.

"We can go tomorrow."

There was nothing to do but get his breakfast and sit down and listen to their chatter.

The mail arrived at that moment. His mother said, "Oh, Penelope got a letter from her grandmother." She passed it down to her.

As she accepted her letter, the corners of her mouth twitched, which was something he'd noticed about her when she was dreading something. He imagined her domineering grandmother telling her to flirt with Henry Gilchrist, but only if he was the wealthiest man in the room.

Just as she'd persuaded Penelope to marry Lord Hampstead.

Jane looked at him. "Perhaps we should take Lady Susan with us."

Lady Susan. He had not parted very well from her at the ball two nights ago. But he'd not been in the best frame of mind that night. She'd been rather cool to him, which he probably deserved.

"Yes, perhaps we should take Lady Susan," he said.

Jane's face froze.

Ah-ha! He knew it. Jane did not actually want Lady Susan to go with them. Was she pretending to try to find Penelope a husband when what she really wanted was for Henry to marry her?

That would work out fine for Jane, since she liked Penelope so much, but he would not be duped again into engaging himself to some poor woman with no options, someone who only wanted to marry money.

"That would be very pleasant, but the carriage will be so crowded with a fifth person," Jane said.

"No, I think we should take her with us," Henry

said.

Henry was enjoying his sister's reaction. She was strangely quiet as her mouth twisted and she stared down at the table.

"I will send her an invitation right away," Mother said.

Still Jane said nothing, but he could tell by the way she was pursing her lips and trying to hide her face from him that she was not pleased.

But he did need to spend time with Lady Susan if he was ever going to make a wise decision about whether to marry her. And he could not be manipulated into being alone with Penelope if Lady Susan was among the party.

CHAPTER TWENTY-ONE

In the sitting room Penelope read the letter from Grandmother while Jane and her mother made plans for their trip to the seaside.

Grandmother set the tone of the letter right away. "You never should have run away with that Henry Gilchrist. Eustace Hammond was beginning to think of you as a possible match, and then you were gone with no explanation. I only hope you are making good use of your time there and engaging Mr. Gilchrist's affections. I have heard his income is fifteen thousand a year now that he's inherited the estate from his brother who died."

Penelope blushed for her grandmother's greed and shallow goals.

Her grandmother, in her letter, demanded that she come back to London as soon as possible, unless she was making advances with Mr. Gilchrist. Then she continued to scold Penelope for leaving in such haste. She never even acknowledged that her life may have been in danger, that she might have been fleeing out of necessity. Her husband was murdered, after all, and a Member of Parliament had been poisoned. Although that might not be common knowledge at this point.

Did her grandmother even care about her? She'd wondered that many times, and the fact that she never seemed very concerned about how unhappy Penelope was in her marriage had seemed to confirm it. She'd even defended him, saying, "All these aristocratic men have paramours, even the Prince Regent and the Duke of Wellington."

"That doesn't make it right, and it doesn't mean their wives are happy."

But Penelope's happiness had never seemed to concern anyone.

If Penelope did win Henry's affections, it would not be because she was flirting or manipulating him. She was more determined than ever to be free of such machinations. After all, she wanted her future husband to love her for who she was, not for how well she flirted.

At least she had the trip to the seaside to look forward to, even though Jane seemed to regret her suggestion of inviting Lady Susan. Penelope had her suspicions that Jane wished Henry would transfer his preference from that lady to Penelope, but it was as if Jane and her brother were playing some kind of passively aggressive game.

Well, she needn't worry about it. Jane was her friend and Penelope would no doubt have a wonderfully enjoyable time with her, getting her first look at the sea.

~ ~ ~

Two days later, Henry found himself in the carriage with his mother, sister, and Penelope, but this time Lady Susan was seated on one side of Jane, Penelope on the other, with he and his mother opposite them.

Lady Susan looked regal, her head high, confident as usual. She was not a talkative woman, but she held her own with Jane, even interrupting her on occasion, as Jane sometimes forgot to take a breath.

Penelope, on the other hand, seemed content to stare out the window, sometimes pointing out sights to his mother, who also was content to let Jane and Lady

Susan do all the conversing.

"You like the mountains more than the seaside, do you not?" Lady Susan addressed him.

"I do prefer rocks and grass to sand, but the ocean has a soothing sort of rhythm to it."

Penelope turned to listen to his comment.

"I prefer the ocean," Jane said, "the very wildness of it."

"I believe I prefer the ocean as well," Lady Susan said, sticking out her chin as if in defiance of his opinion.

"Do you like the mountains, Penelope?" his mother asked, and as there was an unusual lull in the conversation, everyone turned to her.

"I did visit the mountains in Scotland once and liked it very much. The weather was cold, but I liked the castles, the green hills and valleys, the rocks, and the untamed nature of it. Very different from Shropshire. It was beautiful."

"Cold? Scotland is a frozen wasteland." Lady Susan's eyelids hung low, as if she was shuddering inwardly. "I detest the place, myself."

An awkward silence followed. Penelope frowned on one side of her face, but it was an amused sort of frown, as if she was trying to hide her amusement.

"Perhaps it was only the time of year you were there," Jane said cheerfully. "I myself have never seen Scotland. I shall have the season in mind and go in summer."

"I assure you, Scotland is always cold." Lady Susan said. "I have gone there in all the seasons, and it was cold without exception."

Henry found that hard to believe, but having never been to Scotland himself, he said nothing.

"Well, today promises to be pleasantly warm." Jane ducked her head to try to see the sky. "Only a few clouds, and we are headed for the lovely seaside. I can hardly wait to sink my toes in the wet sand."

"Now, Jane, don't go ruining your frock," Mother said. "It's impossible to get the seawater stains out of some fabrics."

"That's why I wore my oldest dress. You know I must be allowed to get my feet wet."

Mother only shook her head. She'd never tried very hard to curb Jane's high spirits. But he was glad they had a kind and loving mother. Penelope had been an orphan for many years, and he certainly could feel sorry that she'd missed out on the love of a father and mother. Perhaps that was why she never stood up for herself to her grandmother.

But Jane was right about one thing. The weather was perfect today. He couldn't help being glad for Penelope's sake. As for Lady Susan, she no doubt had had many opportunities to see the seaside, and would have many more. But once Penelope was back in Shropshire with her grandmother, she'd have little chance to see the seashore or anything else pleasant, if he understood her grandmother . . .

Why was he thinking like this?

He had to admit, he did care about Penelope. Not only was she brave, but she was no thoughtless flirt.

He inwardly sighed. He could already see, this was going to be a long day of arguing with himself.

~ ~ ~

Penelope got her first glimpse of the ocean and gasped. How could it be so impossibly blue?

Jane watched her face as she got out of the carriage.

"Isn't it magnificent?"

"It is, so amazing."

It was a foreign place, with sand and nothing growing on it, next to a body of water so wide and vast that it seemed to have no end. And the color of it was like nothing she'd seen, so blue, reflecting the light of the sun and sparkling like fine-cut gems.

"What do you think?"

"I can hardly take it in. The waves are so loud, and it's so blue. I've never seen anything like it."

"We should take a ride on a boat sometime."

"No boats." Mrs. Gilchrist shook her head.

"Mother is afraid of the water," Jane whispered. Then she hurried to say something to Lady Susan, probably not wanting her to feel left out.

Henry was saying very little and had given his arm to his mother. Meanwhile, Jane had linked her arms through Penelope's and Lady Susan's and was heading straight down to the shore.

When they got close to the water, Lady Susan unlinked from Jane and stood on high ground. But Penelope went with Jane down to the water's edge. They both took off their shoes and let the water wash over their feet, holding their skirts just to their ankles. But that was not enough for Jane. She left Penelope and plunged into the water, soaking her skirt up to her calves.

The water was surprisingly cold, and the sand hard to walk in. But Penelope began to notice a tiny animal walking along the sand. Henry was standing nearby so she asked him, "Is that a crab?"

"It is." He squatted to study it.

Penelope couldn't keep her eyes off the water, and she walked a little way down the shore to a small pool that had gotten cut off from the ocean. Inside were several strange creatures who seemed to be existing happily in the peaceful little pool away from the wild waves.

Jane called out her name. She was running toward her, while Henry and his mother were standing beside Lady Susan, and they seemed to be in conversation.

"What did you find?" Jane bent over the pool, and they watched the animals for a while.

"I feel guilty for running away and leaving Lady Susan by herself."

"Oh, she's very well with Mother and Henry. I'm actually sorry I mentioned inviting her. It was very foolish of me." Jane scowled down at the pool of creatures. "It would be more pleasant without her."

Lady Susan wasn't so bad. Penelope had met much haughtier and prouder young ladies who possessed a fraction of Lady Susan's beauty and wealth. But it was true that they probably would have been more comfortable and easy without her.

"Everything is different here," Penelope said. "Even the birds are different. It's as if we've come to an entirely new continent."

"Yes. Someday I'd like to live in a house right on the sea, so I can listen to the waves crashing every night while I fall asleep. We stayed in a place like that on the Isle of Wight once."

After walking up and down the shore for a while longer, they got back in the carriage and found an inn with an upper room where they could sit and dine. Lady Susan complained about the food, but Penelope found it rustic and filling, certainly nothing to complain about.

But the more Lady Susan complained, the more sober Henry Gilchrist's expression became.

On the way home, Jane began talking of how Penelope had twice escaped French spies who thought she had something they wanted.

"Can you believe, Lady Susan, that she was able to save herself?"

Lady Susan's brows rose as she gazed back at Jane.

"She stabbed her abductor in the back with a letter opener."

Lady Susan's lips twisted into a look of disgust. She stared coldly at Penelope, her face scrunched up as if she was smelling soured milk.

"I think she was very brave," Jane went on, raising her brows. "She did not faint or wait for someone to rescue her. She stood up for herself and did what she had to do to save herself."

Lady Susan's expression stayed the same, but she said nothing. Penelope could feel her cheeks heating, but she did not have to care what Lady Susan thought —although she knew enough to know that most people would take the same view as Lady Susan.

On the drive home, everyone was much more subdued, and Lady Susan was taken to the door of her own home. She made a cursory attempt at inviting them all to stay, but seemed quite glad when they said they would not and needed to go home.

When the carriage was well down the lane, Jane said, "Well, that was a lovely time, was it not?"

"I enjoyed the sea very much," Penelope said. "Thank you for taking me on this lovely outing."

"It was our pleasure, of course, my dear." Mrs. Gilchrist smiled her motherly smile.

"It was a good day for it," Henry said.

"A good day, and good company." Jane grinned at

Penelope.

Penelope settled in for the rest of the drive, about an hour. She did her best not to think about Lady Susan's disgusted look, tried not to think of all the things she might say to that lady if she were bold and didn't care to make everyone in the carriage uncomfortable.

She caught Henry staring at her more than once. What was he thinking in that handsome head of his?

CHAPTER TWENTY-TWO

The next week or so, Penelope and Jane did their usual riding about and even sightseeing, and gradually Henry relaxed the restrictions—many of which Jane was already ignoring, such as having two grooms ride out with them for protection. More often than not, Henry went with them instead of the grooms, and he kept a pistol on his person or in his saddlebag.

Once, when Jane and her mother had left Henry and Penelope alone for a few minutes, Penelope asked him, "Have you heard from anyone in London about the French spies? Have they gone back to France?"

"Everything I've heard is that they continued to see them for a day or two, but haven't seen them since. But we shouldn't let our guard down just yet."

Penelope nodded. "Of course."

On the eighth day of Penelope's stay with the Gilchrists, she received another letter from her grandmother.

Penelope,

Please come back to London right away. I believe Eustace Hammond has decided to make you an offer of marriage, but you must return to London immediately. I cannot trespass on his hospitality forever, and our townhouse is not very near his; therefore I would not be able to keep you at the forefront of his mind if I was not able to see him every day. I demand you cut your visit short, even if you have to say that I am ill. If you do not, you will miss out on the best marriage offer I could hope to get for you, since the unfortunate event of your first husband's passing. Eustace Hammond is even richer than I realized, richer than your first husband was before he gambled away half his fortune.

Was David such a good husband that it was unfortunate that he passed? Certainly not in the way of loving his wife and showing her even a tiny bit of kindness and attention. But kindness and attention had never been her grandmother's strengths either.

The rest of her grandmother's letter was more of the same. Penelope folded it up and took a sip of her tea.

"Is your grandmother well?"

Mrs. Gilchrist asked the question politely as they all, including Henry, took their breakfast together.

"I believe she is well."

"Is she trying to force you to go back to London again?" Jane asked.

Penelope wished she could say no, wanted to reply that her grandmother encouraged her to stay and enjoy herself. "She is, I'm afraid."

"You aren't going, are you?" Jane looked worried.

"No. I said I would stay a fortnight."

"But I want you to stay longer. I know Henry originally said a fortnight, but Mother and I invited you to stay a month at least."

"I want to stay." Penelope felt a knot rising into her throat.

"But you are dependent on your grandmother," Mrs. Gilchrist said sympathetically. "I understand, but we would love for you to stay if you think you can."

She wanted to say that her grandmother would

make her life very difficult if she defied her. But it felt wrong to criticize her, especially to people who didn't know her.

The truth was, she would have to defy her grandmother sooner or later, because she would not accept a marriage proposal from Eustace Hammond. She didn't love him and he didn't love her. Her only hope was that he would turn his interest away from Penelope. But even if he did, her grandmother would still blame her for his transfer of interest.

"Will you stay?" Jane asked.

"I will stay a fortnight."

Jane sat up straighter and opened her mouth to protest.

"I want to stay longer, but as your mother says, I am dependent on my grandmother, and I cannot defy her for long."

Jane balled her hand into a fist. "I wish I were more independent. I would tell your grandmother you are residing with me now."

Penelope wasn't sure what to say. The way Henry was looking at her, she was reminded of how he looked when he was ordering the mercenaries not to lay a hand on her. Was he angry with her? What did she say that he didn't like?

Jane's face was crestfallen. "I don't want you to go. Why can't your grandmother let you stay? Is it because she wants you to marry that Eustace Hammond? Just because he is an earl now?"

Penelope sighed.

"You won't marry him, will you?"

"No. I'd rather die than marry someone who didn't love me."

Perhaps Penelope shouldn't have been so blunt, but it was true. She abhorred the way her grandmother wanted her to pretend and never be herself. With Jane she'd learned to say the truth, even if it would have displeased her grandmother. After all, she was twenty-three years old. She couldn't let her grandmother treat her like a child forever, even if she was dependent on her.

"But what if he says he loves you? What if he does love you? Would you say yes to him then?" Jane leaned toward her.

Even without looking directly at him, Penelope could feel Henry's intense gaze on her.

"No, he is not . . . that is, I don't want to marry someone whose character I don't believe in, without question, someone I'm not in love with. Character and love are the most important qualities in choosing a husband, Jane, but especially character. If I've learned anything it's that."

"Well said, my dear." Mrs. Gilchrist reached over and gently squeezed Penelope's hand. "We also understand that you don't want to upset your grandmother."

"What shall you tell her?" Jane seemed unusually subdued.

"I shall tell her I gave my word to stay a fortnight, and if she insists I come home after that, even though you and your mother have asked me to stay longer, then I will return to London."

Jane sighed. "I don't understand a grandmother who doesn't want you to be happy."

"Perhaps she is thinking of Penelope's happiness," Mrs. Gilchrist said. "Perhaps her idea of happiness is being married to the richest man. But it's not Penelope's idea of happiness."

"Nor mine," Jane said stoutly. "I plan to marry only for the most passionate kind of love."

Henry let out a breath. "Excuse me. I have . . . some correspondence to attend to." He practically ran from the room.

"All this talk of love and marriage sent my brother running." Jane frowned.

"Did I say something wrong? I'm sorry." Penelope searched her mind for something that might have offended him.

"No, no, he's just sensitive," Mrs. Gilchrist smiled and shook her head. "He'll forget his heartache in time."

"Don't let him hear you call it 'his heartache.'" Jane rolled her eyes. "He will say you are mistaken, that he blesses the day that Henrietta settled on marrying his brother instead of him, that he is glad he never will make that mistake again because he's never getting married."

"But he was already considering marrying Lady Susan, so that was just his bitterness speaking," Mrs. Gilchrist said in low tones.

The two continued to discuss their brother and son while Penelope couldn't seem to stop thinking, *In a few more days, I'll likely never see him again. He'll just remember me as the penniless widow who is completely dependent on her grasping grandmother.*

~ ~ ~

Penelope's last full day at the Gilchrist home, Henry was writing a letter in the sitting room while Jane and his mother were looking through a book of botanical drawings, mostly of birds.

He didn't like to think she was leaving soon, but it was surely for the best, since he'd promised himself never to marry a poor woman. And he liked Penelope Hammond very much. Jane was generally a good judge of character, and she never seemed to tire of Penelope's company.

The most dangerous part was that the day they'd embraced next to the stream, with him wishing he could kiss her, was never far from his mind when Penelope was in the room or nearby.

But perhaps that was not the most dangerous element. The most dangerous could be that he was quite bothered by the fact that Penelope never flirted with him. She was kind and attentive when he spoke, but no more than she would have been to anyone else, including Jane's father or any other relative. The danger was that it bothered him.

Did she feel no more affection for him, or attraction to him, than she did for Eustace Hammond?

It was maddening, and even more maddening that he cared.

"Excuse me a moment," Jane said, getting up from her seat abruptly. "There is a book in my room that I want to show you. I won't be a minute." She hurried from the room.

He was alone with Penelope.

He continued writing his letter—or at least he tried to. But he couldn't seem to keep his thoughts on what he was writing. He was thinking of Penelope back in London with her scheming grandmother and Eustace Hammond.

She cleared her throat. He looked up.

"I wanted to thank you," she said, "for inviting me to come here, to get me away from the danger in London. It was very kind of you, and I shall always be grateful, for it also allowed me to make the acquaintance of your sister and mother, whom I shall always think of as the best women I know."

She seemed out of breath at the end of her relatively long speech.

"You are most welcome, and I hope you will be able to make more visits to them in the future." It was the simple, polite answer, rather cold in comparison to her warm words of gratitude.

She simply nodded. He had to say something more.

"I do pray you shall stay safe in London. I shall send word to the other committee members to have the mercenaries to keep a wary eye out for you." He would pay them himself for this service. "If you don't mind, send me your location, whenever you are to leave Eustace Hammond's townhouse."

"Of course. Thank you. I am grateful for all your kindnesses."

In spite of her words, there was a slightly troubled crease in her brow.

"Do let me know if you encounter anything amiss, if you see any of the French spies. You will, won't you?"

"I will."

He turned back to his letter, dipping his pen in the ink, but could not think of anything to write, his mind full of the cool exchange.

~ ~ ~

Penelope's heart was heavy in her chest, as if weighed down with chains, as she listened to her grandmother talk of Eustace Hammond's many good qualities, which consisted mostly of his three homes and his large fortune. At least they were no longer trespassing on his hospitality, as her grandmother had agreed to leave the house that had been Penelope's home for the past five years. Probably because Penelope said she would only come back to London if they stayed in her grandmother's townhouse.

"It is fortunate for you," Grandmother said with a tense flattening of her lips, "that your grandfather is at his house in Cornwall."

As everyone knew, her grandparents were unable to be in the same house simultaneously.

A servant came in with a calling card. "Miss Camille Dupre to see you."

"I am not home." The words flew out of Penelope's mouth. "I will not see her."

Grandmother looked only mildly interested, and said, "I don't remember a Camille Dupre." Then she continued talking of Eustace Hammond, the only subject she ever spoke of, besides Penelope's lack of options and the need to marry before her grandmother was dead and gone and could no longer look after her.

The servant left to tell Camille Dupre that Penelope was not at home. But was that the wrong thing to do? Perhaps she should have pretended to trust Camille. That way she could have learned something from Camille, if the French had accepted the fake plans as real.

"Wait!" Penelope jumped up and ran after the servant, who had not yet reached the front door. "Tell her I will see her. Show her in."

Penelope hurried back to her grandmother and sat down.

"What is this? Who is Camille Dupre?"

"I'll tell you later."

"Miss Camille Dupre," the servant announced.

Camille came into the room looking as confident as ever, this woman who had slept with Penelope's husband, and who had helped the French spies kidnap her.

Penelope's heart pounded as her mind took her to

the moment Camille had led the large man inside her house and they had forced her to go with them, the apology from Camille, who claimed they forced her to help them.

"Lady Hampstead. Mrs. Hammond." Camille dropped a demure little curtsy.

"Camille."

"She is no longer Lady Hampstead," Grandmother informed Camille. "She is Mrs. Hammond now. How is your health, my dear?" Grandmother could be quite polite and kind and friendly to people who didn't know her. And Grandmother obviously either did not know, or did not remember, that Camille had been one of David's paramours. She could be quite cutting and condemnatory with people who broke obvious rules like "Do not commit adultery."

"Of course. Pardon me for the error. How are you, Penelope? I hope you are well."

"I am very well, thank you. Are you well?"

"Yes, I have only been very worried about you, my friend. Your husband is killed in your own home, and then you disappear for a long time. I heard you were visiting friends."

"Yes, I was visiting friends, but I was only gone for a fortnight."

"Only a fortnight? It seemed longer."

A silence ensued. Grandmother seemed to realize, a few moments before, that their visitor had a French accent, for she suddenly grew pointedly uninterested in the conversation.

"I must go and speak to the cook about dinner. Excuse me," she said.

"Why are you here?" Penelope had never spoken so

rudely, but heat boiled up inside her at being deceived by this woman. "Where are your friends who took me from my home and threatened to harm me?"

"Such accusations! They wound me."

"Either start answering my questions or I'll have the servants escort you out."

"Very well. There is no need for such upset feelings. Those men you speak of threatened me as well. They said they would harm my family members who are still in France if I did not cooperate with them. But they said they would not harm you, they only wished to talk to you. You are my friend. I would never do anything to harm you."

Penelope didn't believe her, but even if it were true, the truth of her character was that she had slept with Penelope's husband, then befriended her. That could not mean anything good.

Her blood continued to boil as she stared at the woman, whom Penelope had previously thought was beautiful, but now her every flaw seemed to stand out. Her lips were too thin, her eyes too small, her bodice too low, her chin weak and oddly shaped. But worst of all was her character, and character to Penelope was everything.

Part of her wanted to throw what she knew in Camille's face. But it was probably best to pretend to be her friend, to pretend to believe her, and to pretend not to know that she had been her husband's paramour.

"Have you seen those men since that day? Are they still in London? Because I'm afraid of them."

Camille's gaze shifted to the wall behind Penelope. "I haven't seen them, no. They are no friends of mine, so I don't know if they're still in London. Do you know what they wanted?"

"They wanted information that my husband stole.

But I didn't have it."

"Oh."

Camille then tried to change the subject, asking Penelope about her recent trip, but Penelope refused to tell her where she'd been.

"Will you and your grandmother be returning to Shropshire soon? Or will you be staying in London?"

"I don't know. Grandmother hasn't told me, and I'm entirely dependent upon her." It was easier to keep a certain distance and coolness in her voice when she was speaking of her grandmother.

Camille gave her a sympathetic smile, but it only made Penelope want to punch her in the face. Never had she felt such rage in all her life. But she was enduring this meeting to see what information she could glean. So far, very little.

"I thank you for your visit, Camille, but it has quite upset me, seeing you again. I prefer that you not visit me. Good day."

Camille slowly rose to her feet. "I am sorry you are so upset, *ma petite*. I had hoped we could still be friends. I will consider you a great friend, no matter what you think of me." She pretended to wipe a tear from the corner of her eye.

Penelope wanted to roll her eyes the way Jane always did when someone said something she didn't like.

When Penelope made no reply, Camille walked to the doorway. "Farewell, Penelope."

Still, Penelope kept silent. When she was gone, Penelope muttered, "Good riddance."

"Where is your friend?" Grandmother asked, coming into the room. "She sounded French to me. Why do you have a French friend?"

"She is no friend of mine." Penelope tried to hold back the heat that was rising into her head. Telling her grandmother what had happened was probably not the wisest thing to do. But she couldn't seem to control this rage. After all the unfair things that had happened . . .

"That woman was David's paramour. He was sleeping at her apartments quite often in the months before he died. And she is a spy for the French government."

"What is a spy? What do you mean?"

"She is an evil woman. Please instruct the servants not to let her in, that she is not to be admitted into the house again."

"Of course, child, but there is no need to get so upset. Husbands are rarely faithful these days. If they provide for their wives, that is all most of us can expect." Her voice was cool and emotionless.

The heat inside her increased. She would get no words of sympathy from her grandmother. She should know that.

"I could imagine Eustace Hammond being the most likely gentleman of all our acquaintance to be faithful to his wife. He never gambles, doesn't even have a membership in any of the clubs in town, and he doesn't have any other flirtations at the moment. But that will change. Mark my words, there will be young ladies aplenty who will vie for his hand. He will be quite sought after. A young man of fortune, and an earl . . . he will be quite sought after."

"Will you excuse me? I have to go to my bedroom." Penelope fled the room as if her life depended on getting out of earshot of her grandmother's voice.

In her room, Penelope stared out the window, pressing her hand to her forehead. It was too much. How could she bear it? Bedeviled by her grandmother, her husband's adulterous woman in her face, pretending to be her friend . . . But that was her own fault. She never should have let that woman in the house.

A man walking on the street outside caught her eye. He was looking up at her, and a grin spread over his face. She knew that face and wide body instantly. It was the French spy whom she had stabbed with her letter opener.

All the blood drained from her face. Would he come after her again, to avenge himself on her? There was no Henry Gilchrist in town to save her this time.

CHAPTER TWENTY-THREE

An hour later, Penelope's hand shook as she handed the servant her letter and some coins.

"Please send this letter immediately. It must go out today. Don't stop to talk to anyone."

"Yes, madam." The footman took the letter and was gone.

God, please get my letter safely to Henry. Of course, it would take several hours to get to him, or possibly longer, and then it would take him several more hours to get to London. But she felt a bit more at peace knowing that he would at least be informed that the French spies were in town and were aware of her presence there.

God, save me.

~ ~ ~

Henry was reading the newspaper as he ate his breakfast when Jane suddenly sighed dramatically. "I wish Penelope had not left."

Henry was glad she was gone. At least, that's what he kept telling himself. But he couldn't seem to stop thinking about her—her eyes, her gentle voice, her smile when he said something clever but no one else seemed to notice.

He simply had to forget about her. She'd find some other rich man to marry.

That thought made him shift in his chair. What if her grandmother persuaded her to marry another unfeeling, adulterous man who would make her miserable, or even just some simpleton like that Eustace Hammond? Who Penelope married was not something that was under his control. He should not even think of it.

Penelope might have been easily persuaded, easily influenced when she had received her first proposal of marriage, but she was older and wiser now. Hadn't she spoken of her determination to pay particular attention to character when deciding to marry again? To never again marry someone who didn't love her?

But there were clever men in the world who could fool a woman as kind and compassionate as Penelope Hammond, men who could manipulate her sympathies and make her think he was a man of character when he was not.

His mind had gone over these same thoughts multiple times since she left. But he knew for a fact that it was unwise to marry a woman without any fortune.

"I have nothing to do now that Penelope's gone," Jane stared listlessly at the wall.

"Take a walk with Mother," Henry said. For heaven's sake, she was reflecting his own foolish thoughts back to him, and it was irritating.

"Oh, the post is here." Jane's face brightened as the servant brought in a small stack of letters.

"This came by express courier only a moment ago," the servant said, handing him a letter from a fellow committee member.

"Here's one for me. It's from Penelope!" Jane ripped it open. "But most of it is addressed to you, Henry." Instead of giving it to him, she read it aloud:

"'I was visited by Camille Dupre this morning. I received her, but only because I thought she might impart some information. She did not. But a few minutes after she left, I went up to my room and saw the French spy who had kidnapped me and whose shoulder I stabbed with my letter opener. He was staring up at me. He recognized me, I could tell by the way he looked at me. This may not mean anything, but I thought you should know.'"

Jane looked up. "This was sent yesterday, almost twenty-four hours ago. Something terrible could have happened to her in all that time!"

Henry's heart beat hard, and he stood from the table. Energy flowed through his limbs. But perhaps he should read the letter he'd been sent by Sir Edward, his fellow committee member.

He quickly broke the seal and let his eyes pick out a word here and there until he caught sight of Penelope's name. He went back and read it more carefully.

> *We have a problem. Forgive me, Gilchrist, but I didn't follow your advice and go home. My wife persuaded me to stay in London for a few more weeks. I was probably the only committee member still in town, and that's undoubtedly the reason I was the one who was approached by a very large man with a French accent who strong-armed me and pulled me into an alley and demanded I tell him where the papers were that told of British plans to assassinate Napoleon. I told him those papers were stolen from the home of the late Lord Hampstead. He said the plans that were found in Lord Hampstead's clock were fake. They knew they were fake because of a detail—I didn't quite comprehend. He demanded I give him the real plans. I didn't know what to tell him, so, knowing that Lord Hampstead's widow was with you in Hertfordshire, I told him that she still had*

the plans, hidden somewhere, and that we were also still searching for them. Perhaps it was the cowardly thing to do, but I knew if I told him the truth he would torture me until I told him. I thought it would at least buy us some time and—

Henry stopped reading and slapped the letter with his hand. "Of all the cowardly—" He cut his rant short and started for his bedroom to get his pistols.

"What is it?" Jane followed him. "Is it news of Penelope?"

"She's in danger. The French think she has the plans." He could feel his blood pumping through his veins, heat rising into his forehead. He ought to go shoot Sir Edward for endangering an innocent woman.

"I'm going with you," Jane said.

"Mother!" Henry shouted for his mother as he took the stairs three at a time.

Mother came out of her bedroom. "Merciful heavens, what is it?"

"I'm going to London. Penelope is in danger, and you must keep Jane at home."

"I'm going with him!" Jane cried out behind him.

"No. It's too dangerous. These men are ruthless and will gladly threaten the life of my sister and Penelope's friend to force us to tell them what we know."

"Oh my! No, Jane, you must stay home. How could I bear it if something happened to you?" Mother's voice cracked and he knew she was crying.

"Very well, I won't go." Jane's voice was petulant. Henry had known she wouldn't leave her mother thinking she might be in danger.

Henry grabbed a brace of pistols and hurried from

the room and down the stairs, pausing only long enough to kiss his mother on the cheek.

"Please take care," she said.

"I will."

~ ~ ~

One day earlier . . .

Penelope went through the house and finally found Dolman, the butler.

"Dolman, I know this will sound strange, but I happen to know that some men who were involved in my late husband's death think that I have the thing that my husband was killed for. I need you to make certain that all the servants know that they are not to allow anyone in the house who is not expressly approved by me, at least for the next few days."

"Yes, madam. Of course. I shall endeavor to make certain that this house is safe for you."

But Dolman's expression was rather sour and his words did not give her much peace. She had always sensed that he resented being asked to do anything that he considered to be outside his specific responsibilities. Grandmother often asked more of people than she should, and certainly more than she was paying them for. But Penelope had to do what she could to make the house as safe as possible.

She wished she had her husband's pistols, but she'd left those, along with all of David's possessions. Would she have had the nerve to use a pistol on would-be kidnappers? She'd had the nerve to stab one, so if it came down to killing or being killed, she could probably shoot them.

But she had no pistols, no true weapons.

Glancing around, she found an old lead candleholder that was quite heavy. She set it by her bed. Then she put her letter opener in a small purse and hung it from her wrist. Now she was as ready as she could make herself.

~ ~ ~

Penelope opened her eyes wide, trying to see in the dark.

She was awakened by a noise, but what?

A thump came from the left side of her room. She strained her eyes and noticed something moving, a large, dark form. A man was coming toward her.

She grabbed the candlestick by her bed and something hit her wrist, knocking the candlestick to the floor. A hand slammed over her mouth, pushing her head down into her pillow.

"Don't scream." A man was leaning over her. "If you scream, we'll kill you and your grandmother. Do you understand?" He was grinning, his face so close to hers she could smell his musty, greasy odor.

Penelope couldn't answer. His hand was crushing her lips to the point of cutting them with her teeth.

"You're coming with us, very peaceable-like," said a second man, the one whom she'd seen coming toward her.

They yanked her up and out of bed. She'd been so afraid when she lay down the night before she'd worn her dress to bed. So at least she was dressed and was not in her nightgown in front of these men.

She also still had the small purse around her wrist.

The man with his hand over her mouth whispered, with his stinking breath, "If you scream, we'll have to kill anyone who comes to help you. Do you understand?"

Penelope did her best to nod.

The man took his hand away and immediately put a cloth in her mouth and tied it around the back of her head.

They pulled her out into the hallway and guided her down the stairs and out the front door into a waiting carriage.

What would they do to her when they realized she didn't know what the real plans were? That she had never read them and didn't know what they said? They would simply kill her. What else could they do? She'd seen them, could identify them and testify against them.

They must have bribed one of the servants to leave the front door unlocked. She wasn't surprised. Her grandmother paid her servants so little.

If she got out of this alive, and if she ever had the means, she vowed she would pay her servants what they were worth, not the pittance her grandmother paid.

It must be past midnight and no one seemed to be about, from the glimpse she'd seen of the street. Now she was riding in a carriage with three other men, one of whom had a pistol in his hand, lying in his lap.

No one spoke. They rode for what seemed about half an hour and finally came to a stop.

One of the men said, "Stay here," and opened the carriage door and went out. Penelope did her best to see what she could of her surroundings, but it was too dark and he shut the door too quickly. But as she sat there, she heard the sound of water, as if gently lapping against something solid, and she guessed they had taken her to the docks by the Thames.

She tried to glean what she could from the expressions on the men's faces, but they were all stone-faced.

The carriage door opened and the man who left

filled the open space. He leaned over and pulled a black hood over her head.

"Let's go."

The men pulled her up and half carried out of the carriage; her feet never touched the steps. Then they dragged her, causing her to lose her footing on the gritty path, and she was hard-pressed to keep any semblance of balance, though the men were holding her up, with their huge hands painfully gripping her arms tighter than necessary.

She could see nothing inside the dark hood, but she felt the ground beneath her feet change to wood. A door creaked open. The men stopped pulling her, yanked the hood off her head, and she found herself being stared at by four men.

She steeled herself against losing her self-control in front of these evil men. She would not let them get the best of her. She'd be brave and make Jane and Henry and their mother proud of her, even if she died.

God, please help me. Don't let me die.

"You're a clever little minx, aren't you?" A man she'd never seen before came around to stand in front of her.

Penelope only glared at him.

"Your own people killed your husband, but perhaps you planned it that way," he went on. "Perhaps you killed him yourself. For women like you, it's better to be a widow. Is that it?"

He was baiting her. She knew this, but it still stung that he would so misunderstand her. She never, not in a thousand years, could have planned her husband's death.

"Not talking, eh? Well, we have ways to make you talk. We know you have the plans. If you tell us where they are, we won't have to torture you. But we will find out eventually."

If she told them she didn't have the plans, they would still torture her, in case she was lying. But if they tortured her and discovered she didn't have the plans, if she revealed what she knew, which was that the committee had the plans, then they would kill her. After all, they'd have no further use for her.

He slapped her across the face.

Tears gathered in her eyes. Her cheek burned, her vision blurred, and her jaw ached.

"Now tell us what we want to know or that will feel like a kiss from your sweetheart."

Penelope could hardly breathe, and yet, something inside her rose up and made her want to defy them. Pride? Spite? She wasn't sure, but she had to be wise. Think. What would Henry tell her to do?

Perhaps the wisest thing was to tell them the truth. She knew very little, but she could tell them what she did know.

"The truth is, I never even saw the plans. We finally found them in a clock in my husband's home—"

"Those plans were fake."

"We found the real plans in the clock, then the committee members decided to plant fake plans in the same place, in the clock."

"Where are the real plans?" The man spoke through clenched teeth, leaning in close to her face.

"The committee members have them. That is all I know. They have the plans."

"I talked to one of the committee members, a Sir Edward, and he said you have the plans."

"That is not true." The breath went out of her. How

could that man say such a thing? "He was lying to save himself. I don't have them, never even saw them, only the outside of the folded paper, before the committee members took them." She refused to say his name, to even think it.

The man grunted. "If you are lying to me..."

"I am not lying. I know nothing. The committee members know what the plans are. They are the ones who wrote them."

The man twisted his mouth and rubbed his chin. "What you say makes sense. But if you're lying, I will come back here and make you wish you were dead. Do you understand?"

"I'm not lying. And yes, I understand."

He turned as if to leave, then pointed his finger at her. "Don't make any noise." Then he looked at the men around him. "If she makes any noise, kill her."

They nodded, then one of them smirked at her.

The men left the room and shut her inside. A key grated in the metal lock and clicked.

CHAPTER TWENTY-FOUR

Penelope listened in the pitch black of the room but heard nothing.

They had not said they would release her if she was telling the truth. Why would they? They could kill her and go straight to France and never be held accountable for her murder.

She needed to escape.

She still had her letter opener in her little purse on her wrist. They obviously hadn't thought she was enough of a threat to search her for weapons, even after she stabbed the one man.

They'd taken the light with them, so the room was completely dark, with only the tiniest bit of light coming through a large crack high in the wall.

She could see nothing around her, but from what she remembered, the room was empty. She rubbed her arms, wishing she had a cloak or a blanket, but these men were ruthless. They'd hardly care that she was cold.

She headed toward the place where she remembered the door being, disoriented in the total darkness. Holding her hands in front of her, she found the wall and felt around until she could feel the door and the keyhole.

Taking out her letter opener, she whispered, "God, please let this work."

Was God listening to her? If these men killed her, she believed she would go to heaven to be with God. Was that God's plan for her? She was so lonely with her grandmother, and the thought of spending the rest of her life with her in Shropshire was a dreadful prospect.

"God, please let me live. If you do, I will not let my grandmother continue to make me miserable. I know I am dependent on her, but I can make friends. I can find good friends like Jane Gilchrist. I can do things for other people instead of thinking only of myself. I can cheer the cheerless, sell my paintings for money and take food to the poor. I can make my life mean something and stop being so pathetic. Help me, God. I'm telling you this as a promise of my future behavior if I do get out of this alive. I am determined not to be the same woman I was."

Penelope finished her whispered prayer and sat on the floor. She inserted the letter opener in the keyhole and moved it around inside the hole, twisting and pressing the sharp tip against everything it touched in the attempt to make it work like a key. She worked at it so long, her arms got tired and she had to rest. She prayed and then worked at it some more.

After what seemed like half an hour of fighting with the lock, something inside gave way, the lock clicked, and the door opened.

She kept the letter opener in her hand as she opened the door enough to peek out. But it was too dark to see anything. The men must have gone.

Carefully, her skin tingling as if the hairs on her arms were trying to detect any danger around her, she moved out of the room and into the larger area.

A tiny bit of light shone around a rectangle on one wall. That must be a door. She walked toward it, trying not to make any noise.

Was it the door to the outside? Or a door into another room, where the men were waiting for her? With any luck, the men had gone out, looking for the committee members.

A pang stabbed her stomach. Perhaps she shouldn't have told them that it was the committee members who had the plans, knew what was in the plans. It was true, of course, and should have been obvious. She would not feel guilty for not sacrificing herself for a bunch of men who had not protected her. Even Henry Gilchrist, who had been so kind to help her and protect her in the past, had left her with only the mercenaries to watch over her. And obviously, they weren't doing a good job of that.

She felt no ill will toward Henry. He'd protected her and had offered to let her stay longer. It had been Penelope's decision to go back to her grandmother, knowing that the longer she stayed away, the angrier her grandmother would be. And she didn't want to suffer the consequences of her grandmother's wrath.

But wasn't that the response of a child? Making decisions motivated by fear of her grandmother's disapproval?

She was an adult, and she'd been offered money before for her paintings, but her grandmother said it was beneath a lady to sell her artwork. Instead of spending her time reading books, Penelope could use her time to make money for herself. Then she wouldn't be so dependent on her grandmother, like a child.

The solution had been right in front of her. She simply had to make the hard decision to change her behavior—to stop being afraid of her grandmother's disapproval and make provision for herself.

But first, she had to get out of this place and find somewhere to hide.

She reached the door and stood still, listening. A

voice sounded as if it was coming from far away, outside on the street. She put her eye up to the crack around the door and saw a dimly lit alleyway.

Penelope tried to open the door, but it wouldn't open. She felt around for the keyhole and used her letter opener again. She worked at it for a few minutes, but remembering how she had opened the one before, she got this one open more quickly.

She opened the door and stepped out, holding her breath. If only her dress wasn't such a pale cream color, which made it stand out in the dark night.

She saw no one, so she walked quickly and quietly down the dark alleyway, heading away from the river, which she could see at one end, and deeper down the dark alley.

Her heart beat hard and fast as she looked from left to right, right to left constantly as she walked.

Something moved near her feet. She drew in a quick breath and saw it was a man, hunched over and mumbling to himself. The smell of strong drink wafting up told her he was drunk.

She walked on, hurrying faster now, as the darkness seemed to hide her the further away she went from the dark building that had been her prison.

She turned a corner and heard men's voices singing a bawdy drinking song. She went the opposite way, not wanting to encounter a group of drunken men.

Her bare feet kept stepping on and in things she didn't recognize, and she cringed but kept going. Filth could be washed off, but a stab wound or bullet to the chest . . . not so much.

Her heart lifted more and more the farther she went. She had got away from them! But where was she?

She didn't recognize any of these streets. The buildings were old, from medieval times, and the streets were dirty and full of refuse.

She hurried down street after street, hoping she was going in the right direction but still seeing nothing familiar. None of the shop signs looked familiar.

Her feet were becoming sore, and she was sure she had a few cuts from stepping on sharp objects. But she had to keep going. What choice did she have?

After walking around for an hour, at least, and still seeing nothing familiar, she started to look around for a place to hide for the night. Once the sun was out, she could see the taller buildings—the White Tower at the Tower of London or St. Paul's Cathedral—and then she could get her bearings. She could also ask for directions and wouldn't have to worry about running into drunken men. But where could she hide?

She turned down yet another alley and found the mews of a large house. She managed to squeeze past a gate that was slightly ajar and get into the stable where a few sleepy horses stood in their stalls. She found an empty stall and lay down in the straw on the floor.

Never had straw felt so good. She mounded it around herself in an attempt to get warm. Shivering, whether from nervous energy or the cold, she wasn't sure, she lay on her side and used her hands as a pillow.

~ ~ ~

Penelope startled awake to the smell of horse manure. Where was she?

The straw surrounding her and the pain in her feet brought it back to her—the night of terror, running through the streets of London in bare feet.

It must be dawn, for there was a gray light seeping

into the horse stall. She stood up, wincing at the pain of the straw in the cuts on her feet. She hurried out before the servants came to tend the horses.

How humiliating to be seen in her bare feet, no doubt looking dirty and afraid. She just wanted to go home, but she wasn't sure she was safe there.

She tried to think of some acquaintance to whom she could flee. How few friends she really had! If only she could go back to Hertfordshire. If only she had never left! What was there for her with her grandmother? Nothing but scoldings and constant pressure to marry well.

But even though Jane was a good friend to her, there was nothing for her in Hertfordshire either. Henry had made it abundantly clear that he cared nothing for her, was not interested in developing any affection for her.

Tears of pain and exhaustion welled up in her eyes. But she remembered the promise she'd made the night before—to take control of her life and her own happiness, to make friends, and to work to provide for herself.

She walked out of the mews and hurried down to the street. It was indeed dawn, and many people were milling about. Penelope ignored their stares. As well they might stare at a woman dressed the way she was but with mussed hair and bare feet.

There was the Tower of London! She knew where she was, or approximately.

She kept going. But again, she tried to think where she should go. She'd been taken from her grandmother's home. She'd been taken from her old home that Eustace, the new Lord Hampstead, now occupied. And Henry was not at his home.

The more she walked, the more people stared.

Eventually she would come upon someone who recognized her. What would they say, seeing her so bedraggled?

She was so footsore she was limping now too. And then she realized, Henry's townhouse was on this street.

She kept going, only feeling that she would be safe there. But when she arrived, she couldn't bring herself to knock on the door. She went around to the back. Would the servants let her in? Surely not, if there were even any servants about, since their master was not home.

Finally, weary and near tears, she managed to slip into the mews behind the Gilchrist house.

Penelope checked all the stalls in the early morning light coming through the windows. There were only two horses inside, leaving plenty of room and fresh straw and hay. Grateful tears pricked her eyelids, and then she had to hold back a sob. How pitiful and pathetic was she, that she was grateful for an empty horse stall to lie down in?

She lay her head on an old feed sack in the clean straw, as she had done before, and cried until she fell asleep.

~ ~ ~

Henry rode hard and fast to London, but it only seemed to him that it was taking too long to get there. What had become of Penelope by now? It had been so long. Anything could have happened to her.

Why had he let her go? He should have gone with her, intervened with her grandmother, anything to stop her from going back to London to get attacked again.

If something terrible had happened to her, he'd never forgive himself.

He rode to her house and knocked on the door, still holding onto the reins of his horse. A servant girl answered.

"Henry Gilchrist to see Penelope Hammond. Is she home?"

"No, sir. She and Mrs. Whitewood went to stay in Mrs. Whitewood's house."

"In Shropshire?" His heart stopped.

"No, sir. In London."

Her grandmother did have a house in London. He'd nearly forgotten. But it would have been better if they'd gone to Shropshire, farther away from the spies.

He thanked the servant and mounted his horse. But he immediately got back down and went to the door and knocked again.

The same servant answered. "Can you give me the direction to Mrs. Whitewood's home?"

"Just a moment. I shall ask."

She left and Henry waited on the step, holding his horse's reins, shifting his feet. What was taking her so long? *O God, let her make haste or I shall burst into the house —*

Eustace, Lord Hampstead, came to the door.

"Ah, Mr. Gilchrist. Won't you come inside instead of standing out of doors? It is—"

"No. I have no time to lose. What is the direction to Mrs. Whitewood's?"

"Oh." Lord Hampstead looked taken aback. No doubt he thought Henry very rude.

"Forgive me, but it is a matter of life and death."

"I see." His expression fluctuated for a few moments, then he gave Henry the street name and number.

"Thank you." Henry was off again as fast as he could mount his horse and spur him forward.

Unfortunately, her home was halfway across London, but he arrived without running anyone over or breaking his own neck, for which he thanked the Lord above.

Again, he knocked on the door and waited, chafing at the seconds it took for someone to answer the door, at the delay in finding Penelope.

But perhaps he was overreacting. She was probably home at this moment, sipping tea or writing a letter.

A servant girl answered the door, covering a yawn, then blushing.

"Henry Gilchrist for Mrs. Penelope Hammond."

The girl's eyes went wide. "Pardon, sir, but she's not home."

"Not home? Where is she?" He put his hand on the door to push it open and force his way inside.

"Who is there?" Penelope's grandmother's voice came from inside.

While the servant was looking behind her, Henry did brush past her into the house.

"Henry Gilchrist, madam."

"Mr. Gilchrist, do you know where my granddaughter is?" A strange tone marked Mrs. Whitewood's voice.

Henry's stomach melted into his boots. *O God.*

"I'm searching for her. She's in danger. Where did you last see her?"

"She went to bed last night and now she's gone. There is no trace of her, no note—"

"Did any of the servants see anything?"

"If they did, they're not talking." She glared in the direction the servant girl had scurried.

Henry's heart pounded and his hands tightened into fists. He would murder whoever had taken her.

CHAPTER TWENTY-FIVE

A pain went through Henry's chest as Penelope's grandmother stared at him with a look he'd never seen on her face before. But he had to think, be calm and think.

Where to begin searching? They'd been informed that the French spies seemed to have been headquartered somewhere along the docks. He'd start there.

"If you hear anything from her, send me word." Henry turned to leave.

"Mr. Gilchrist," Mrs. Whitewood said with an outstretched hand. "Please find my girl."

"I will, ma'am."

He hurried from the house, believing his own words. He would find her.

He rode to the docks, wondering if he should have changed horses at home first, but he didn't want to waste any time.

At the docks he searched every face he saw, peered into whatever doors were open, looking for something suspicious. He talked to some roughly dressed people, asking questions that might lead him to the French spies or to Penelope. But no one seemed to know anything, and many looked at him as if they wouldn't tell him anything if they did know something. No doubt they didn't like outsiders and thought he should stick to his wealthy section of town.

He had to keep looking, but the more eyes looking, the better. He'd go find the mercenaries and enlist their help. And he needed a fresh horse.

He headed toward his house, praying silently.

God, help me find her. Forgive me for rejecting her because of her poverty. That was never your way when you were here on earth. Forgive me. Now she's in trouble and it's my fault. You put a wonderful woman in my path, a woman of goodness and integrity, beauty and sweetness, and I was wrong. All this time, for the past two years, all my bitterness . . . Forgive me. I will never believe my "wisdom" over yours again.

He dismounted at his mews only to find the servant who came every day to feed and water his horses standing outside scratching his head, his hat askew.

"Sir, I'm glad to see you."

"What is it, Gates?"

"There's someone asleep in the stable."

Henry handed him the reins and pushed open the door of the stable.

"At the back," Gates whispered. "The last stall."

Henry strode toward the back of the stable. If this was some drunk man . . . He didn't have time for this. But something told him to keep going.

The stall door was open, and when he was standing in front of it, he saw Penelope lying there, half buried in the straw, her eyes closed.

Please, God, let her only be asleep.

"Mrs. Hammond?" He bent over her and her eyes suddenly opened. "Thank God I found you."

She blinked up at him. "I was kidnapped," she said.

"Are you all right?"

"Yes. I escaped. That's why I'm such a mess." She was running her hands over her hair as she sat up, removing the straw.

"You're a beautiful sight to me."

He reached down to help her up. When she stood, she winced.

"You're hurt."

"Just my feet." She lifted a bare foot in the air. "They took me from my bed. No shoes."

He lifted her in arms, so swiftly she sucked in an audible breath.

"Forgive me." He held her as tenderly as he could. She put her arms around his neck and gazed into his eyes, and his heart soared. "Can you ever forgive me for letting you go back to London?"

She just stared up at him with wide eyes and her mouth slightly open.

"I'm so sorry that you ended up in danger again."

"That is hardly your fault. I chose to leave."

He carried her the short way from the stable to the house. "Send for Mrs. Bleeker," he ordered the manservant who watched over the house when he was in Hertfordshire. "And bring me a bucket of warm water."

As he was carrying her up the stairs, he noticed a faint smile on her face.

"What?"

"You are always saving me."

"It seems to me, you usually save yourself. I am only there afterward to get the credit for saving you."

"No, you have no idea how frightened I was this morning. You saved me from having to walk all the way to my grandmother's house in bare feet, looking as if I fell in a pigsty."

"You don't look as if you fell into a pigsty. Although you do still have some straw in your hair."

She looked embarrassed and started patting her

hair, which was long and flowing over her shoulders. It looked messier and more beautiful than he'd ever seen it.

He set her down in a chair and picked out the straw that was still tangled in her lovely dark blond hair.

The servant came in with a bucket of water. "Is this warm enough?"

Henry tested it. "Perfect."

The servant left and Henry poured some water into a basin.

"What are you doing?"

"I'm going to wash your feet."

"No, no, please." She drew her feet under the chair.

"My female servants aren't here, so all you have is me."

"I can wash my own feet."

"Sh." He placed the basin on the floor. He knelt in front of her and dipped a cloth in the water. Then he picked up her foot and placed it in the basin.

Strange as it seemed, this felt right and good. The modest, meek, and yet brave Penelope, blushing in front of him.

~ ~ ~

"No, you mustn't."

Penelope's cheeks stung at the intimate, humble scene before her—Henry Gilchrist, Member of Parliament and wealthy gentleman, kneeling and bathing her feet.

He used the cloth to dribble warm water over her feet. She wouldn't have admitted it, but it felt so good—not only the warm water on her cold feet, but having a handsome gentleman perform such a loving act for her. It was like nothing that had ever happened to her before.

He even examined the bottom of her foot.

"You have several cuts," he said, frowning.

"I'm so embarrassed at you doing this."

"Why? There was no one else here to do it."

She wasn't sure what to say. "People were staring at me on the street. My hair was messy and I suspect there was some dirt on my face."

"Only one little smudge." He reached up and wiped her cheek with his thumb. "There."

Her cheeks burned anew as he continued washing her feet.

"How did you escape? What happened? Did they harm you?"

"I am well." She started telling him the story, and the way he seemed to hang on every word she said made her heart expand inside her, filling up her chest. *O God, please let me have a husband someday who looks at me the way Henry is looking at me now.*

"Go on," he said, making her realize she'd stopped talking to stare at him.

She continued explaining what the kidnappers said to her and how she escaped, once again with the help of her letter opener.

"I must remember to carry a letter opener with me at all times," he said with an ironic grin. "It is a very useful tool."

"I will not disagree with that." She allowed herself a smile as he dried her feet with a towel and moved the water basin out of the way.

"Penelope—may I call you Penelope?"

He wanted to call her by her Christian name? It wasn't proper at all, but she wasn't sure what to say. When she didn't answer, he continued, still kneeling on the floor in front of her.

"I want to tell you again how sorry I am that I

let this happen. You have suffered quite enough due to the sins of your first husband. You should not have to continue to suffer, to be threatened and forced to walk through the streets in bare feet. I want to tell you I'm sorry. I will not leave you at the mercy of evil men again."

She wondered how he planned to do that, but she was too surprised to speak.

"Mr. Gilchrist?" a woman's voice called from somewhere outside the open door of the room.

"In the guest room, Mrs. Bleeker," Henry called out. "She's my housekeeper," he explained.

A woman who looked to be in her fifties came bustling into the room. "What is it?" She was quite out of breath.

"I'm sorry to send for you without any notice."

She waved her hand as if to say it didn't matter.

"This young lady has been through a terrible ordeal at the hands of evil French spies."

"Oh, good Lord!" she exclaimed, pressing a hand to her breast.

"And I wonder if you could take care of her. She has several cuts on the bottom of her feet from being forced to walk on the streets without her shoes."

"For heaven's sakes alive, of course." She waved him away from her. "I shall take good care of the poor lassie."

"Thank you."

"Let me go get my bag of remedies and send for the other servants. She must have a hot bath and a good deal of strong tea." She hurried out of the room before she was finished talking.

"And I shall make sure you have two guards to watch over you at all times," he said, "guards with guns who are brave and loyal."

Why was he behaving this way? He'd been so cool to her when she'd left his Hertfordshire home for London.

"Sir?" A manservant was standing in the doorway. "An express just came for you."

Henry took the missive out of the servant's hand and read it aloud. "Jane is coming here today. She was too worried about you not to come right away, she says."

Wonderful Jane. How good she was to be so concerned for her.

"This is good," Henry said. "Now you can stay here and we won't have to send for your grandmother."

He wanted her to stay at his house?

Just then Mrs. Bleeker came back, and Henry hurried out before she could say a word.

The kindly woman slathered her special salve on all of Penelope's cuts, then bandaged her feet, clucking over the ordeal she must have endured. Meanwhile, Penelope's thoughts seemed to spin around in a strange whirl.

Never had she felt so cared for.

When Henry returned, he had two menservants with him.

"Mrs. Hammond, these men are Jones and Culpepper and they are here to protect you. Please don't go anywhere without them. They are each armed with a pistol." They lifted their coats to show the gun strapped to their hip. "They have made a vow to me to protect you with their very lives, if necessary."

Penelope covered her mouth as a laugh bubbled up and threatened to escape. The thought of someone being willing to protect her with their life, as well as Henry Gilchrist being so determined to protect her, felt ludicrous. But the next moment she was tearing up in gratitude.

"I thank you, all three of you," she said. "I am very

grateful and humbled by your kindness and courage."

She let her gaze settle on Henry. He wore a gracious smile.

"Now, get out of here with you," Mrs. Bleeker said. "It's time for our lady's bath, and then she's going to drink my medicinal tea and take a nap."

The men stationed themselves in the hall on either side of her door, and Henry left, closing the door with an intense look straight at Penelope.

She couldn't help thinking how much better this day was ending than it had begun.

CHAPTER TWENTY-SIX

Henry was busy for the rest of that day and the next, requesting—and being granted—twenty members of the king's guards to help him round up the French spies who had kidnapped and imprisoned Penelope in a building at the docks. Through her memory and direction, they found the building where she'd been threatened.

They carefully hid, lying in wait, and ended in capturing five of the spies who had so bedeviled her.

Inside the building, they found Sir Edward bound and gagged. He'd been beaten, then left with the promise of more and worse beatings when they returned.

Sir Edward said he hadn't told them anything, but there was no way of knowing if he was telling the truth. For that reason, Henry planned to ask Parliament and the military leaders to scrap the entire plan. It was never a very good idea anyway, in his opinion.

And now that Henry had dealt with the men who had endangered Penelope's life, he could get started with another plan, quite different from the plans he and his fellow committee members had been tasked with.

He sought out his sister and Penelope and found them together, as he'd expected, in the sitting room.

"Ladies," he said, "would you do me the honor of accompanying me to the park this afternoon, weather permitting?"

Jane's mouth fell open. Penelope was the first to recover enough to speak. "We'd be delighted, I'm sure."

Jane gave him a sidelong stare that slowly turned into a smile.

He'd expected her to react that way, so it was of no consequence.

"Shall I call for you in an hour?"

"Thank you, yes." Again, it was Penelope who answered him.

An hour later, both young women were ready with walking apparel and parasols. Jane was strangely quiet and allowed him and Penelope to carry the conversation with only minimal input from her. But every time he chanced to glance at his sister, she was smiling.

What had Penelope said to Jane to keep her so quiet? Or was Jane so intent on his seeing her friend's good qualities that she was keeping herself in check, not talking, but allowing the two of them to speak?

Penelope thoughtfully asked after Sir Edward's health.

"He is mending well at home."

"I do feel terrible."

"Why?"

"It's my fault he is suffering!"

"It's not your fault."

"It is. They were torturing him because of my saying that it was the committee members who knew what the plans were, that I had never even seen the plans."

"It is more his fault than yours for saying that you were the one who had the plans. You could blame him for your ordeal of two days ago."

"He didn't know I was in London. He thought I was with you."

"Still, it was unchivalrous of him, very badly done."

"I would never have wished him to be beaten and

maltreated."

"You are very kindhearted." He wanted to call her Penelope, but he didn't dare in front of Jane. Still, it was necessary for his sister to be with them. He wanted to do this properly and show how much he respected her.

She was beautiful, never more so than when he complimented her. She would smile up at him with that bashful look of hers, her head down to the point that she had to open her eyes wide to see him. Many women attempted that demure expression, but Penelope's was authentic. Even though she was a widow, she had a tenderhearted, innocent air about her that most other women, young and old, married and unmarried, did not possess.

By the end of the walk, Jane was talking a bit more, as both he and Penelope included her and drew her out.

He'd never had to "draw out" Jane Gilchrist before.

When they arrived back at home, they were taking off their gloves and hats when Jane suddenly said, "I have to go up to my room, but I'll only be a moment."

She was halfway to the staircase by the time she finished speaking.

Penelope shook her head as she laid her bonnet and gloves down.

"My sister . . . there is no one like her."

Penelope smiled. "I like her very much. I've never met anyone with such a good heart and so high-spirited at the same time."

"I will not argue with you about Jane's good qualities." Penelope was obviously a loyal friend. But there was something he was wondering. "I saw you were painting something in the sitting room."

"Yes. I've decided to try to work and paint portraits for wages. I already have my first commission. Lord Seagrove has asked me to paint a portrait of his daughter."

"I have not seen your paintings. You must be very talented."

"Lord Seagrove saw one I painted of my former governess a year or so ago and told me if I was ever willing, he would commission me to paint his daughter. My grandmother was offended by the offer, but I was not. And since I don't want to be dependent on my grandmother forever, I have accepted. His daughter is to come and sit for me next week. And hopefully I will receive more, similar commissions."

This was Penelope standing up to her grandmother and refusing to be persuaded by her. She was not waiting for an offer of marriage. She was working toward supporting herself.

The way he had treated her, she had no reason to believe that he had any interest in marrying her. But this changed nothing, except to make him respect her even more.

They wandered into the sitting room and she showed him the painting she was working on.

"This will be the background of Lord Seagrove's daughter's portrait."

He complimented her use of color.

"I know it doesn't look like much yet. But Jane offered me the use of her painting supplies and I thought I might as well get started."

"Yes, Jane certainly isn't using her paints. She could never sit still long enough to complete anything. Her art lessons were torture, both for her and for her instructor."

Penelope only smiled. "She has other good qualities and talents. She doesn't need to paint."

"Fortunately for her."

But Penelope did need to paint. She needed to have a way of supporting herself. And it seemed as though she'd rather do something like this than marry again. But if he could make her fall in love with him . . . He was getting ahead of himself.

"I'm sorry you've been through so much." He wasn't sure if he'd said that to her, as he'd been so busy trying to make sure her kidnappers were locked away so they could never hurt her again.

"Oh, thank you, but it's over now. I will be all right, now that the shock is over." She suddenly sucked in a breath and covered her mouth, turning wide eyes on him. "You meant the kidnappings. I thought you meant . . ."

She thought he meant what her husband, Lord Hampstead, had done to her.

"I'm sorry he treated you so badly. I hope it doesn't . . . that is, I hope you will not be afraid to marry again because of how he behaved."

She acknowledged his words with a slow nod but did not speak right away. Finally, she said, "I was very young and foolish when I married him. And it does make me fearful that I'll be naïve again. Mostly it makes me determined to choose more wisely next time. But if I'm honest, there is a lot of fear, fear of making the same mistake again, of being trapped with someone who not only doesn't love me, but makes me feel as if he despises me. I never want to go through that again."

Her voice grew quieter and quieter the more she talked, and she stared at the tea table between them.

"Forgive me if I'm making you sad by mentioning this."

"It's not your doing. You were asking me about the kidnappings and I misunderstood. And I don't mind." Already her face had brightened. "The kidnappings were very frightening, but also not your fault. That was the fault of my husband, who stole the plans and attempted to sell them, to the detriment of his own country, and because of his sin of gambling away most of his wealth." She smiled, as if amused at the irony in it all. "But we must forgive him, if we ourselves wish to be forgiven."

He smiled back at her. "I admire you, Penelope." He said her name quietly, so that even if a servant were passing by the room, they wouldn't have heard him. "Forgive me for calling you by your name, but it is such a lovely name, and it suits you much better than 'Mrs. Hammond.'"

The bashful look came over her face again. "You are very kind and complimentary today, Mr. Gilchrist."

"I never give insincere compliments."

Just then, a movement by the doorway caught his eye. Jane was lurking there.

"Come in, Jane," he said. His silly sister. He'd been enjoying his intimate conversation with Penelope, and Jane would have sneaked away if he hadn't called out to her. But perhaps it was best. He was probably making Penelope uncomfortable, with all his compliments and calling her so familiarly by her Christian name. He feared she was easily startled, and he didn't want to send her running, like a skittish colt.

She was such a paradox—seemingly timid, but fierce and strong when the occasion warranted, as now, when she was determined to support herself to be independent of her grandmother's influence. *Brava*, Penelope.

~ ~ ~

Penelope's heart leapt when he called her by her name.

His manner toward her now was so strange and different. He'd been very solicitous when he'd come that first day, when David's body was laid out in the drawing room, when she was still in shock at what had happened. And he'd been kind but rather businesslike when she was answering the mercenaries' questions and when he took her to his house in Hertfordshire in his carriage. But now he was different somehow. And it had started when he found her asleep in his mews.

He'd picked her up so tenderly, gazing into her eyes with such compassion. It had reminded her of the moment by the stream when he'd held her in his arms. But that had only been a moment. He'd been rather cool to her after that, as if he'd found her wanting and had decided to reject her.

Rejection. That was a feeling she never wanted to feel again. And when she looked into her heart, she saw a bit of resentment toward Henry for making her feel that when she left his home in Hertfordshire.

She could explain his compassion and wish to take care of her as owing to his guilt over allowing her to return to danger. But when he'd bathed her dirty, bloody feet with his own hands . . . she could still feel the same warmth flowing through her when she remembered his gentle hands, the way he knelt in front of her, the expression on his handsome face.

Was all of that due to his guilty feelings?

And now, all of his compliments, his smiles, his intensity when he said he never gave insincere compliments . . . It was probably good that Jane was here with them now, for Penelope didn't want to embarrass herself by showing how he was making her feel now.

"Have you seen any of Penelope's portraits she's

painted? They are so very good, better than most painting masters' portraits."

"Jane, you exaggerate." Penelope shook her head at her friend.

"I have not seen any of her portraits," Henry said, "but I would very much like to. Where are they?"

"There were some in her home. I do hope you took those when you left." She turned back to Penelope.

"I did. They're now at Grandmother's townhouse."

"We should go and see them. You will be so impressed, Henry. Our Penelope was born with at least two great talents—painting and playing the pianoforte."

"Which she perfected with careful study and practice, no doubt."

"There you go, trying to make me feel guilty for not practicing the pianoforte, but I will admit this time that you're right. Penelope is much more disciplined than I am, and she has practiced to perfect her talents."

It was as if they were trying to outdo one another in complimenting her. Penelope pressed her hands to her warm cheeks. "You must stop all this flattery and talk of something else."

"Very well. What should we talk of? Parliament is no longer sitting so there won't be very many balls, but there were a few invitations in that stack of mail. I shall go fetch it and we shall choose a party to go to."

Even though she could have rung the bell for a servant to send to fetch the letters, Jane jumped up and went after them herself. Was it because she had not the patience to wait? Or because she wanted to leave Penelope and Henry alone again?

"Is it safe for me to go to a ball now?" Penelope asked Henry.

"I believe you are safe now. Your attackers have been apprehended."

"Will you go to a ball with Jane and me?"

"I will. And if you wish to go to a lecture, a concert, or the theatre, we shall do those things also. I am pleased to escort you anywhere you wish to go."

Penelope's heart fluttered at the intense way he was looking at her while he offered to take her anywhere she wished to go. Could he truly be so interested in squiring her around town?

Probably he was only wanting a way to entertain Jane, who loved attending parties and balls. Or perhaps he was still feeling guilty.

When she didn't say anything, he asked, "What do you like? I've offered you lectures, concerts, and the theatre. Which do you prefer?"

"You are very kind to concern yourself. I do enjoy concerts, and lectures as well, depending upon the topic, but theatre is my favorite."

"Shakespeare?"

"Of course." She felt a little giddy at being asked what she enjoyed.

"Christopher Marlowe? Ben Jonson?"

"Yes, and some more modern ones, as long as the subject matter is not vulgar."

"Very good. I shall see what is scheduled in the near future, and if you find something you wish to see, just let me know. You are our guest, and my time is yours to command."

"Thank you, but you don't have to be so solicitous. I don't hold you responsible for any evil events that have befallen me."

"Penelope!" Jane hurried into the room with a stack

of invitations. "You silly girl. If Henry wishes to take us to a ball, you should just say thank you."

"Forgive me. I didn't mean to offend." Penelope had seen the clouded look that came over his face when she told him he didn't have to be so solicitous.

"I think, dear Jane, that Mrs. Penelope Hammond cannot accept that someone wants to do something just for her, for her own enjoyment and pleasure."

The look on Henry's face when he spoke was hard to make out.

"Penelope, let Henry do something for you. He is sincere in his offers. I know my brother. He wouldn't offer to take you somewhere if he didn't wish to."

Her breath was shallow and she actually felt tears threatening to flood her eyes. Oh dear! She couldn't let them see her cry. They'd ask her what was wrong and she honestly didn't know. She only knew that they were staring at her, that they were being much too kind, and she wasn't sure how to respond.

"Truly, thank you. You are both so kind." She remembered yearning for just one tiny bit of kindness from her husband. And then the stares of people on the street after she'd escaped from her kidnappers, wandering around, lost on the streets with no shoes on her feet. And Lady Susan's look of disgust when they told her that Penelope had stabbed her captor in the back with a letter opener.

"What invitations do you have there, Jane?" Henry asked.

They both seemed to sense her consternation and started looking through the letters and invitations. Thankfully, her tears dried up when they were no longer staring at her, so concerned and attentive.

Jane held up an invitation, waving it in the air.

"Here's one from Lady Fairweather to a ball tomorrow night! Is it too late to say yes?"

"No, not if you write back today." Henry actually sat down at a desk against the wall and took out paper and pen and ink.

Jane continued to look through the invitations, then asked for the newspaper to search the lectures, concerts, operas, and plays that were being put on in the next two weeks.

Penelope pressed her back against the cushions of the couch, a posture her grandmother would have scolded her for, and listened to Jane's excited chatter and answered her questions about what Penelope would prefer—this play or that concert? This lecture or that lecture? This ball or that ball?

A handsome man of integrity wanted to take her wherever she wanted, and Jane was making sure she took him up on the offer.

The world had obviously turned upside down, and she might as well enjoy it while it lasted.

CHAPTER TWENTY-SEVEN

Penelope was finding it hard to work on the painting she'd been commissioned for, since Jane always had an idea for something they should do or somewhere they should go, and her stamina was boundless, it seemed. And Henry was taking them somewhere every night—or at least for the last three nights. They'd been to a concert, a play, and an opera.

She'd enjoyed them all, so she was not complaining.

Sometimes she wondered what David would say if he could see her now, so happy with her friends, Jane and Henry, enjoying herself, no longer feeling as if there was an invisible fist around her stomach as she waited and wondered if her husband would come home, if he would even speak to her or notice her, wondered why he hated her.

But she knew that if David could see her, he wouldn't care.

That had been the hardest thing for her to accept when he was alive—that he just did not care about her. At all.

And so, last night after they'd gone to see the opera *La clemenza di Tito*, her mind was full of the nobility of a man of high morality and character. How different David had been, how opposite and dark and ugly his behavior appeared when compared to Henry's.

She took out a small box she brought with her

when she left David's home. Inside were the two letters that David had written her before they were married. She untied the blue velvet ribbon that held them together and stood before the small fire in her bedroom grate.

She stared at the flames for a long moment. She whispered, "Purified by fire." Then she threw the letters in and watched them burn.

She waited for a sense of satisfaction, but none came.

"God, I forgive my husband for his cruelty to me, the wife he was commanded to love and cherish, and I ask you, please give me a real love someday, someone of good and noble character who truly will love me. And please don't let me make another mistake by marrying someone who isn't good and doesn't love me."

She lay in bed remembering how kind and loving Henry was to his mother and sister, how he'd held her in his arms, both in the woods by the stream and when he'd carried her in the house after finding her asleep in the straw.

"God," she whispered, "Henry is a man of noble character." But she stopped short of asking God to make him love her. Would God take offense to her asking for such a thing? God always knew best. And since she'd done something before that hadn't seemed quite right—agreeing to marry David—she couldn't bring herself to ask for the thing she wanted.

"God, you know best. So I pray for your best for me and for Henry."

When she went to bed and closed her eyes, her body relaxed and, in contrast to most nights since David was murdered, she fell asleep almost immediately.

~ ~ ~

More and more Jane was leaving Penelope alone with her brother. But he was always respectful, and he seemed to open up to her more when they were alone. So the next day, when Jane made up a flimsy excuse to leave the sitting room while the three of them were having tea, Penelope decided to ask him a question.

"You have mentioned before that you were engaged to be married, and the lady married your brother instead. People say a man's first love is strongest. Do you think you would ever wish to marry that lady in the future?"

It was a bold question, to be sure, but if what he was doing—taking her to every play, concert, or opera that she wished to go to—was his idea of courting her for marriage, then she wanted to know his feelings for that lady. And if he became angry with her, that would also be helpful information. Though she had a horror now of marrying a man who was cold and unfeeling, she'd also vowed never to marry a man whose temperament was angry.

"That is a good question," he said, his voice calm and his eyes on the floor, as if he was thoughtfully contemplating his answer. "I can honestly say that I do not love that lady, and probably never did. But only because I did not know her. I loved who I thought she was, not who she actually was. And no, I would not marry her. She is not the kind of lady I admire or could ever fall in love with."

Penelope nodded.

"You do believe me?"

"I have no reason not to believe you. You are an honest, trustworthy man."

"A wise person once said, 'Character and love are the most important qualities in choosing a husband.' And character and love are the most important qualities in choosing a wife as well."

Was he speaking of what she'd said to his mother and Jane? Yes, she remembered saying that one morning at breakfast when he was present. Was he only flattering her again, calling her wise? Her mind was spinning. Was she being foolish and gullible? She needed to get alone and think through this.

"I know you went through something terrible in your first marriage. It must have felt like a prison, and worse."

"Yes. It was so much worse than being kidnapped by those men and threatened. It was a slow, painful torture of an existence." She glanced up at him, suddenly feeling sheepish. "You must think I'm being overdramatic."

"Not at all."

His gaze was so full of compassion, she couldn't look away. His eyes captured her, and she felt it deep inside her.

"No one should be treated as cruelly as you were. You deserve to be loved."

Her heart stopped. It was too much. She jumped up.

"I need to go . . . get something . . . and make sure Jane is all right."

As she was hurrying away, Henry said quietly, "Forgive me."

Penelope stopped and looked over her shoulder. "There is nothing to forgive. All is well." But she hurried away.

By the time she reached her room, she was so out of breath she was gasping for air, her heart pounding against her chest.

She groaned and fell across her bed. How strange she must seem, running from the room! But she'd become so frightened by his words. But why? She couldn't understand it. She only knew that when he'd looked her in the eye and said those words, that she deserved love, she became so overwhelmed she couldn't face him.

"O God," she whispered, "am I losing my sanity?"

No. She was just afraid. Living with David had created a wound inside her, and obviously that wound was not healed. And the thought of Henry pretending to love her and asking to marry her when he didn't truly love her . . . it touched that wound and made it bleed.

There was also the very real possibility that he did love her, that he was sincere in his regard for her. But every time she considered that possibility, she remembered how cool he was to her when she was leaving him at Hertfordshire. And she could not bear his coolness, not if they were married. Because, in stark contrast to how she felt when she married David, she was in love with Henry Gilchrist.

"Oh dear." How could she be in love with him?

It was true, though, and she knew it. She'd been falling in love with him for weeks now, with his kindness and goodness and integrity, not to mention his beautiful face. He was so handsome it made her chest ache.

She pressed her hands against her hot cheeks. She couldn't let him know. She had to think this through.

A knock came at her door. Jane's voice said, "Penelope? Are you well? May I come in?"

Penelope sat up. "Yes, come in."

Jane rushed to her side. "Henry said you came up to your room, but he was worried about you. Are you all right?"

"I am perfectly well, but I . . . Jane, tell me the truth. Do you think . . . ? I can't even say it."

"Say what? Say it."

"No, no." What if she was wrong? She couldn't bear to lose Jane's friendship. She was the best friend Penelope had ever had.

"Penelope, if you're wondering about my brother's feelings for you, I can say that he would never, never ever pretend to feel more than he was feeling. And I have seen the way he looks at you and heard the way he speaks of you when you're not present. He adores you, Penelope."

"Jane, no. Adores me? I can't believe that."

"Well, then, believe that he admires you, for it is so, and I assure you that I've never seen him look at anyone the way he looks at you. I would never say this if I wasn't convinced, but I believe he is in love with you."

Henry in love with her? That was too good to be true, surely.

"Henry would not go to balls and operas and plays if he was not trying to impress you, to make you happy. He certainly has never done so much before. He has always enjoyed outings, but not to this extent. And have you noticed how he always asks you which play you are most interested in? How he asks your opinion first and lets you choose where we go?"

"This is only because I'm your guest."

"It is not only for that reason, I assure you."

She tried to take in what Jane was saying. Was it true?

Jane sat quietly beside Penelope for a few moments, then said, "What are you thinking?"

"I'm afraid, Jane. I love your brother's attention, and you are the best friend I've ever had, but I'm afraid of making a mistake again. You must hate me for that, since you're never afraid of anything."

"Of course I don't hate you. Penelope, you had a terrible experience, both during your marriage and since. I'd been unfeeling indeed if I didn't understand that you'd have some fear."

They sat in companionable silence for a few more moments. Then Jane turned to look Penelope in the eye.

"Forgive me for asking, but . . . Do you think you might one day overcome your fear and come to love Henry?"

"Oh, Jane." She sighed and wiped away a silly tear that escaped her eye. "Yes."

They both laughed.

When Penelope was breathing normally again, she asked, "What will you tell Hen—your brother? You won't tell him what we talked of, will you?"

"I won't tell him anything. But I have full hope that you will one day be my sister, and everyone's happiness will be great from that day forward."

A tiny wave of fear lapped at her mind to hear Jane make that prediction. But the next moment she remembered a verse she'd memorized as a child. *God hath not given us the spirit of fear; but of power, and of love, and of a sound mind.*

"But if you ever feel that either I or Henry are pressing you, or that we are being impatient with you, then you have every right to speak out and tell us to stop. Henry can be impatient when he wants something, and you must tell him plainly that you will not be rushed."

"So far he's been only kind and gentle with me."

"Good." Jane smiled. "But you must be honest with him. I know that when I'm not completely open and honest with someone, I begin to dislike them. So remember to be brutally honest with Henry. He can take it. He is not a child."

"Yes, I will. Thank you." And she determined in her heart that she would be completely honest with Henry, even if it made him angry. Better that she know his true character and temperament now than when it was too late.

CHAPTER TWENTY-EIGHT

The next morning, Penelope found herself in the breakfast room alone with Henry.

"Where is Jane?" he asked.

"Jane left me a note under my door saying she stayed up very late reading *Udolpho* and was planning to sleep late."

"That's my sister. Unpredictable."

"She is never dull, though."

"Very true." He smiled. "How would you like to take a walk this morning?"

"I would like that very much. I believe I've grown quite strong since having Jane for a friend, as I never walked so much before."

"Jane is a much greater walker than reader, but I suppose it was too dark last night to go for a walk."

"There now. We mustn't abuse your excellent sister—my most excellent friend—when she is not here to defend herself."

"You are right. Come. Are you ready for our walk?"

"I'm ready."

They collected their hats and gloves. Then Penelope took his arm and they walked toward the park.

"I want to tell you I'm sorry for making you uncomfortable yesterday. Please forgive me."

"No, there is nothing to forgive. You did nothing wrong."

He gently squeezed her hand. "I hope you will tell

me if I say something that makes you uncomfortable."

"I will. Yesterday I was only a bit overwhelmed by your words. But that does not mean I didn't enjoy hearing them." There. She'd been completely honest.

Henry was looking down at her with a most tender expression. "I am glad to hear that."

They continued at a slow but steady pace, talking of the weather and which houses were the most appealing and the types of architecture they liked best. In the park they remarked on the flowers and trees and then began to talk of when he came to her home for the first time and their impressions of each other, how he had looked through all her husband's belongings looking for the plans. He'd thought her so trusting then.

"I must have seemed very naïve. I was still in so much shock, and I think in my mind, I was protecting myself by letting a Member of Parliament get involved in solving my husband's murder. Besides that, I'd seen you at church. I felt as if I knew you, at least a bit."

"That is reasonable. Besides that, I just have a very trustworthy face, don't you think?" He turned his head from one side to the other, allowing her to examine him.

"You do have a trustworthy face, I suppose, if there is such a thing." Penelope hid her smile behind her hand.

"Ah, I hear the doubt in your voice."

They teased each other a bit, talked of Camille Dupre and the other spies and how Penelope had escaped from them three times.

"They aren't the most competent spies, to have allowed me to escape three times."

"You don't give yourself enough credit. I think you are just very good at escaping."

"I suppose I am, when you consider that my upbringing did not involve lessons in the art of escaping kidnappers." Penelope smiled up at him. "Truly, you shouldn't flatter me so much, Mr. Gilchrist."

"It isn't flattery."

He didn't look angry or even perturbed, but there was a serious expression on his face.

"I don't think you understand how much I admire you."

They were standing under a large oak tree in a rather secluded area of the park. Few people were around, as it was raining a sort of misty, drizzly rain. Anyone might have thought they were taking shelter under the massive, low-hanging tree branches.

She was facing him now, and his hand was under her elbow, holding her gently. A drop of rain was on his temple. She reached up and wiped it away with her gloved finger.

They were very close now, their eyes locked on each other.

"Not much time has passed since my husband's death, and I'm still afraid. But no one has ever told me I deserve to be loved. It was good to hear you say it, but it just reminded me how afraid I am to make another mistake."

His gaze drifted down to her lips, and she couldn't help following suit. Her own husband had kissed her so rarely. How would it feel for this man, Henry Gilchrist, to kiss her?

"I hadn't planned to say this now, here, in the rain," Henry said, his voice unusually gruff.

Her heart skipped a beat, then beat so fast it stole her breath, as the whole world seemed to depend on what he would say next.

"I love you, Penelope, and I couldn't wait any longer to tell you. I beg you to say you will make me the happiest man in the world by accepting my offer of marriage. Will you marry me?"

"Yes. I will." She said the words almost without thinking. And yet the thought went through her mind, *You can change your mind later if you need to.*

"You will?" A smile was spreading across his face. It was in his eyes and in the way he held onto her arm.

"I will." The caution in her head said again that she could change her mind. "But I need more time. I hope you will not be angry with me, but I'm not ready yet."

His eyes were so clear and so dear. He'd been so good to her. But it was difficult to stop remembering how he was cool to her when she was leaving for London. It was the only time Henry ever put her in mind of her husband David.

"I know it is soon, but do you love me, Penelope? I need to know."

"I do. I love you." Admitting that she loved him was both exhilarating and terrifying. And she did love him. He was impossible not to love, with his good nature and the way he had always protected her, even when he didn't know if she was a loyal British citizen or a French spy, due to her French mother.

The way he was looking at her, she could almost believe he truly loved her. But she wanted to be sure.

He touched her cheek, gently smoothing her cheek with his thumb.

Penelope moved her parasol so that it would block their faces from view should anyone chance to walk by. Her heart fluttered. She wanted him to kiss her, wanted to feel his arms around her and his lips on hers, longed for warmth and passion.

"Will you allow me to kiss you?" he asked, as politely as if he were asking her to dance. But there was an edge to his voice and a light in his eyes that made her knees weak.

"Yes."

He leaned in and pressed his lips to hers.

The air seemed to rush back into her lungs. How utterly sweet was his kiss—eager and yet controlled, gentle and yet firm.

It was a brief kiss. She did not pull away from him, and he kissed her again. Her stomach turned inside out and she clung to him with the hand that wasn't holding the parasol.

David's kisses had always been so tepid and even annoying. But this was different. So different. He kissed her as if there was nothing else in the world except the two of them, as if he was intent on nothing but convincing her of his love. Best of all, he kissed her as if she was the most important thing to him.

Even after the kiss ended, her head was still floating in the clouds. She opened her eyes to find him gazing at her with the most tender look she'd ever seen. Her heart crashed against her chest.

"You will think me scandalous," she whispered, the first words that came to her mind.

"Why would I think that?" His voice was warm and deep, and he drew a fingertip across her temple, as if to smooth back a strand of hair that had come loose.

His attention was so intoxicating, the way he continued to gaze at her so intently.

"Because I allowed you to kiss me here, in the park, so publicly."

"If you are scandalous, then I am just as much so."

He was smiling now. Did he know how scattered her thoughts were?

"Are you sorry you let me kiss you?" His voice was just above a whisper and he was leaning very close to her.

"No."

"I won't hurt you, Penelope. I'm not like your first husband. I won't leave you alone, or ignore you, or make you wonder where I am."

"Truly?" Her heart was in her throat.

"Truly. I want to love you, forever."

"Do you promise to never stop loving me?"

"I promise."

He leaned down and kissed her again. His kisses were glorious! How had she lived in the world without knowing that this was how it felt to be kissed?

When they left the park and walked back to his home, she was still thinking of his kisses. How shameless she was, to let him kiss her in the park! It was raining and few people were out. She only hoped no one saw them or recognized them. Was it so very bad, since they were engaged to be married? Truly, she would do it again.

Engaged to be married. Was she mad? She was not ready to remarry. Her husband had only been dead for a month and a half. What would people say? She'd be called every derogatory name there was, especially by the mothers who were hoping their daughters had a chance to wed the wealthy and handsome Henry Gilchrist.

"Shall I ask your grandmother for permission to marry you?" He was gazing down at her while they walked.

"Perhaps we should wait."

"Wait? Why?"

"Because it has only been a short time since my husband died."

"We can wait, if you wish. How long would you like to wait?"

"Is six months too long?"

Would that give her enough time to be sure, to settle in her mind that she was not making a mistake?

He hesitated, and she saw his throat bob as he swallowed. "No, that is not too long. But are you so worried about what other people think?"

Would he understand her fears? Would it hurt him to know the real reason she wanted to wait? But she had to be honest with him, had to make sure that his love for her was real and enduring.

"I'm just afraid. And I think I would be less afraid if we waited six months."

"Afraid of what?"

"Of making another mistake. Are you not also a bit afraid? After what happened before?"

"I thought I would never trust again, and I vowed I would never marry a poor woman."

"I am a poor woman."

"Yes, and that is why I was willing to let you go back to London. You might have wondered why I was a bit cool to you then."

"I did think you were very cool, and I felt hurt. I thought you were like David—cold, uninterested, and unfeeling."

He grimaced. "I deserve that, I suppose. And just as you say, I was afraid of making another mistake. The coolness was also because I didn't trust myself. That day in the woods, when I held you in my arms, all I could think about was kissing you."

Her heart fluttered. Was that truly what he was thinking?

"But I'd vowed never to marry a poor woman. I told myself poor women weren't to be trusted, that they would never truly love me, only my money."

"And that's what you thought about me?"

"Not you specifically. As you say, it was fear. Just as you fear marrying someone like your first husband, I feared marrying someone who could easily transfer her feelings to someone else with more money."

"Feared? You don't fear that anymore?"

"Perfect love drives out fear." He gave her an ironic smile. "Only God's love is perfect, but I do love you, Penelope. It sounds strange, but I did feel as if God was telling me not to let you go, that he had provided you for me, but I let you go because of my fear. And then when I got your letter, and the letter from Sir Edward, I realized you were in great danger and it was my fault for not listening. Now, that was real fear—fear that something terrible would happen to you, or even that you would be killed."

"You were worried about me?"

"I was mad to get back to London and find you. I rode at a frenzied pace all the way here."

She liked thinking of him being worried about her.

"So when you are remembering me being cool to you that day in Hertfordshire, just replace that memory with an image of how wracked with remorse I was, how frenzied I was to get to you and save you from the danger you were in."

A good thought.

"You are brave and good, gentle and kind, and I do love you, Penelope Whitewood Hammond. You have been through a great shock and a painful marriage, but to be honest, I don't want to wait six months to get married. I will wait, though, if it puts your mind at ease."

"Thank you, for being willing." It was all she could offer him. The fear was still there.

CHAPTER TWENTY-NINE

The next week, Lord Seagrove's fifteen-year-old daughter Euphemia came to sit for Penelope. She would paint for an hour and a half every day, as that was as long as Euphemia could bear to sit still. Henry and Jane would usually go for a long walk or a drive so that Penelope could work uninterrupted.

The only person they told of their engagement, besides Jane, was Mrs. Gilchrist, who also came to stay with them to protect against accusations of impropriety.

Today Mrs. Gilchrist was sitting quietly with some embroidery while she watched Penelope paint. Euphemia seemed calmer when Mrs. Gilchrist was present, and the two of them could have short conversations while Penelope concentrated on painting.

When Penelope told Henry she planned to continue with and finish painting Euphemia's portrait, Henry said, "Of course. You may paint as much or as little as you like, for money or not, just as you wish."

"You don't mind, then?"

"No, of course not. You will not need to make her own money now that you are marrying me, but if you wish to, I see no reason why you shouldn't, if you enjoy it."

Instead of pressing her not to do the work, he often said encouraging things about how well the portrait was turning out and how talented she was.

Grandmother had been to visit them a few times,

and they had made the obligatory return visits to Grandmother's house, with Penelope showing Henry and Jane her portraits.

Penelope was sure that if her grandmother had been able to get her alone she would have asked if she was making good use of her proximity to Henry to flirt with him, and to ask if she was making any progress toward securing his affections. So Penelope made sure never to be alone with her.

To receive money for her own work of art was a pleasure Penelope hadn't anticipated. Lord Seagrove had given her half the promised sum upon Euphemia's first sitting and would give her the balance when she was done. But it was her own money, not given to her begrudgingly by a guardian or unloving husband. She was earning it herself and no one could tell her how to spend it.

With Euphemia coming only three days a week, it would probably take Penelope six months to complete the painting, the time she had told Henry he would have to wait to marry her.

But waiting was not proving as easy as she'd thought.

Nearly every evening, Henry was able to walk her to her door and sneak a kiss goodnight. But on the evenings when she was prevented from kissing him, it felt like punishment and even torture.

Jane did discreetly leave them alone together quite often, but his kisses and the sweet things he would whisper to her were so divine, she never wanted to stop. She was beginning to realize they would need to make their engagement public or risk the tarnishing of her reputation.

Every day she became more convinced that Henry was nothing like David and never would be. Why did she need to fear?

One morning Penelope awakened and realized she'd slept later than usual. She dressed herself and left her room, immediately hearing voices downstairs, coming from the front door.

Penelope started down to see who was there, and the closer she got, the more convinced she was that there were two voices, a male and female, and they belonged to Henry and Camille Dupre.

"I can assure you, Miss Dupre, that Penelope Hammond does not wish to see you."

Thank you, Henry, Penelope thought, as she ducked into a small room not far from the front door.

"You will take a message to her, then."

"Make it brief."

Henry had told Penelope that they did not have enough evidence against Camille to imprison her with the other French spies. But the committee members all believed she was aiding the spies and was guilty of treason. They were working on getting her sent back to France.

Camille said something, but Penelope couldn't make it out. She crept closer, trusting the shadows to hide her, until she could actually see Camille Dupre and Henry framed in the doorway.

Camille suddenly leaned close to Henry and put her hand on his chest.

Penelope's blood boiled. How dare that woman be so bold?

Penelope watched as Henry took hold of Camille's wrist and thrust her back.

"I can be your courtesan," Camille was saying. "I can make you happy, just as I made Lord Hampstead happy. I don't ask for any money for the first week."

Heat invaded Penelope's forehead as her breath rushed out of her. The woman was shameless.

Henry's voice was firm. "Those services are not wanted here, Miss Dupre. You should go now."

"You would not be sorry." Camille voice had a sing-song quality, and she swayed, making Penelope wonder if she was inebriated.

"I am already sorry I came to the door. Farewell, Miss Dupre." Henry shut the door even as Camille tried to hold it open. Then he locked it.

Even though he was very firm with Camille Dupre, Henry was not as cold and cruel as David had been to his own wife. He was nothing like David.

Henry turned and sighed heavily before walking away from the door.

Penelope stepped forward, revealing herself.

"Penelope. Camille Dupre was here to see you, but I told her you did not wish to see her."

"I know. Thank you for sending her away."

"You heard the exchange?"

"A bit of it." Penelope threw her arms around Henry. "Thank you."

"Of course. I knew you wouldn't want to see her. She asked me to tell you that she's still your friend."

"I know that to be a lie." Penelope huffed out a breath. "I heard her tell you she could be your courtesan. What nerve! And that the first week was no charge. The audacity of her."

"I'm sorry she ever pretended to be your friend, but I do pity her."

"Pity her?"

"Yes. The life she lives couldn't possibly make her happy."

"That is true enough." Penelope huffed again, then pressed her face into Henry's strong, broad shoulder.

Henry was right. Penelope was so blessed to have the love of a good man, to be cherished and loved by a man like Henry Gilchrist. Camille Dupre would likely never know such love. And once people realized her moral character, Camille could never go out in polite society again.

Henry had handled the situation well. He was not cruel, but he had firmly rejected Camille's brazen offer.

"I'm ready," Penelope said, lifting her head to look into his eyes.

"Ready?"

"To marry. I want to marry you, whenever you wish."

"When do you wish it?" As usual when he spoke to her, his eyes were tender and his expression gentle.

"As soon as possible. And you may ask Grandmother's blessing today if you like, and notify our parishes of our intention."

"We could be married within the month."

"I would like that very much."

They kissed, a mutual meeting of lips and hearts and minds, tender and passionate at once.

"I love you, Henry Gilchrist. You are the best man I know."

"And I love you, Penelope Whitewood Hammond, soon to be Gilchrist. You are the best woman I know."

EPILOGUE

Four weeks later, Henry and Penelope were married in a small ceremony attended by Penelope's grandmother, Jane, Mrs. Gilchrist, and a few other relatives and friends.

Penelope thought the flowers outside in the churchyard uncommonly bright and cheerful, and the stone church was old and romantic, as if a Medieval knight might come marching up to the door next to a beautiful lady wearing a flowing gown and Medieval headdress.

Penelope's happiness was only dimmed by her difficulty in believing her good fortune. Was she truly marrying Henry Gilchrist? He gave her such adoring looks and treated her so well, she had to believe in his love for her. Truly, she'd never felt so loved in her life, and that changed everything—the way she thought, felt, trusted, and believed. She was reborn, no longer a child of disapproval or scorn, a child for whom no one cared. She was a woman loved and cherished.

"A threefold cord is not quickly broken, Ecclesiastes the fourth chapter," the rector said. Then he recited: "'Two are better than one; because they have a good reward for their labour. For if they fall, the one will lift up his fellow: but woe to him that is alone when he falleth; for he hath not another to help him up. Again, if two lie together, then they have heat: but how can one be warm alone? And if one prevail against him, two shall withstand him; and a threefold cord is not quickly broken.'

"It is not good for man to be alone," the rector continued, "and that is why God instituted marriage. God has said that he who finds a wife finds a good thing and gains favor with God. Now go, you who have found this good and favorable thing, and be blessed in your union."

Besides these words the rector spoke, the wedding vows were the same as they ever were, read and recited from the Common Book of Prayer. But Penelope did not feel common. She felt as if what was happening to her in marrying Henry had never happened before, and that her moment of happiness, when the rector proclaimed them man and wife, was a singular moment, as she turned to Henry and he embraced her, and she him.

Joyful and at peace, the two emotions so often at odds, mingled inside her as she whispered, "I love you," and Henry whispered them back to her, kissing her forehead, before turning to the small group of well-wishers.

God had been very good to her, indeed.

The End

A TREACHEROUS TREASURE

Book Two in the Imperiled Young Widows Regency Romance series

Coming Soon!

In Book Two of Melanie Dickerson's Regency Romantic Suspense series, Imperiled Young Widows, **Rebecca Heywood** finds herself a widow at the age of twenty-two. Her husband Arthur was a philanderer who got himself killed in a duel by the husband of one of his paramours, so why does someone wish to kill his wife? Arthur did owe a lot of money and had bragged he had fortune in gold doubloons his sea captain father had left buried on the family estate. Some desperate men want it, and they believe Rebecca is the one who knows where it is.

Lieutenant Thomas Westbrook is a soldier just back from the war. After the death of his father, he has sold his commission and plans to live a quiet life of building up his family's estate, helping his tenants, and hunting in his massive deer park. But then he helps a young lady who is being chased by ruffians—never realizing by doing so that he will have to fight for his life and the life of the lovely widow, who will quickly complicate his quiet life.

Rebecca has long despaired of having a loving relationship with her own husband, and has even grown almost accustomed to the embarrassment of his many dalliances with married women all over England. Having come from a family of ten children, her parents were all too pleased to marry her off to Arthur Heywood, a wealthy gentleman of large fortune and a great estate in Derbyshire. Rebecca, young and foolish, with dreams of romantic love, had believed his flattering words to her.

Before she knew his true character, she was married and was pregnant with his child. But having lost the baby in the middle of the pregnancy, she fell into a depression and was almost glad of the paramours who kept him away from home, for he frowned and sneered at her when he was there.

Now that Arthur's dead, Rebecca can't imagine ever trusting anyone again. But suddenly she is running for her life from her husband's murderers, and she runs right onto Lieutenant Westbrook's country estate, and right into the path of its owner.

Thomas doesn't take lightly to being shot at. And no one will harm a woman if he can stop them. He was not trained as a soldier for nothing. As he takes it upon himself to protect the young widow, he is intrigued by the tales of pirate treasure buried on her late husband's estate--and intrigued by the beautiful widow of his rival, the man who was his playmate when they were children but who grew up to betray him in adulthood. It would be beneath him to fall in love with that man's widow.

While you wait for *A Treacherous Treasure* to release . . .

Read Melanie Dickerson's other sweet

and clean Regency romances:

REGENCY SPIES OF LONDON SERIES
A Spy's Devotion
A Viscount's Proposal
A Dangerous Engagement

And the rest of Melanie Dickerson's historical romance titles:

THE DERICOTT TALES
Court of Swans
Castle of Refuge
Veil of Winter (Coming June, 2022)
Fortress of Snow (Coming Dec., 2022)

A MEDEIVAL FAIRY TALE (THORNBECK) SERIES
The Huntress of Thornbeck Forest
The Beautiful Pretender
The Noble Servant

FAIRY TALE ROMANCE (HAGENHEIM) SERIES
The Healer's Apprentice
The Merchant's Daughter
The Fairest Beauty
The Captive Maiden
The Princess Spy
The Golden Braid
The Silent Songbird
The Orphan's Wish
The Warrior Maiden
The Piper's Pursuit
The Peasant's Dream

SOUTHERN SEASONS SERIES
Magnolia Summer

WANT TO HELP AN AUTHOR?

As you all know, authors depend on book sales to keep writing. And one of the best ways to get the word out about an author's books, besides telling all your friends about it, is to write a review.

It's easy to leave a review on Amazon. Just write what you liked about the book, or how it made you feel, or whether or not you would recommend it to others. Even just a few words, with a rating of 4 or 5 stars, will help get the book in front of readers searching for their next read. To leave a review, click the Write a Review button.

Also, please consider putting your review on Goodreads, Facebook, or Instagram, or wherever you hang out online!

WANT TO STAY IN THE KNOW?

If you want to stay in the know about my next book and all my latest news and updates, sign up for my newsletter here and check out my website, www.MelanieDickerson.com

Another great way to stay in the know is to follow me on social media, particularly Instagram www.instagram.com/melaniedickerson123, Facebook www.facebook.com/MelanieDickersonBooks, and you can also follow me on Book Bub https://www.bookbub.com/authors/melanie-dickerson and Amazon https://www.amazon.com/Melanie-Dickerson/e/B003BAAJG6/ to follow me in order to get a notification when I have a new release.

Thanks! I look forward to connecting with you!

DISCUSSION QUESTIONS

1. In what ways did Penelope's husband make her feel unimportant? In what ways was this a reinforcement of how her grandmother had treated her?
2. Why did Penelope marry Lord Hampstead after initially refusing his offer of marriage? Have you ever been pressured into doing something you didn't want to do? If so, would you handle that situation differently if you could do it over? How?
3. Henry Gilchrist states at one point that Penelope is "timid." Why do you think he would think that? Is it true? Why or why not?
4. Penelope said she had been mourning a long time before her husband was killed. What did she mean by that?
5. How does Penelope disagree with her grandmother's—and society's—idea of what makes a good husband? What does Penelope say are the most important things to look for in a spouse? Do you agree?
6. Penelope decides, when she's been captured and is trying to escape, that she will stop allowing

her grandmother to treat her like a child and will endeavor to make her own money and provide for herself. How does she plan to do this? This is a breakthrough moment for her. Have you ever had a breakthrough moment when you realized something profound enough that it changed your life? What was it?
7. Henry Gilchrist has his own breakthrough moment when he realizes he needs to fully forgive his brother and his sister-in-law. What has he lost because he did not forgive and held a grudge?
8. Henry also realizes he has been trusting his own judgment instead of God's by making a rule never to marry a poor woman. Are there any vows that you've made to yourself about things you will or won't do? Have you ever revisited these and asked yourself if they're wise? Have you ever trusted your own judgment instead of God's? How did that turn out?
9. Penelope accepts Henry's marriage proposal but she wants to wait six months because of her fear. Why does she have so much fear about marrying again? Does this seem reasonable to you? Why or why not?
10. Henry had said that he wanted to become a Member of Parliament in order help people. Do lawmakers have the ability to improve people's lives? Why do you think we hear very little about politicians and elected officials making a difference in a positive way?

ABOUT THE AUTHOR

Melanie Dickerson

Melanie Dickerson is the Christy award-winning and New York Times bestselling author of Regency romantic suspense and Medieval fairy tale romances.

Growing up about 50 miles from Harper Lee's hometown in rural Alabama, Melanie wrote stories in notebooks for her friends, who read passed them around in class as soon as she finished a scene. (And no, they didn't get in trouble—much.) These stories always involved adventure, danger, and a hero and heroine falling in love, with a happily-ever-after ending.

She's been a romantic for as long as she can remember!

Melanie lives in North Alabama with her husband and sometimes her two young adult children, who have (mostly) flown the nest. You'll find her sprint-writing with her friends on video chat or hanging out with her handsome husband, watching movies with her oddly calm Jack Russell terrier, or daydreaming about her book-in-progress.

Printed in Great Britain
by Amazon